LETHAL
JUSTICE

Has a cruel killer met his match?

ROBERT McCRACKEN

Published by The Book Folks

London, 2021

© Robert McCracken

ISBN 978-1-913516-12-3

www.thebookfolks.com

Lethal Justice is the fifth novel in the DI Tara Grogan mystery series. Details about the other books can be found at the back.

Prologue

Laughter filled the night as the flames reached up into the darkness. His eyes watered from the sweet but sickening smoke, and tears ran down his cheeks until he smudged them away with his grubby hand. Bottles clinked as figures stood, arms around shoulders, lovers kissing and drinking, unsteady on their feet. His eyes never left the flames, his young face glowing from the heat that penetrated the flimsy denim of his trousers and warmed his legs. A few feet away, close to the stone wall, a woman lay on the ground, moaning, while the heavy frame of a bearded man writhed awkwardly between her legs. Through the flames he watched a man strum his guitar, while a woman in her nightdress danced barefoot, a rolled fag in one hand, a beer bottle in the other. Another man ambled toward the guitarist and joined in the music with a tin whistle, and the sounds of a folk tune cut through the night. More joined in the dancing. All were drunk, or drunk and stoned. And still he peered into the flames, into the glowing of embers forming from the combusted remains of the lifeless body. His mother.

And they danced around the pyre. Singing, laughing, embracing. Women, young and not so young, gave themselves to the men, drunk men with only the strength now to fondle breasts and squeeze bottoms. Other kids copied the adults, drinking, smoking, fondling. Men chased young girls around the yard, feigning a silly game when all they wanted was sex. And he peered into the fire, thinking only of his beautiful mother. Why were these people rejoicing when he had lost so much? They ignored him as the music played. Some eased away from the fire, holding hands, moving to darker corners of the farmyard, a few were entering the big stone house and others the hay barn. They had no time for him now. He didn't belong here anymore. But he would remember them. He would never forget what they had done. He would run. Run for his life. He hoped for a new one, a fresh start. He would find someone to love him, just like his mother.

The blonde girl, half his age, in a white lace dress entrenched with dirt and the smoke from the fire, clutched her Jemima doll. She didn't understand. She didn't know her mother was gone forever. That her body now fuelled the fire and sent the smoke that stung her eyes. She didn't know anything. He clasped her hand and stepped back slowly from the flames. No one in the yard seemed to notice as the pair edged further into the darkness. A few more backward steps. He shushed his sister and tugged her gently away from the outbuildings. Soon they were on the lane, and he began to run, encouraging her to keep up. The noises from the party faded, and he told his sister not to look back. They had to keep going. He would never stop until they reached safety. He would find someone to look after them far away from the fear they'd left behind. But he would never forget.

The glow from the fire was hidden now as the trail wound into the woods. No one was coming after them, he told himself. They had nothing to fear from the darkness. He longed for rest but knew he must keep going. His sister cried and shivered at his side. He pulled off his coat, only a light anorak but he made her put it on. He tucked her doll inside and closed the zipper. All the while he spoke words of comfort, promising that wonderful times were coming. Soon they would have a new family, a new mother, a beautiful house with a garden and a swing and a fishpond. All the food they could eat, burgers, ice cream and chocolate buttons. They just had to get away. She listened, and his promises helped her fear, and the coat warmed her arms. And they moved further into darkness, away from the light.

He would never forget.

CHAPTER 1

Present Day

She had never stood quite so close to Detective Superintendent Harold Tweedy before. He seemed to draw comfort from their touching arms. To be honest, she did too. Never particularly strong at a crime scene, Tara shivered in the night frost. Her toes were frozen and felt detached from her feet. Weariness from being roused from her night's sleep prompted the urge to yawn continuously, but she managed to stifle them. Everyone present had to endure the lateness of the hour and the freezing air; she was no one special. Lights had been strung up above the body of the victim as the medical officer, Dr Brian Witney, set about his examination. Neither detective could bring themselves to look away from the body, stripped to the waist and stretched out, open arms and open legs across a circular wooden frame that resembled an old cartwheel. Hands had been strapped to the frame with fine rope, but flat-headed nails, four inches of cold steel, had been hammered an inch or so into the open palms. The feet, bare, had been attached to the wooden ring by nylon rope with nails penetrating below the ankle bone. Besides the macabre, it was to Tara a puzzling scene, raising question after question. The entire wooden frame rested against the trunk of a tree with the feet of the victim uppermost.

'He's been dead around five or six hours,' said Witney, a pathologist of fifty-something, with a functional manner and a middle-age spread. 'We'll know better when we get back to the lab.'

Tweedy nodded, remaining silent. Sometimes it was best to simply absorb the scene, save questions for later, for the cold light of day.

'What's that attached to the wood, Brian?' asked Tara, stepping towards the frame. The pathologist had taken no notice of such things, he being more concerned with the condition of the corpse. 'Can we get more light on this?' she called out to the forensic team.

Someone adjusted the angle of one of the arc lights, and Tara moved closer to the frame. At the uppermost portion of the circle several lines of text typed on a sheet, within a polythene sleeve, had been stapled to the wood.

> *Therefore shall they eat of the fruit of their own way,*
> *and be filled with their own devices.*

She glanced back at Tweedy, who merely nodded slowly. She'd never seen him look so disturbed at a crime scene. He had years of doing this, all hours of the day and night, in all weathers. His experience helped him cope better than most. But under the lights, within the canopy of trees, his lined face betrayed his age. He was, it seemed to Tara, an officer weary of his job, his responsibilities. Perhaps weary of life itself.

'What do you think, sir?'

He pulled a handkerchief from his anorak pocket and wiped his nose.

'Let's leave it till we get back to the station, Tara. We've seen enough for now.'

'Sir.' She watched him pick his way through the detritus of autumn, reaching the narrow trail that led down the hill to the melee of police vehicles assembled on the lane. Her curiosity was piqued not only by the gruesome sights before her but also by the reaction of her boss to this latest case. If she didn't know him better, she would suggest that he was frightened by what he had witnessed.

Standing alone as the forensic team continued to gather the evidence, they would need to plan a strategy to solve this mystery, her own fears surfaced. Seldom did she look strong enough to endure such challenges, merely five foot one inch tall, with a young-looking face. The grip of a shiver ran through her lower back, all the more intense in freezing temperatures where your breath condensed in front of your face. She pushed a lock of golden-blonde hair away from her eyes, tucking it behind her ear, waiting for Brian Witney to issue his final comments before departing the scene. She scribbled down the inscription she'd read into her notebook, already forming an opinion that it held some religious significance, a biblical phrase perhaps.

'A few injuries to the torso,' said Witney, stepping close to DI Tara Grogan, his breath mingling with hers as he spoke. 'At least one broken rib, and then the spikes through the hands and feet. Very sadistic.'

Tara studied the body as Witney continued.

'Of course, Tara, you don't need me to tell you the cause of death. Goodnight.'

'Thanks, Brian.' She smiled thinly as the pathologist walked off between the white tapes that now showed the way onto the trail through the trees. For the last time she surveyed the frame with the body cruelly attached, but, as Witney had said, she didn't need to ponder on the cause of death. She stared at the lower part of the frame. The victim's head was missing.

CHAPTER 2

By tomorrow I'll be out of this dump. Business as usual. Lots to do. Places to go, people to meet and, of course, girls ripe for the picking. Can't wait. OK, so I've had my wings clipped, my card marked. They know who I am now, but they don't know what I've done. Not really. I got banged up for snatching that pretty wee cop, DI Tara Grogan, but then I didn't get to finish the job. That big eejit DS Murray put the dampers on my party of a lifetime. And Tara lived to tell the tale. Except she didn't remember much, dear love her.

So now they know my name. James Guy, or Jim to my friends, except I don't have any of them. Not for a long time, not since I was a kid. I'll be on the sex offenders register, so in theory the police can keep tabs on me. Watch where I go, what I do, who I meet. I'll have to be careful when I get out. Always was careful, it's just that I overstepped the mark with Tara Grogan. All my years of experience went out the window when I met her. Strange that a girl can have such an effect on a poor soul like me. More so when she was a cop. You see, what I like doing is taking a nice wee girl, giving her a shot of China White, fentanyl, so she's out of it. I do my business with her and then, just to be tidy, I finish her off with a lethal dose. Dump the body at sea and I'm in the clear. Simple. But I made a balls of it with DI Tara Grogan.

Didn't think I would survive prison at first. Place is full of frigging weirdos. And that's only the inmates. Bloody screws aren't much better. There are blokes in here that have done some pretty disgusting stuff. Most of the kiddie fondlers are in the next wing, but I have to put up with

6

blokes who've been violent with women, beating them up to get their way with them. Some of them just beat up women, and that's it. That's their bag. And I never realised before that it's a specialised activity. Some guys beat the crap out of their girlfriends but never touch the face. They just kick the poor woman in the stomach and back. Other eejits do the opposite, deliberately try to take away her good looks. There's a boy down the hall from me who poured acid on his girlfriend's face while she was sleeping in their flat. Ronnie, in the cell next to mine, stalked some woman who'd been on *Big Brother*, and when she refused to have anything to do with him, he drove his car into her, broke her hip and one of her legs. I told him to catch himself on. He's fifty, and she was only nineteen. Didn't like me judging him. I got a black eye for opening my big mouth.

I've got worse than that in here, though, just for being Irish. The screws don't like that I come from across the water. I get the blame for every IRA bombing in England and the death of every British soldier in Northern Ireland. Really, I think it's because they don't like my cheek. They don't like me talking back to them. You see, I regard myself as different from the other hallions in here. I'm classed as potentially violent because I got done for aggravated assault. Same as most of them. But nobody knows what I've really done. I'm no reckless woman-beater. I'm a seasoned collector of exquisite totty. I've worked hard to develop the ultimate method for taking women, drugging them, having great sex with them, and disposing of them when I'm finished. I suppose you could call it the perfect crime. So far, it's worked well for me. I've had dozens of pretty women who've never been seen again. Not a thing can be traced back to me. My only failure was my little friend DI Tara Grogan. Finest looking woman I've ever seen. Her bloody fault that I got banged up. But when I get out of here just try and stop me from having another go at her.

My plans this time have been well thought out. I've had little else to do in prison except dream up strategies to enhance my career. Sounds very businesslike, doesn't it? I am in possession of a business strategy, a way ahead, a new development process. Firstly, I'll choose a few easy targets, nothing too difficult, just to get my mojo working. Seems a bit like a footballer coming back after a long-term injury, playing a couple of warm-up games before stepping into the big time. Test the water, see if I still have what it takes. Then, when I'm up and running, into cruise mode, I'll start picking the good stuff, enjoy myself. And all the while you can be sure of it, I will keep my eyes on wee Tara. I haven't finished with her. Not by a long way.

CHAPTER 3

When a new case emerged it was usually Superintendent Tweedy who first took charge of a whiteboard to note the early findings of the incident. This morning at St Anne Street station, however, it was Tara standing by the board jotting down what little they had so far learned from this bizarre killing. Tweedy was not himself. Tara could see it, and she reckoned that even Alan Murray sensed it too.

'Anything significant about the location?' Tara asked. DS Murray, DC John Wilson and Tweedy were seated in the superintendent's office. Murray scanned a page in his notebook.

'Rough ground, under trees.'

'Yes, but why Rimrose Valley Country Park?'

'No idea so far,' Murray replied.

'Any news on ID?'

'Not yet. Nothing found at the scene,' said Wilson.

'We have an estimated time of death between eight and ten last night. Anyone come forward who was in the area at this time?' Tara was already frustrated, having so few details to record.

'Get an appeal out for information, Alan,' said Tweedy, surprising his colleagues by speaking for the first time since the meeting had begun.

'John, can you tell us again about who made the discovery?' asked Tara.

'Yes, ma'am. Six teenagers, four lads and two girls found it at approximately one thirty this morning. Girls are only fifteen, the lads sixteen to seventeen. They'll not get over the sight easily.'

'What on earth were they doing traipsing about the park at that hour of the morning?'

'They had a few bottles of vodka with them. Having a bit of a laugh, I think.'

'But it was minus two last night. Don't they have school or college today?'

The broad-shouldered Wilson merely shrugged at Tara's suggestion.

'Any possibility that the kids were involved?'

Tweedy was already shaking his head.

'Judging by the state they were in,' said Wilson. 'I very much doubt it.'

Tara was still wearing the clothes she'd worn when called to the scene in the middle of the night: slim jeans, T-shirt and a dark-green roll-neck jumper. She didn't feel clean, her hair hastily tied back with a scrunchie, no make-up, and all the worse for lack of sleep.

Having also attended the scene, Tweedy and Wilson were more casually dressed than Murray who hadn't been there. He had managed a good night's sleep and was more presentable in a light grey suit, pink shirt and striped tie. Mid-thirties had brought with them a swelling neck size and waist, not helped by his appetite for snack food and the demands of his job. Still, Murray remained a handsome officer, tall, fresh-faced with large eyes, a man not long divorced and once again playing the field. Tara could tolerate him as a colleague; beyond that he wasn't her type. Not that she dwelt on the subject, but it had been quite some time since she'd had any type when it came to men. Again, the demands of her job, although she was becoming proficient at using this as an excuse not to go on dates. Her recent experience at the hands of a date rapist hadn't helped stir enthusiasm to pursue anything close to a romantic relationship.

'Can we discuss the MO?' Tara continued.

'Weird, to say the least,' said Murray.

'Seems like a ritual killing,' said Wilson.

'Or made to look that way,' Tara suggested. 'Going by the amount of blood on the ground, the victim was killed at the scene and the head, apparently, taken away by the killer. For what purpose?'

No one, including Tweedy, was prepared to offer any reason. Tara thought it very strange. She was used to her boss making suggestions, giving advice, issuing orders. He was a gentleman among coppers. Now in his late fifties, he'd seen it all through Merseyside Police, and he managed his team with a calm and respectful air. He didn't shout, certainly did not swear, and yet managed to get results from his officers. His pale, wrinkled and long face belied his compassion. One had to look closely to see the caring nature and the happiness hidden in his blue eyes. He derived great comfort from his Christian faith and was often to be found reading the leather-bound Bible that he kept on the left-hand corner of his desk. This morning, Tara had noticed him glancing several times at the book. She wondered.

'What about the message pinned to the wood between the legs of the victim?' she asked.

'Religious wording of some kind?' said Wilson. Tara saw Tweedy give a slight nod in acknowledgement.

'The work of a religious nutjob, a Bible-basher,' said Murray. Tara cleared her throat, and the realisation of what he'd just said in front of Tweedy registered with Murray. He blushed red.

'*Therefore shall they eat of the fruit of their own way, and be filled with their own devices*,' Tara read. 'Do you know if it is biblical, sir?'

Tweedy got to his feet.

'Yes, it is indeed. I checked when I first got back. Old Testament, Proverbs, Chapter one, verse 31.'

'What do you think it means, sir?'

Before he could answer, Paula Bleasdale, a young female detective constable, tall, with long brown hair pinned up, appeared at the window of the office door and beckoned Murray to join her. He rose from his seat and went to speak with the DC. The others in the office looked on as Bleasdale spoke to Murray.

'Any news?' Tara asked when he stepped back into the office.

'Yes, they've found the head.'

CHAPTER 4

Free at last, free at last. Hey, hey they let me go. I've served my time for what I did to wee Tara, and now I'm on probation. It's not so bad, really. OK, I'm a registered sex offender; they know who I am. I have to attend regular meetings with my supervisor, and there's a whole list of things I'm not allowed to do and places I'm not allowed to go. For instance, I must stay well away from DI Tara Grogan. But they've set me up in a flat, and I can claim housing benefit and job seeker's allowance. It's a one-bed affair in Wavertree. Doesn't bother me in the slightest. I could live anywhere so long as I have the opportunity to see beautiful women every day. Some charity that looks after ex-prisoners gave me a single bed, an armchair, a fridge and a TV. There was already a cooker in the flat, so I've got all I need. My supervisor has arranged a couple of job interviews. I've a wee bit of money saved that'll keep me ticking over and I still have my boat, *Mother Freedom*. The last I heard, she'd been taken from the harbour at Penrhyn and stored in a boatyard. I probably owe some money for that, but I can't wait until I can get her back in the water and use her for what I like doing best.

I realise I can't go within a beagle's gowl of Tara Grogan, but I can deal with that later. For now, I'm happy to get back into my groove. I can take my time, set everything up the way I used to, buy a van, set about choosing some wee honey and having my wicked way with her. Of course, I'm more than happy to go the conventional route, meet a nice girl, take her out for dinner, a few drinks, bit of a chat, get to know her. The only problem is that it might get awkward when she asks what I do for a living, when she decides maybe to check me out and discovers I'm an ex-prisoner, a man on the sex offender list. It doesn't bode well for an intimate relationship. And besides, I'm supposed to inform my probation supervisor when I'm planning to have an intimate relationship with someone. Now, I can't see that happening. Spoil the mood, wouldn't it? Let's not forget that my last attempt to go the romantic way with young Tara ended with me near losing it and then spending eighteen months in the nick. No, for now, everything is back to basics. Good planning and careful choosing of my girls. Get back on my bike. And maybe, when all has settled down, I will do real homework on DI Tara Grogan and make sure that next time I take her the right way and do the business.

CHAPTER 5

Priory Road had been closed to traffic. To her left, Tara had Anfield Cemetery and to her right, Stanley Park. A team of Scene of Crime Officers, SOCOs, were already at work on the pavement by the park railings. But Tara, along with Tweedy and Murray, were focused on the appalling vision of a male head impaled upon one of the spikes of the railing.

'Sick bastards,' said Murray, out of earshot of Superintendent Tweedy, a man not given to expletives.

'I really don't like this, Alan,' said Tara. 'Why here? Why remove the victim's head and bring it here?'

'Whoever did it must revel in the shock value. Last night a group of kids had the fright of their lives, and this morning two elderly ladies walking their dogs came across this.'

Tara's mobile burst into life, 'Moves like Jagger' attracting several glares from others standing close by. Her friend Aisling was calling.

'Hi, Aisling, what's up?'

'Tara love, you won't believe the shoes I've just seen in Harvey Nic's.'

'I'm a bit busy at the moment, Aisling.'

'I won't keep you. They're black leather sandals, exactly what I've been looking for.'

'Uh-huh.'

'They're *Francesco Russo*.'

'How much?'

'Only six-twenty.'

'You've more money than sense, Aisling love. I'll have to go.'

'Should I get them? I don't know what to do.'

'Yes, you do, Aisling. If I say yes, you'll get them, and if I say no, you'll phone Kate and ask her. And even if she says no, you'll still go and buy them.'

'Will you come with me, this evening?'

'Can't, Aisling, I'm working. You're a big girl, you're quite capable of going on your own. Got to go.' Tara cut the call, exasperated yet slightly amused that the dilemma of her friend's day was deciding whether or not to buy a pair of shoes, while her friend, Kate, worked in a cardiac ward at the Royal Hospital and she, Tara, was standing in the middle of a road looking at the severed head of the victim in her latest case of murder.

Her last investigation of homicide, before her month lay-off, had involved two killings and frenzied slashing of the victims. And no sooner had the case been put to bed when she almost suffered at the hands of a date rapist.

Thoughts of that evening seldom left her now despite her having little memory of what occurred. She'd been abducted. She'd been drunk at the time, out for an evening with Kate and Aisling. The man, James Guy, had injected her with fentanyl. Fortunately, she'd been rescued before he could do anything more than removing her clothes in the back of his van. But still she was left with a peculiar trauma as if she lived permanently in winter, a cool wind constantly blowing through her and she flapping uselessly like the grass.

She'd been informed two days ago that Guy had been released from prison on probation. At night, alone in her flat at Wapping Dock, Tara pondered another case that had never actually been a case. Absurd, she realised, but she couldn't shift from her mind the pictures of missing women she'd found in the flat of murdered journalist Terry Lawler. At first, she'd thought that Lawler was responsible for abducting the women until she discovered that the journalist had been searching for his missing sister and possibly had stumbled upon the work of a serial killer.

But Terry Lawler had been murdered by someone close to him, and she'd had to focus on finding his killer. It wasn't her job to go searching for a long list of missing women. No trace of any of them had ever been found, and she doubted that any police officer in the entire country was even looking for them.

She felt a hand on her shoulder and turned around to face her boss, Harold Tweedy.

'Tara, I would like a quiet word when you get back to the station.'

'Yes, sir.'

Without elucidating Tweedy strode off, waving acknowledgement to the crime scene manager.

Tara watched and pitied the young forensic officer charged with removing the head from the spike. She realised too, that at this moment, they had to assume this head belonged with the body recovered from Rimrose Park. She shuddered to think there could be more than one victim of such a killing.

'What did the old man want, ma'am?' asked Murray, who had been speaking with the two women who'd made the gruesome discovery. Tara thought it strange that, at the time, no passing motorist had stopped at the scene.

'He wants a quiet word back at the station,' she replied.

'What's going on, Tara? He's been acting very odd this morning. You don't think he's had enough of the murder game, about to pack it in?'

Tara never ceased to be amazed at how her detective sergeant could switch from the formal to the casual in the same breath. She was well aware that he coped poorly with her being a detective inspector, eight years younger and half as many years in policing. It wasn't that she was a stickler for protocol but, in Alan Murray, she couldn't help feeling that he did it deliberately just to get up her nose. She chose her moments carefully to remind him of her seniority.

'No,' she replied, 'I think he has an inkling as to what's going on here. Maybe it's personal, close to home.'

'You think he knows the victim?'

'No, but I think the MO is familiar to him. I've never seen him so shaken at a crime scene before. It was like he was reliving some horror from his past.'

CHAPTER 6

Superintendent Tweedy had retained a pensive look on his face when Tara entered his office an hour later. He was pacing around the room then seemed to bounce back to reality when Tara sat down.

'What's the problem, sir?'

Tweedy took his seat and placed his hands upon a buff folder.

'I'm sorry, Tara. I should have explained at the outset. This murder, the MO, I've come across it before. A killing like this one happened twenty-five years ago.'

He opened the folder. There were several typed sheets inside, some handwritten notes and several black-and-white photographs.

'This is my personal file on the case.'

He handed the picture to Tara.

'His name was Alastair Bailey.'

Tara examined the photo of the man. She guessed that he was in his early thirties, with short hair, a bright smile and a clear complexion.

'What happened to him?'

'He was a member of my church, a youth leader and quite a scholar of theology. He questioned everything. What I mean is he was keen to discover all he could about his Christian faith. He studied theology at university; he wanted to become a full-time pastor. But his inquisitive nature was perhaps his downfall. He explored many faiths, Islam, Buddhism, Roman Catholicism, paganism and Hinduism. I believe that he was really a soul in turmoil. He sought an absolute truth that he was never going to find. Eventually, having dwelt upon all kinds of religious and atheistic philosophies, existentialism, Gnosticism, Judaism, he began to investigate much darker theologies, firstly, ideas such as dualism and mitigated dualism, and then somehow, he began a study into the occult and satanic practices. I remember he came to me at one point trying desperately to explain himself. You see, some of the church elders didn't approve of his dabbling in non-Christian faiths and practices, and he was coming under pressure from them regarding his continued leadership of our youth ministry.

'He was married and had two young children, and I was growing concerned for them as Alastair became more preoccupied with his faith journey.'

'His faith journey?' asked Tara.

'That's how he viewed things. His research, his investigation of these religions, was all a part of his faith journey. He believed, and at the time I could understand his viewpoint, that one day he would find something that would add so much credence to his Christian faith that he would be stronger and more able to represent Christ in this world. But they were difficult conversations between us. I advised him to tread very carefully and to think first of his wife and children. Some of the elders were not so understanding, and eventually he was asked to relinquish his role as youth minister within our church. I could see how much the lack of trust displayed by his Christian brothers hurt him. The day he left our congregation was the last time I saw him alive.'

Tara could see Harold Tweedy reliving those events in his mind. She realised that he would have been of similar age to Alastair Bailey at that time. For a few moments there was silence as he sat gazing at the open text before him.

'What happened to him, sir?' she ventured.

'Well, I didn't hear much from him for a year or so, although I saw his wife, Janet, occasionally at school PTA meetings. Sadly, one day she told me that they had separated. A week or so after hearing that news, he telephoned me sounding more upbeat than I should have thought given that he had just split from his wife and family. But he told me that he had at last found real hope in his faith. He'd joined a group called...' Harold reached for the folder and retrieved a sheet of paper. 'The Church of the Crystal Water. There was not much ever known about this church, but it was thought at that time to be an occultist group. It was mostly centred in Britain: London, the Midlands and one cell in Lancashire.

'About five months after that conversation, I attended the scene of a murder. I was a DS then. The victim had been dead for several weeks before he was discovered in woods at Croxteth Country Park. The body was nailed at the hands and feet to an old cartwheel which rested against a tree. The body was upside down, completely naked, and the head had been removed. We never found it. Alastair was identified through his fingerprints and DNA.'

'Did you find the killers?'

Tweedy shook his head slowly.

'Sadly, no. Obviously, I was of the opinion that his murder was related to his activities within this church he had joined. But all attempts to track down other members came up blank. Investigations into occult practices, and those involved, failed to shed any light on this Church of the Crystal Water.'

'Do you think the same people could be involved in this new killing? It has been twenty-five years.'

'The MO is the same, except for us finding the head of the victim.'

'Have you heard anything about this church since that time?'

Again, Tweedy shook his head.

'There is one further similarity between both cases,' he said. He produced an 8 x 4 photograph from the folder. 'A biblical inscription was attached to the body.'

He passed the photo to Tara. It showed a rough plank of wood hanging from the cartwheel with an inscription upon it.

None that go unto her return again.

* * *

Murray was eager to hear the latest when Tara returned to her desk.

'What's happening then?'

'He's just invited me to dinner at his home.'

'My, my, you're privileged. Didn't think Tweedy was one for mixing business with pleasure.'

'He wants to discuss the case. Away from the station.'

CHAPTER 7

Jason Collywell, my probation officer, suggested that if I wanted to buy a car, get my PSV licence, I could get a job as a taxi driver. So far, my only job prospects are a kitchen porter or labouring on a building site. Not great. The labouring job is only temporary, but it pays better than the kitchen porter. Do you know the only qualification required to be a hotel kitchen porter is that I must be able to speak English? What the fuck? This *is* England for goodness' sake.

When I met the catering manager, he was less interested in my prison record and more concerned with my ability to string a few words together in the mother tongue. So, I've got the job. I will mostly work evenings, with some early morning shifts to cover breakfast. It's minimum wage, but it'll do for now. I'll certainly have a go at the taxi driving once I get enough money to buy a car. Good idea that. Might be useful for a certain hobby of mine. Collywell is not such a bad lad, getting me a job so quickly. And he isn't the sort to sit in judgement of my past. He's full of the joys really, a glass-half-full type, look to the future and all that shit.

'Mr Guy,' he said. Calls me mister, dear love him. 'I'm not interested in what you've done in the past. We all make mistakes. I'm concerned for your future. Getting you a job, a decent place to live. I measure my success by keeping you out of prison. If we both work at that then my job is made very easy indeed.' Apart from the 'mister' bit he spoke to me like we were mates. I suppose we are of similar age. He could be a good mate if he weren't my supervisor. He seems a typical lad, pictures of the Liverpool team on his walls, a scale model of a Ferrari GTO sitting on his desk.

As long as I keep out of trouble, he says, I should do all right. Bless him. If only he knew what I've done and what I'm planning to do, he might not be so understanding. But hey, at least I can speak the Queen's English.

My boss, the hotel catering manager, is Romanian. He's a bit serious, very keen to impress the powers that be but well organised. Unfortunately, most of my time is spent in the kitchen, and the master there is the head chef. What an asshole. It's all 'yes chef' this and 'yes chef' that. I reckon he's one of those narcissistic twats who thinks he should be famous, on the telly and that. But I've told myself to keep my head down. Do as I'm told, don't draw attention to myself. Most of the other workers are foreign, Polish, Romanian, and a couple of Lithuanians. Makes me wonder why I wasn't asked if I spoke a language other than English.

I've only had one day off so far, but I got out and about around the city centre letting my eyes wander. There was lots of talent about, plenty to take my fancy. I spied this wee thing coming out of Lime Street station. She looked Asian, more like Thai, dressed in black jeans and boots and a fluffy white coat. Perfectly formed. I couldn't resist a wee dander as she headed towards an office block. Haven't had a Thai girl yet, but she certainly whetted my appetite. I have to think of an appropriate name for her. Then a devilish thought struck me. I hope she is female and not one of those Thai ladyboys that you hear about. Doesn't float my boat, and not something I want to discover when I'm about to do the business. I'm not into those kinds of surprises.

It didn't take me long to start wondering what Tara was up to. Was she still a police detective? Did she still live at Wapping Dock? I took a stroll down there, just on the off chance that I might catch a glimpse of my elusive treasure. I should've known that I was going to have a long wait. There was no sign of her coming or going. Maybe it would be better to start at the cop shop. I know it's not going to be easy. For now, I think I'll concentrate on my little Thai girl.

CHAPTER 8

Harold Tweedy appeared perfectly relaxed within his home. He greeted Tara at the front door of his bungalow on Allerton Road in Calderstones, one of Liverpool's leafy suburbs, wearing brown slacks, an open-neck shirt and suede moccasins.

'Tara, come in, come in, welcome. Terribly cold night out there.'

'Another frosty one,' she replied, stepping into the warmth of the hallway.

'I really appreciate you coming, especially after such a difficult day. But we'll talk later.'

He led her into a sumptuous living room containing two cushioned sofas and an armchair, the room lit by uplighters in opposite corners. It was a more contemporary setting than she had imagined, judged only by Tweedy's demeanour at work of all things classical. As she was about to remove her coat and take a seat on one of the sofas, the lady of the house, Lorraine, barged in with a gracious welcome.

'For goodness' sake, Harold, take her coat. Hi, Tara, great to see you again. You're looking well. How've you been?'

'I'm fine thank you, Lorraine.'

'Managed to settle back into work again? That was a dreadful business.'

'Keeping busy is the best way to deal with things, I suppose.'

She slipped off her black overcoat and red scarf, both instantly whisked away by Harold. For a second, she felt examined by Lorraine. She'd managed to dash home from the station and change into a red lace, mid-length dress and a pair of black sandals. Not the most appropriate for the cold evening, but she didn't have much of a choice. She really should take a leaf from Aisling's book and let shoes become the centre of her world.

Lorraine Tweedy, despite home ground, looked glamorous in a navy-blue dress. But it wasn't difficult to like the woman, Tara had always thought. She had a cheery smile that said, whatever the weather we have to get on with things.

'Oh, I nearly forgot,' she said, 'this is for you.' She handed Tara a large glass of red wine at the correct temperature. 'Harold can get his own drink.' Her husband rolled his eyes at Tara as he left the room.

Despite the friendly welcome, and again from experience, Tara knew she would have difficulty getting a word in. She would have thought that working as a university lecturer in sociology she would tend to give her mouth a rest after a day's work, but Lorraine seemed to have deep reserves of energetic chat.

'So, what's it about tonight? Harold seemed very pensive when he called me to arrange dinner. I hope he's not expecting you to work all evening. Really, the man sometimes doesn't think before putting one foot in front of the other.'

'Something about our present case,' Tara replied rather sheepishly.

'Mmm. I've warned him, no shop talk until dinner is over.'

When dinner had ended Harold led Tara across the hallway to a room he and his wife used as a study. It was warm, a gas fire burning in the fireplace, long curtains and wall space entirely swallowed with books, CDs, vinyl records, and family photos. The only other pieces of furniture were two solid desks of dark wood, one presumably for Harold, the other for Lorraine, placed such that husband and wife could sit facing each other. Both desks held laptop computers and reading lamps. Tweedy fetched a chair from the dining room and invited Tara to sit next to him at his desk.

Lorraine Tweedy pushed open the door of the study and carried in a tray of coffee. Harold Tweedy was on his feet browsing his bookshelves, while Tara helped by pouring the coffee into two cups from a coffee pot.

'I'll have mine in front of the telly,' said Lorraine in a playful whisper. '*Silent Witness* is just starting.' With a smile at Tara, she closed the door.

While Tweedy proceeded to leaf through books, Tara sat in silence wondering exactly how this was going to help them with a case of murder.

'Take a look at this picture, Tara, see how it resembles our poor victim.' Tweedy passed an open book to her. Tara studied the drawing, the figure of a man within a circle or a wheel, his arms and his legs outstretched. A straight line was drawn from each outer point, left leg to left arm, to the head, to the right arm, right leg and back to the left leg.

'I've seen this before, sir, the lines forming a pentagram. Wasn't Da Vinci renowned for drawing something like this?'

'It has certainly been associated with the artist, but throughout history it has taken on several meanings.'

Tweedy placed his finger on the image of the pentagram.

'A man drawn in such a position actually forms a five-pointed star. Simply put, the symbol of the five-pointed star is a pentagram. When placed within a circle it is usually referred to as a pentacle, but the terms pentagram and pentacle are at times nowadays regarded as the same thing. There are five points, each with its own meaning. The upward point of the star represents the spirit, while the other four points signify an element: earth, air, fire, and water. Some people wear a pentacle as a piece of jewellery. It supposedly expresses the wearer's feeling of a connection to the elements and their respect for the Earth.

'The number five has always been regarded as a mystical and magical number, and yet at the same time there is a human association. We have five fingers, five toes, and five senses: to see, touch, hear, smell and to taste. There are five stages or initiations in life: birth, puberty, congress, parenthood and death.

'In Christianity, there were five wounds of Christ on the cross. There are five pillars of the Muslim faith and five daily times of prayer. The Wiccan Kiss is fivefold: feet, knees, womb, breasts and lips. Five is a prime number. The simplest star, the pentagram, requires five lines to draw it, and it is unicursal.'

'Unicursal?' asked Tara.

'It is a continuous loop.' Tweedy lifted a pencil and traced out the symbol without lifting the pencil from the paper. 'If we place the figure of a man on a pentacle with head and four limbs at the points and the genitalia exactly central, it can be said to represent man in the microcosm, symbolising our place in the macrocosm or the universe.'

'But what has this got to do with murder?' She hoped she didn't sound impatient, but she was beginning to wonder where all this information was taking her. Tweedy was obviously very knowledgeable on the subject, but she was going to have to extract the points relevant to her and this case.

'The pentacle has also been regarded as a protection against evil. The Christian church at one time used it before eventually choosing the cross as a more significant symbol for Christianity. But the pentacle may also be inverted with one point down and two points upward. This is how our crime scene looked. It implies that the spirit is subservient to matter, of man subservient to his carnal desires. The inverted pentacle has come to be seen by many pagans as an evil symbol. Fundamentalist Christians see any form of pentacle as such.'

With the heat of the room and after eating dinner, Tara was beginning to wilt under the barrage of information. So far, she couldn't see a reason why someone would want to kill their victim in this manner. What on earth was her boss trying to say?

'But it has been suggested that the symbol originated much earlier with King Solomon. Then, of course, what I think is relevant to this case is that some people regard it as a magic symbol. But what is significant here in our crime scene is the pentacle's orientation. With a single point upwards, the pentagram is regarded as spirit presiding over the four elements of matter: earth, air, fire and water, and is essentially "good". Writers such as Eliphas Levi describe it as a sign of evil whenever the symbol appears the other way up. A reversed pentacle, with two points projecting upwards, is believed to attract sinister forces. It overturns the proper order of things and demonstrates the triumph of matter over spirit. It is the goat of lust attacking the heavens with its horns.'

'A goat?'

'Yes. The flaming star, when turned upside down, is the hieroglyphic sign of the goat of black magic, whose head may be drawn in the star, the two horns at the top, the ears to the right and left, the beard at the bottom. It is the sign of antagonism and fatality.'

'I'm sorry, I don't understand. Are you suggesting that the murder is linked to black magic?'

Harold Tweedy nodded, and a cold shiver gripped Tara's lower back in much the same way as she felt whenever she viewed a horrific crime scene. But this seemed like talk of fiction, murders caused by witchcraft? This was Liverpool for goodness' sake. Surely such things did not happen here in this day and age?

'But what does all of this mean?' she asked.

'The pentacle and particularly one showing the head of a goat is a classic satanic symbol. It is a logo for the Church of Satan.'

'So, you are suggesting that a satanic cult is responsible for this murder?'

'No, Tara, at least not yet,' said Harold. 'I just want to give you some background. There is symbolism of some kind going on here. I want you to be aware of it as you proceed with the investigation.'

'Fine, sir. Can you explain about the goat? I don't see how that fits in with what we saw in Rimrose Park.'

Tweedy gave an understanding smile then moved another of his books under the desk light.

'There are many "cults", as we call them, using various symbols for their own purposes. The pentacle has been used to portray both good and evil, the upturned variety most commonly associated with the occult. I didn't mean to suggest that a goat has anything specifically to do with our case, but there is a high degree of symbolism occurring in the crime scene. Look at this, for example.' He indicated a painting that sparked another shiver coursing through her.

'This is the Hindu goddess Kali. There is a similarity between this depiction and one of the so-called Dark Goddess Baphomet. She is presented as a mature woman carrying a severed head.'

CHAPTER 9

'I find it hard to believe that this sort of thing could be going on in Liverpool.'

'You need to believe it, Tara,' said Harold. 'Our city is no different from anywhere else in this world when it comes to murder.'

'But, sir, are you suggesting that our murderer is into devil worship?'

'Tara, devil worship, satanic cults, they are really just terms of ignorance that we use to pigeonhole certain groups of people. Our perception is of witches dancing around a fire, casting spells and calling upon a devil with horns and a trident. It's not necessarily like that. The word "Satan" simply means, from the Hebrew, "opposer" or "he who questions". It's more like an atheistic position. It doesn't mean that all such people worship a deity, but it does result in many, and varied, philosophies and practices. Some take the form of cults, as we call them, where a certain mantra is followed, but others are no more than personal and privately held beliefs. From time to time some practices bubble to the surface and find an outlet in subversive groups. Anarchists, people who try to disrupt normal government, protesters at G8 summits, terrorists, Islamic extremists, neo-Nazis, those who claim to practise magic, sex magic, those who attend sex orgies and even human sacrifice.'

'Do you think our murder is a case of human sacrifice? All these similarities,' said Tara. 'And we don't have a motive?'

'In the case of Alastair Bailey, I believe it comes down to two possible reasons. Either this Church of the Crystal Water took against him because of his Christian background and saw him as a threat, an interloper, or it was a case of human sacrifice.'

'You really think that sort of thing goes on, sacrificing a human being in some devil worship?'

'It does happen, Tara,' said Tweedy. 'Usually such a killing doesn't come to light. The bodies are buried or cremated. The victims are quite often vagrants, homeless people, addicts or people of low value as they have been described in some satanic literature. Most often, of course, it is likely to be the sacrifice merely of a lamb or a goat.'

'There have been murders associated with the occult in recent years. A case last year in Wales was linked to the occurrence of a blue moon, another in Yorkshire where the victim's beating heart was removed and eaten by the killer. There have been several instances of vampirism, individuals believing they can attain immortality by drinking human blood.'

'In both our cases the removal of the head would suggest ritual killing and human sacrifice.'

'Can you deduce anything from the biblical inscriptions left with the victims?' asked Tara, looking at Tweedy and hoping to at least take some comfort from what she had learned.

'Both inscriptions were extracted from the Book of Proverbs, written by King Solomon,' he said. 'One of the main themes in the book is the learning of wisdom. It seems like a hijacking of a biblical text for the use of justifying the teachings of whatever cult has done this. Or it may simply be a mocking of Christianity or indeed Judaism. Many of these groups, especially those with neo-Nazi leanings, would also be anti-Semitic.

'Sorry to have kept you so late, Tara,' said Harold. 'But we have a lot of work on our hands.'

'Yes, sir. Hopefully we can get an ID soon on the latest victim, and it may help in establishing motive.'

'We'll talk some more tomorrow after you have briefed the remainder of the team. Goodnight, Tara, drive carefully.'

'Goodnight, sir.'

Tara got the feeling as she left the Tweedy household that her boss had already connected the two cases. Although they were separated by twenty-five years, she guessed that Tweedy was intending to solve the mystery of both killings, the first of which was somewhat of a personal issue.

On her drive home to her flat at Wapping Dock, as was usual, her mind strayed into the findings of her latest case. She shivered to even consider that ritual killing was involved. The idea of human sacrifice taking place in this day and age and in a city such as Liverpool filled her with a fear that if there was one such killing then there would be more to follow.

CHAPTER 10

I decided just to call her Thai. A name like Carol or Ann wouldn't suit her. You see, I always give the girls I choose a name. It saves me from telling you their true identity. Like I said before, I'm careful, I'm meticulous. I don't want any murders traced back to me. Thai is one of those types that look less Chinese; she may even be of a mixed East-meets-West race, if you know what I mean? Maybe her da was one of those loners, Norman-no-mates types, took himself off to Phuket and got himself a nice wee Thai bride cos he couldn't get a woman the normal way. And young Thai is the product of his investment.

At this stage I know she lives in St Helens and gets the train every morning into Lime Street. She works for an insurance company in Renshaw Street, not far from the station. Some days she goes for lunch with colleagues, at other times she stays put in the office all day. See what I've sussed out already? I'm beginning to get back in the groove. From what I've learned so far, I think it will be easier to lift her in St Helens rather than from the city centre. It'll take a bit more reconnaissance.

Tonight, I'm going to an auction down by Ellesmere Port. I might get me a nice wee van that I can kit out for the lovely Thai. Then I have to get *Mother Freedom* back in the water, although this is really the wrong time of year. I will probably have to move her from Penrhyn in case it attracts some nosey parkers. And, of course, I have to find my old mate, Janek. My supplier. I'm sure he's forgotten all about me after such a long time with me not bringing him any business. I don't have his number, so I will just have to keep a look out for him in the street or keep tabs for coded messages in the papers or online. That won't be easy, but I can't do my women without his gear. It was the best stuff around Liverpool.

In the meantime, I will finalise all my plans for taking wee Thai, and in my spare time I'll continue to check up on Tara. You can be sure I won't be telling my new friend, Collywell, what I'm up to.

CHAPTER 11

'Morning, ma'am, we have an ID for the victim.'

Murray had reached her desk before she had and certainly before she had the chance to remove her coat. He looked his cheery self, always on the verge, it seemed, of throwing in a witty quip where usually it was not welcome.

'Good,' she replied, as brightly as she could manage with less sleep than normal after a night pondering a gruesome killing. 'Let's hear it.' She sat at her desk, switched on her computer and leaned back in her chair to look up at her DS. He had resumed his eating of a Mars bar.

'The name we have is Derek Greasby, aged fifty-eight, originally from Widnes.'

'How did you come by the name?'

'This is the good bit, he's on the national computer. He served three years for sexual assault and a further ten for the rape of a fourteen-year-old girl.'

'Had he been reported as missing?'

Murray shook his head, all he could manage at that point, his mouth full of the chocolate bar. Tara had a file containing photos from the crime scenes open in front of her. The body had been slight, no excess fat, his ribcage quite prominent in the stretched position on the wooden frame. The picture of the head told her little of what kind of man Derek Greasby had been. He had a thin face and longish greying hair. It resembled as much a death mask as it did a human head.

'Do we have an address in Widnes?'

'Yes, ma'am.'

'Let's get over there.'

From experience, she realised the address they were headed to and the one listed on the police national computer may not have been the victim's last abode. The chances were it was an address of convenience, provided to the court when Greasby was released on probation, or even the one given prior to his last trial. When the elderly woman answered the front door of the mid-terraced house in Foster Street, Tara had her assumption confirmed.

'I haven't seen or heard from him in nearly two years,' said the woman, who was slightly built, with wiry grey hair and a pinched face. 'What's he done this time?'

'May we come inside, Mrs Greasby?' said Tara.

Without a word the woman, dressed in a pink cardigan and navy trousers, turned to her left and stepped from her tiny hallway into her sitting room. Tara and Murray followed her indoors. The house reeked of cigarettes and fried food, with not a window open to allow some fresh air. Tara tried not to show her discomfort, but Murray wasn't quite so discreet.

'What a pong,' he whispered.

The woman sat herself down in a crumpled armchair and indicated a two-seater sofa with wooden armrests for Tara and Murray.

'You don't look old enough to be a detective, love. Or am I just getting older? Seventy-four last birthday. I was only sixteen when I had our Derek. Not my finest hour with me not married. His dad got back on the ships as soon as he found out I was in the family way. Caused a bit of a rumpus in those days. So, what has he done that you're looking for him?'

'We're not looking for him, Mrs Greasby. I'm afraid Derek is dead. We found his body yesterday morning. He's been murdered, Mrs Greasby. I'm very sorry.'

The woman was silent for a moment, staring directly at Tara as if struggling to absorb the news.

'Can I get you some tea, love? You look worn out.'

'No thanks, we just want to ask you some questions. We won't take up much of your time.'

'What about your friend?'

'No thanks, love,' replied Murray.

'What happened to him?'

'We found his body in the woods at Rimrose Park in Liverpool.'

'Was that the story that's been on the news?'

'I'm afraid it is.'

'The head found on railings?'

'I'm very sorry, Mrs Greasby.'

'Don't be sorry, love. My Derek was always going to meet a bad end. Spent his whole life up to no good, and that sort of living catches up with you.'

'Do you know where Derek was living?'

'Can't say for sure. Somewhere in Liverpool.' She rose from her chair and went to a letter rack sitting on a cabinet with glass doors beside the fireplace, where an old electric heater burned a single element. The wooden letter rack, 'A Gift from Skegness' emblazoned on the front panel, exhumed all of its contents as the woman searched for an address. 'This is the last note I had of where he lived. He told me he had a girlfriend after he came out of prison. Said he was nice and settled. I didn't believe a word. No woman in her right mind would ever have taken him.' She handed a folded scrap of paper to Tara.

'Thank you, Mrs Greasby. Is there anyone we can call to come and be with you?'

'Oh, don't worry, love. My friend, Winnie, lives next door. We'll be going to bingo later.'

'If there's anything you can think of that might help us catch whoever killed your son, Mrs Greasby, please let us know.' Tara handed her a card.

'Oh, there won't be, love. And you don't have to call me Mrs Greasby. I never did get married.'

* * *

Murray drove them to the address in Toxteth, a narrow dead-end street of red-brick terraced houses with ground-floor bay windows.

'Doesn't look to be anyone at home,' said Murray, peering through the sitting room window. They checked the houses on either side, Tara taking the right and Murray the left. A youth who answered the door to Murray confirmed that a bloke lived next door, but he hadn't seen him for ages. An elderly man with a walking frame told Tara the house had been quiet for weeks. Tara got Murray to force the lock on the glass-panelled door of the house. Once open, they stepped through a pile of mail scattered over the floor. The house had front and rear sitting rooms. Murray headed for the back, while Tara wandered into the front. The place felt cold and had an odour of damp and stale air. The walls of the room were painted cream but had no pictures hanging. A tattered suite of furniture, from as far back as the seventies, a sofa and two armchairs, was all that occupied the room. It didn't appear to have been lived in. Tara joined Murray in the back room which led onto a small kitchen. Purple walls this time that did little to improve the light which came from a single window that looked onto an enclosed yard. A single armchair and a table and three chairs sat upon the linoleum floor, a few newspapers and magazines were scattered over the table. In the corner by the window sat a small, flat-screen TV.

'A bit spartan, to say the least.'

'Not much in the kitchen either,' said Murray. 'Usual stuff in the cupboards, tea, tinned soup, corned beef. Fridge has milk, eggs and cheese.'

'Upstairs then.'

There were two bedrooms, only one of which contained a bed. It was covered with a black flower-pattern duvet, and a flimsy hanger stand served as the wardrobe. Tara was surprised to see both male and female clothes hanging: a pair of men's trousers, a pair of jeans, a couple of plain shirts, three flowery dresses and a black skirt. On the floor were a pair of brown brogue shoes and a pair of ladies' heels in black suede.

'Nothing much to learn here about Derek,' said Murray as he stooped to peer under the bed.

'Unless he enjoyed women's clothes.'

'Hold on, we might have something now.' Murray slid a plastic storage box from under the bed. He got down on his knees on the carpet and flipped open the lid. When Tara saw what had been uncovered, she joined Murray on the floor.

'Looks like Derek was up to his old tricks,' said Tara.

CHAPTER 12

I traced Janek without a problem. He was still doing business through a convoluted ad on a website that only his customers would recognise. Then I made two phone calls. One to a staging post where I got a note of the second number which got me straight through to the man himself. Janek is Estonian, and he gets his hands on a lot of China White from contacts in his home country. That wee drug seems quite popular in those parts. It's always been my drug of choice for dispensing with my girls.

We met up in the city centre, just as he likes to do. Janek prefers a busy spot, plenty of people around, rushing about, minding their own business. He hadn't changed a bit. He had the same greasy hair, thin unshaven face and the boggin' leather jacket. He obviously doesn't spend his profits on looking dapper.

'Mr Guy,' he said. 'You been on holiday?'

'You could say that, Janek, mate.'

'I thought I'd lost a good customer.'

'No, mate, had some shit to deal with. Just getting back in the swing of things.'

He nodded at that, and I realised he probably didn't get the turn of phrase.

I didn't have that much dosh to spend, but I had enough to buy some China White sufficient to see off my wee Thai. The rest of my money went at the auction in Ellesmere Port where I managed to get an old beat-up Ford Transit. I'm praying it holds together long enough and doesn't fall to bits when I'm doing the business with the girl. As I'm used to doing, I parked it well away from my flat in Wavertree. Don't want any smart arses linking me to the van.

My supervisor asked me how I'd spent my weekend. Couldn't tell him the truth, could I? Told him I was trying to get fit by doing a lot of walking. Wasn't exactly a lie, I suppose. I was walking some of the time. Watching what Thai gets up to on her days off. Plays badminton, dear love her. She walked to a sports centre not far from her house, early on Saturday morning. Didn't reappear until late afternoon around four. She went home and didn't come out again. On the Sunday a young lad stopped his customised Seat, metallic blue, dropped suspension and twin exhausts, outside her house and a few minutes later she stepped out in jeans, boots, a heavy overcoat and with a big smile for her boy. I didn't have to follow them for long. Soon realised they were going to a rugby league match at Langtree Park. After the game, when they returned to the car, I followed them to a Burger King, and afterwards they went to a cinema. Talk about trying to squeeze it all into one day. Finally, to cap it all, the lucky wee bastard gets his hole when they parked in a lay-by out by Knowsley. Steamy windows, the heap. It was just coming up to midnight when he dropped her off at home. Such a lovely romantic day for some. I reckoned now that I had to base my snatch on a weekday, probably taking her on her way home from work. Hopefully, I can manage it before the boy racer gets his leg over again.

CHAPTER 13

Maurice Young lived alone these days. He never thought it would ever happen to him. He'd always had something on the go, a woman to share his bed, a mate staying over until he got sorted, a few of the lads to meet in the pub or at the match. Even when he'd been inside, he had company. There was banter, joking and conversation. He hoped his solitude wouldn't last – that he would walk into his local one day and the next woman of his dreams would be waiting for him. But he realised that the older he became the less chance he had of landing a good one. He'd have to lower his standards, be less choosy. And the older he got the more he had to make the effort to raise himself from his seat in front of the telly and go out into the city among people.

His home was a dreary flat, three floors up, a living room, a bedroom, kitchen and bathroom. That's all he had. No job, not that he cared. He hadn't worked much anyway over the years. He didn't have much money either but enough for a few beers and the odd takeaway meal. His days seemed to drag and his nights even more so. Not much to do, nowhere to go. But last time he was inside, he had learned how to use a computer. Now that was his lifeblood, his gateway to the world. He could get anything he wanted online. He'd bought drugs, not the hard stuff, but weed and some blow. He could watch porn when he was bored, and he could gather all kinds of useless information. Rock music and movies remained his interests from his teenage years. Led Zeppelin, Black

Sabbath and Pink Floyd. Clint Eastwood and Christopher Lee. He'd love to get back to the old days, to a time when there seemed to be no rules. When he got together with friends, they took over a squat, an old farmhouse or simply camped in the woods. And they would drink and sing, play music, smoke weed and fuck their brains out. Now all his mates had moved on. Some had settled down into plain, ordinary lives, some were dead from fast living, drink and drugs, and some were inside, serving much longer sentences than he ever had to endure.

But tonight, he had hope. Thanks to his computer, provided by social services to help him make his way when he returned to society, he had made some new friends. His kind of people. People who liked to enjoy themselves. People with a passion for wild things. And best of all, they had found him. Thank God for social media. Not your Facebook or Instagram. It was the dark web for him, and soon he'd made the kind of contacts he'd longed for.

Tonight, he was going to meet them for the first time. He'd received a party invitation by post. On the face of it a nice evening meeting new people in a relaxed setting. But he knew it would be more than that. He would be invited to join their group, to get involved in their activities, and then he would be back living the dream.

Another night chilled by a descending frost, but he'd wrapped up warm in his anorak, scarf and bobble hat. He paced slowly by the corner of the road waiting for the car to arrive. Just like he'd imagined, they wouldn't disclose the location of the party. He might even be blindfolded for the journey. But once he was inside, a member, and he had gained their trust, he could learn their secrets. It was all part of the fun, the excitement.

After waiting ten minutes by the roadside a dark car, quite large, a Mercedes, drew up and a woman got out of the back. A man was at the wheel.

'Maurice?' she said. She had blonde hair, swept back in a ponytail, rosy cheeks and a prominent nose. Wearing a short black dress, leather jacket and black ankle boots, she was just as he'd hoped.

'That's me,' he replied.

'Great to meet you at last,' she said. On her heels she was taller than he was, but she threw her arms around him, kissing him on both cheeks, her red lipstick leaving its mark. 'Are you ready for this?'

'Can't wait.'

'Good, let's go.'

He climbed into the back seat, and the woman followed, taking his hand in hers as the car roared away.

Maurice Young was fifty-seven, and of mixed race. He wouldn't see fifty-eight.

CHAPTER 14

'Morning, ma'am. We have the contents of Greasby's house ready to look at.'

'Thanks, Alan,' she replied, following him to a side room where dozens of photographs, taken from the storage box found under Greasby's bed, had been laid out on a desk.

'All young, pretty women, ma'am. Some are pornographic and others look as though he'd taken them himself. Voyeuristic, I'd say.'

Tara scanned the array of photographs, printouts and magazine articles, all showing young women, mostly teenagers she reckoned. Her mind returned to the vision of the pictures they'd found on the bedroom wall of murdered journalist, Terry Lawler, eighteen months ago. All of them were women who had disappeared without trace, and she had initially believed that Lawler was responsible. She soon discovered, however, that Lawler's sister was among the missing, and he had been searching for her. Tara wondered if they had now found the man responsible. Did any of the women in this collection match any of those found in Lawler's flat? But how many men, loners, sex offenders, kept pictures such as these? Quite a few, she imagined. It was still worth checking.

'John,' she called. DC John Wilson came to the door of the room. His huge frame, number two haircut, chubby face and narrow eyes belied his gentle manner.

'Yes, ma'am.'

'I want you to go through these photographs, see if any match those taken from Terry Lawler's flat. Also, if you can, I want you to gather some info on satanic groups on Merseyside.'

She met a surprised look on Murray's face.

'Have to start somewhere. We need to establish a motive beyond the theory of human sacrifice.'

'Human sacrifice?' Now Wilson had alarm written on his face as he wandered back to his desk.

Tara invited Murray for coffee at the station canteen and explained to him the information she'd learned from Harold Tweedy two nights ago.

'It's one line of inquiry, Alan. Such a strange killing, the head placed on a spike, this pentacle thing and the biblical inscription. It's either a ritual killing of some kind or else the killer wants us to believe it is.'

'Doesn't explain why Greasby specifically.'

'Historic cases of sacrifice have usually involved someone of dubious character, say a vagrant, a homeless person or an ex-con. Greasby fits into that mould, being a convicted sex offender.'

'If it isn't a ritual killing, who would want us to think that it was?'

'I've no idea. Perhaps it is connected to Tweedy's friend from years ago.'

Tara and Murray spent the morning looking into the life of Derek Greasby. They had little to work from besides the police files relating to the two cases of sexual assault for which he was jailed, the box of pictures taken from his house, and the forensic evidence gathered from the murder scene.

Murray reviewed the forensic report, while Tara read the file they held on Greasby. His first conviction was for sexually assaulting a nineteen-year-old woman after she had left a nightclub in Liverpool. Greasby was thirty-seven at the time of the attack. It was revealed in court that he had stalked Tina Jeffries for several weeks, following her home from work, calling her, sending her letters and on two occasions, bouquets of flowers. On the evening of the assault, Greasby had approached Tina while she was with a group of friends. She had resisted his advances twice while in the nightclub. But Greasby had waited until she was outside and walking alone towards a taxi rank. He pulled her into a shop doorway and forced himself on her, kissing her several times and putting his hand up her dress. He served fifteen months of a three-year sentence in Altcourse Prison.

His second conviction was for the rape of a fourteen-year-old schoolgirl. Again, it began with him stalking her as she walked to and from school, but this time he managed to befriend her, and he gave her several pieces of jewellery as presents. One afternoon he picked her up from school in his car and drove her to a forest park nearby where they had sexual intercourse. In court the girl claimed that he forced himself on her, but Greasby maintained that it was consensual. Nevertheless, in view of the girl's age, Greasby was found guilty of rape, and in consideration of his previous conviction was sentenced to ten years. He served nearly six. Tara continued to wonder if Greasby could be the man responsible for her collection of files on missing women. The murdered journalist, Terry Lawler, had found something to link all the disappearances, suggesting that one man was responsible. Could Derek Greasby fit the bill? His two convictions were for sexual offences against young women. He'd always denied that he'd forced himself on the fourteen-year-old. A man such as this had probably committed many more offences without being caught. But aside from the court files, there was little other background to the life of Derek Greasby. Since his release from prison on probation, he'd lived alone at the house in Toxteth that Tara and Murray had visited the day before. They'd found his collection of pictures, and they'd found some female clothing, but there was nothing to suggest that he was embarked upon the abduction of women or that he had any involvement with cults or with devil worship. Why then had he been killed in such a strange and brutal manner?

'Find anything interesting?' Tara asked. She had wandered across the operations room to Murray's desk.

'Not much beyond what we saw at the scene. Traces of barbiturates found in his system. His hands and feet had been nailed to the wood using a heavy-duty nail gun. Witney reckons the head was removed using something like a heavy sword or a felling axe. It probably took only a single blow. No prints found on the wooden frame or on the poly-folder that held the inscription. A few footprints and tyre tracks were lifted from Rimrose Park that have not been accounted for. We still have to eliminate the possibility that the footprints belong to the kids who found him.'

'And we have no indication of motive. Unless we're looking at a revenge killing for his previous crimes.'

'It's not impossible. Where do we go from here?'

'Firstly, I think we'll take that line – that it's a revenge killing. We'll look up the victims of Greasby's past convictions. Secondly, we had better look at the files on Tweedy's old case. Maybe we can connect the two.'

CHAPTER 15

Joanne White was now twenty-four and worked as a fitness attendant at a leisure centre near Walton Park. She was a slight woman, similar in build to Tara, with brown eyes, brown hair in a ponytail, and wore a navy polo shirt and shorts. Understandably, Tara thought, she was nervous being confronted by police officers at her workplace. Tara had read the details of her case, how Greasby had groomed her with the promise of money and travel, how he had charmed her to the point where he expected sex. When she had resisted, he'd gone ahead and forced her, raping her twice in his car and once in his house.

Every day since James Guy had abducted and drugged her, Tara shuddered at what else he might have done. She remembered nothing of the incident. How much worse must it be for Joanne White, who had suffered as a young girl at the hands of a rapist and probably remembered every tiny detail of her experience?

'What's happened?' Joanne asked, above the shouts and screams of children enjoying a birthday party in the adventure play area of the leisure centre. When Tara explained about the death of Derek Greasby, the colour drained from the woman's face.

'We were wondering if you had seen him since his release from prison.'

Joanne looked confused by the question and merely continued to stare at Tara as if waiting to be prompted further.

'Had he tried to contact you in the last few years?'

Joanne shook her head, and tears appeared in her eyes.

A tall man in his twenties, wearing a white T-shirt and navy sweatpants approached. He had short hair, the remnants of acne on his cheeks, and tattoos on both arms. He was a man with a well-developed physique. He put his hand on Joanne's shoulder.

'You all right, Jo?' he said, glaring suspiciously at Tara and Murray.

'I'm fine.'

'And who are you?' Murray asked.

'I'm her boyfriend. Who are you?' It was clearly a defensive stand by the young man. Murray wasn't one for diplomacy in such situations.

'Do you have a name?'

Tara intervened. She wasn't there to referee petty gamesmanship.

'I'm Detective Inspector Grogan. We are here to speak with Joanne.'

'It's OK, Martin can stay,' said Joanne, touching her boyfriend's hand, still resting on her shoulder. Murray and Martin continued to glare at each other.

'Can I ask of your whereabouts two nights ago?' said Tara.

'We were at home,' said Joanne.

'Can anyone vouch for that?'

'No. You think we had something to do with him dying? You think I killed him to get my own back?'

'What the hell is this?' said Martin.

'We need to eliminate you from our enquiries, that's all.'

'We were at home, all right? Jo was working here till six, and I was at home. Now why don't you leave her alone?'

Tara handed her card to Joanne.

'Thanks for your time. If you think of anything that might be helpful to us, please give me a call.'

Joanne smiled weakly and Martin, fuming, guided her away.

'That went well,' said Murray on the way to the car.

'Sometimes, Alan, you should know when not to dive in on the offensive.'

'What do you mean?'

'That was a rape victim we were talking to. Show some understanding?'

'But the boyfriend was an arrogant sod.'

'No, he wasn't. He was just being protective of his girlfriend. If you're not going to be helpful just keep your mouth shut.'

* * *

Tina Jeffries, at forty, was a mother of two girls and living in a semi-detached house in a quiet cul-de-sac in Widnes.

'I don't know how I can help you, Inspector Grogan,' she said. 'I haven't set eyes on Greasby since his trial.' Tina was not a tall woman and had evidently put on some weight, Tara thought, recalling a picture of her at nineteen at the time Greasby assaulted her. She had large brown eyes, wide nostrils and long, dark brown hair, well-brushed down her back. Twin girls, about eight years old stood either side of their mother tugging at her grey jumper to gain her attention. 'Not now, Jessica,' she said to the one on her left. 'You and Janine go watch TV while mummy is talking.' The pair stropped off from the hallway to the living room.

'Did Greasby attempt to contact you after his release from prison?' Tara asked.

'If he did, I never heard about it.'

'Derek Greasby has been murdered, Tina.'

'Good riddance to him, that's what I say.'

Tara handed the woman her card.

'If you think of anything that may help us find his killer, please get in touch.'

'If I found his killer, Inspector, I'd shake him by the hand and say well done. Greasby got what he deserved.'

Tara had no words in response to such a comment. Faced with a victim of a sex crime it was difficult to counter the argument. She thanked Tina for her time. The woman remained by her door and watched them drive off.

Tara and Murray stopped for a coffee on the way back to St Anne Street station.

'I suppose,' said Murray, munching on a caramel square, 'Tina Jeffries and Joanne White may not have been Greasby's only victims. He may never have been caught for other offences. If we're looking for a victim out to get revenge, we aren't going to know who they are.'

'Then our main lead is to investigate the devil worship angle.'

'By looking into Tweedy's old case?'

'Yes, let's hope that Wilson has found something to get us started.'

CHAPTER 16

She was hardly the best piece of skirt I ever had but, to be fair, it wasn't entirely her fault. I'd spent a few more days working out her routine, more of what she did when she was at home, figuring out times when her family might expect to see her and when the wonder boy with the fancy wheels was feeling randy and took her out. In the end I decided the best time, as with many of my snatches, was to lift her when she was on her way home from work. It was best also that I met her when she was off the train in St Helens rather than taking her in the centre of Liverpool when she only had to walk from her office to Lime Street station.

Usually, she arrived at the station in St Helens about ten past six; she walked down Shaw Street by the blocks of modern apartments then turned left into Cansfield Street, passing by a funeral parlour. I decided that was my best spot to snatch her. In the dark, with no houses fronting onto the street, there would be few people about at that time.

I parked the van half on the pavement and half on the road. When Thai walked by there would only be a narrow space between the van and a brick wall. The evening was just as I'd hoped, rain and wind. People didn't hang about in this weather. They didn't take the time to notice a van parked in a street. I sat waiting. Several people passed by, more than I liked to see, but presumably on their way to or from the station. Couldn't help feeling nervous, like I was about to meet a girl for a first date. Tingling in my stomach, sweaty palms. It had been a long time, and even during those boring days in jail I never once considered that I wouldn't be doing this again.

I had no doubt in my mind until she rounded the corner. She was bang on time. For a brief moment, I considered allowing her to walk on by. That I should catch myself on. But just as quickly the thought vanished and the familiar urges stirred. I jumped out of the van so that as she entered the narrow passage between the van and wall, I met her as she emerged. She stopped instantly, startled more than afraid. I didn't give her time to think. No time to scream. I rammed my hand tight under her chin, squeezing the soft tissue of her neck. It was a delicate little neck. She tried to scream, like they all do, but it came out as a gurgle. I marched her backwards, opened the rear door of the van and pushed her inside. Her arms flailed trying to fight me off but, as I've said before, when you control a body by the head, you control all of it.

Still gripping her under the chin, I forced her down onto the mattress, reached for my strip of gaffer tape that I had hanging from the roof, and stuck it over her tiny mouth. I'll give her that, she was a feisty wee thing. I had a few bruises to prove it after she kicked out as I reached for the cable ties to secure her hands and feet. Then came my first problem. She was struggling so much I lifted the wrong syringe from my bag. It was the one containing the lethal dose of China White, the one I was supposed to use after I'd had my way with her. I'd injected nearly half the volume before I realised. I pulled the needle out of her leg and looked into her eyes. She was crying and still trying to put up a fight. I knew I didn't have much time. I may not have given her enough drug to kill her straight away, but she might be too far gone for me to have any fun.

I drove the van quickly to some wasteland outside the town. It was close to a road, but there wasn't much traffic about. Thai wasn't moving when I climbed into the back. Her breathing was very shallow. I didn't want to waste a second. I cut the ties at her hands and feet, stripped her naked and did what I do best. By the time I'd finished with her, I reckoned she was close to death. I gave her the rest of the shot and tidied up. Her clothes and mine went into a big sports holdall, the type with wheels, followed by her wee body. But I was not happy. I'd messed up. Badly. My first time since getting out of prison. I'd been looking forward to it for months and now this. I had a dead woman in my van and no thrill. Already I was edgy. Visions of wee Tara Grogan flashed through my head.

I dressed in my spare clothes so that I wouldn't be contaminated by the girl. Late in the night I drove into Wales, and at first light I made for the harbour at Caernarfon. It was a bloody rough morning when I sailed *Mother Freedom* out from her mooring. The previous week I'd managed to get her into the water at Penrhyn. That took the last of my money and caused a few heads to turn at the sight of some plonker putting his boat into the water during winter. But needs must. I motored her to Caernarfon, where she didn't look so conspicuous among other boats in a more sheltered harbour.

Waves broke over the bow at times, but I had to get far enough out to sea to dump Thai. It was nearly two years since I'd been out so far, and I was sick as a dog. At the first opportunity I toppled the bag, filled with rocks and Thai inside, into the drink and headed to shore. When I reached the harbour and tied up, I lay down in the cabin bunk and went to sleep. It was into the afternoon before I dumped the mattress at a refuge site and then power-hosed the van at a service station. I had to hurry because I didn't want to be late for work. That gobshite chef would not be happy. The whole experience was a bollocks, to say the least. None of my urges had been quenched. Months I'd been looking forward to my next girl, and I'd made a hash of things. I needed another one, and soon.

CHAPTER 17

Maurice woke, freezing cold, stiff, unable to move. Gradually, his eyes focused on a grey sky; dusk or dawn, he couldn't tell. What leaves remained on the trees rustled in the wind, many losing their grip and falling to the ground. He shivered. Suddenly his confusion switched to fear. He couldn't move his hands or his feet. Turning his head to one side and then the other, he saw his wrists fastened to something wooden, a wheel of some kind. He tried to pull free, but the nylon rope seemed to tighten with his effort. His feet, too, were held firmly in place by rope. He was splayed, his bare arms and legs open wide. There was something, tape of some kind, over his mouth, and he drew deep breaths through his nose taking in the smells of the forest – damp fusty odours of moss and dead leaves. His head throbbed; he remembered little from his evening with the girl and the man who had driven the car. Everything was blank. They'd given him a few drinks. Beyond that he remembered nothing.

He tried to call out, to make a noise through his gag. This surpassed weird for him. He realised he'd entered a world where anything goes. Was this his initiation? His pathway? Did he have to prove his worthiness to be one of them? He'd heard stories of guys forced to live in a cave for weeks, naked, alone, in darkness, starved, just to prove themselves worthy of the church. Others had to commit rape, assault or robbery to become a full member of the congregation. And now this. How long would he be like this? How long before somebody came? And was there more to follow?

'Ah, Maurice, you're awake at last,' said the voice of a man. An educated voice; confident. But he couldn't see him. He heard his feet brushing through the deep carpet of leaves. He tried to speak out, to ask for his freedom. His body shook on the frame as he tried to break free. 'Now, now, settle yourself. It won't be long. It'll be over soon.'

In one way the man's words seemed to promise his freedom, in another it signalled a threat. That he was near his end. In panic he tried to wriggle his hands free, and his frustration and fear jumped several degrees. Suddenly the face of the man peered downwards into his, but it was silhouetted against the dim light of the sky.

'You don't remember me, do you, Maurice?'

Maurice looked hard. He didn't know what he was supposed to do, and he couldn't speak. His eyes watered, pleading for mercy.

'And my assistant, you don't recall her either? I realise it's been an awfully long time.'

He glanced at the woman standing over him. She was holding something in her hand, hanging by her side. A machine, a drill of some kind. He thought he detected a caring smile on her lips. A smile like that of a nurse when she is about to stick a needle in your arm or take a blood sample. Mildly sympathetic. Fear and hope was all he had.

She stepped over him, her legs astride his face. He saw her naked beneath her short skirt. She smiled, and his spirit rose.

'Do you like what you see, Maurice? I'm sure you do.'

Then she crouched beside him, and he gazed pleadingly at her. He felt her take a gentle hold of his left hand, caressing it in hers. Smooth warm skin touching his. He tried to take hold. Then it felt like she was pressing his hand to the wood. He heard a click then a thud. He screamed, but little sound escaped through the tape on his mouth. Searing pain engulfed his hand. He steeled himself to look. Maybe his hand was gone. Then he saw the nail and he yelled for release.

'A little something,' said the man, 'to remind you of the pain you inflicted on your victims.'

He saw his hand stained red. Instinctively, he tried to bring it closer to him, but it was held fast and the pain was too great. And now she was crouching to his right. The wooden frame shook with his attempts to break free. There was another click and thud as the steel pierced his palm. Tears poured from his eyes. Her exposed crotch meant little to him now as she stooped over and punched a nail through his right foot. Quickly, she did the same to his left.

The man smiled down on him.

'Not long now, Maurice. Thank you for being so patient.' He seemed to step away, but Maurice didn't want him to go. Then his voice spoke in a low drone. He was reading something aloud. But Maurice wasn't listening, the pains in his hands and feet overwhelming his thoughts. He didn't see the woman as she swung the axe.

CHAPTER 18

She arrived at the station in a sprightly mood. A night in the company of her friends, Aisling and Kate, always lifted her spirits. John Wilson was already busy in the office when she floated in.

'Morning, John. Any news?'

In a flash he was up from his chair, following his DI across the room to hers.

'Morning, ma'am. A list of possible contacts for occult groups around Merseyside.' He set a piece of A4 on her desk as she removed her coat.

'Did you get any matches from the pictures of the women from Greasby's house and those we had from Terry Lawler?'

'I'm afraid not.'

'Worth a try, I suppose.' She felt a little deflated by the news. It had little to do with her present workload, but each day she couldn't help wondering what had happened to all of those missing women that Lawler had been trying to find. 'So, what about these satanic groups? Any names?' She lifted the paper from her desk. 'Two. Is that all you've got?'

'Couldn't find anything else that was current.'

She read the names.

'Elsie Greenwood and Carl Sloan.'

'Yes, ma'am. Elsie Greenwood owns a shop that sells Goth fashion. Sloan is a lecturer at Liverpool University.'

'I suppose we should have a word. Maybe they can provide another dimension to this ritual killing theory.'

She had hoped to see the Church of the Crystal Water mentioned. A contact name, a reference, anything. Sitting down at her PC, she ran the name through HOLMES, the Home Office Large Major Enquiry System, and then Google. She turned up only references to a Christian church on a Greek island and a Crystal Waters bar in the Caribbean. Nothing in the UK.

* * *

When they entered Dead Nice on Bold Street, not far from Liverpool Central station, Tara introduced herself and Murray to a teenage girl dressed in black with immaculate Goth make-up, pale flesh, black eyeliner and black lipstick. Looking startled by the visitors, the assistant quickly fetched the shop owner, Elsie Greenwood, from a room at the back of the shop. She also wore black: baggy T-shirt, leggings and trainers. On first meeting, Tara found it hard to put an age on the woman. She had waist-length, straight and shiny black hair, a bony face and a narrow mouth. She wore little make-up except for eyeliner and shadow around her eyes but had a very pale complexion and sported several piercings, a silver ring above her left eye, one through her lower lip, and a diamond stud through her nose. When she spoke yet another was revealed – a silver bar through her tongue. Looking good for fifty or poor for thirty-five? Tara wasn't sure. An accent akin to Essex didn't help in deciding what to make of the woman. Murray was intrigued by the array of clothing on show, dresses, trousers, skirts and jackets, all Gothic style and invariably black. He'd commented to Tara as they'd approached the shop that he reckoned it was just a fancy-dress store. Tara smiled bemusedly, fairly sure that he was expecting something akin to Ann Summers. She saw the disappointment on his face as he looked around.

'What can I help you with, Inspector?'

Tara felt herself examined by the woman who did seem quite daunting, with dark eyes and a focused stare.

'I was hoping that you could provide me with some information on occult or satanic activities around Liverpool.'

'That's a very wide net you are casting. Can you be more specific?'

'We're investigating the murder of a man who seems to have suffered a ritualistic killing. Our inclination is to believe the killer has some leaning towards occult practices.'

The mouth of the young assistant who had remained, dropped open.

'And you think I have knowledge of such practises?'

'Or that you may know of someone who does.'

'I am a witch, Inspector. I follow the laws of nature, the seasons, the stars. I deny the existence of God, but I don't go around casting spells and cursing people.'

Tara produced a couple of prints from her bag.

'You may find these images shocking, Elsie. What can you tell me about them?' She set the pictures on the counter.

'Wow! You do have a problem, don't you, Inspector?' Elsie examined the picture of the headless body of Derek Greasby nailed to the circular wooden frame. The second picture showed a close-up of the biblical inscription. Tara was drawn to the woman's hands as she held the pictures. There was a ring on every finger and a heavy charm bracelet dangled from her left wrist. 'Well, it's a pentacle,' she said. 'Was it found upside down like this?'

'Yes, and the head of the victim was found a few miles away, placed on a spike.' The woman shook her head.

'I don't know of anyone who is likely to do this kind of thing.'

'Have you ever heard of the Church of the Crystal Water?'

There was a slight hesitation as the woman glanced at Tara. She handed back the photographs.

'No, sorry, can't help you.'

Can't help or won't, Tara thought as they left the shop.

* * *

Dr Carl Sloan, a forty-five-year-old lecturer in ancient history, sat at his desk in a modern faculty building off Abercromby Square. An intense expression on his bearded face, he held one of the two reprinted photographs that Tara had presented to him. Fair-haired, with his beard in need of serious trimming, he was of light build and not quite filling his tan corduroy sports jacket. Tara was taken most by his deep-set blue eyes that seemed to suck information from the page before him. As with Elsie Greenwood, he remarked on the inverted pentacle but instantly recognised the inscription as coming from the Book of Proverbs.

'Definitely a ritual involved here,' he said in a soft voice and an accent reminiscent of the Scottish Borders. 'What the killer means by it, I can't say. If a satanic group of some kind is responsible, they will have their own peculiar reasoning and justifications behind it all.'

'Do you think it was a human sacrifice?' Tara asked. Sloan gazed amusedly, another perhaps surprised that this young-looking woman could be a detective inspector.

'Looks like it. Such things do occur, you know? The bodies, however, are not usually discovered and certainly are not put on public display like this poor soul.'

'Have you heard of the Church of the Crystal Water?'

The man snorted at the question.

'Yes, I have indeed, but good luck to you if you are trying to connect this killing with such a name.'

'Why do you say that?'

'These kinds of groups, even if this one still exists, hold more secrets than the CIA, MI5 and the Vatican combined. You'll be very lucky if you are able to identify a single member. They don't walk around wearing badges, and I very much doubt if they would put a dead body right in front of Merseyside Police.'

'But they are capable of killing people?' Murray asked.

'As I say, the Church of the Crystal Water may no longer exist, and if it does there is no way of telling who is a member. They might just as easily be high ranking officers of the police as bloodthirsty neo-Nazis. You'd be surprised by the names of the famous who participate in occult practices. Why do you ask about this group in particular?'

'It's a name that came up. There was a similar style killing twenty-five years ago allegedly connected to this church,' said Tara.

'And why come to me?'

'Your name also came up in our research.' Sloan fixed a more serious stare upon Tara. He didn't seem to appreciate her reply. 'You have spoken for the *God is Dead* campaign.'

'Yes, I have. But it doesn't make me a devil-worshipper, Inspector. I have a keen interest in ancient rituals associated with Wicca. Perhaps that is how you stumbled upon my name.'

Murray's phone ringing broke the silence and Sloan's deep stare at Tara. He answered the call and in a second reported his news.

'We have to go, ma'am. Another find.'

Tara bid Sloan a hasty goodbye and hurried out with Murray.

When the police had departed, Carl Sloan picked up his phone and dialled a number.

'Hi, it's me,' he said. 'I think we may have a problem.'

CHAPTER 19

It was to the rear gate of Liverpool's Anglican Cathedral on St James Road that Tara and Murray had been summoned. A crowd of bystanders had been ushered out of the way as the place filled with police and forensic team vehicles. On the spiked railings, by the open gate, the head of a brown-skinned male had been impaled, and it sat at a crooked angle, the face with open eyes looking towards the cathedral building. A biting wind funnelled through the narrow roadway where Tara stood beside Murray, leaving them both cold and increasingly perplexed by the events unfolding. They'd taken a closer look at the head of the victim but then stepped away to allow the SOCO team to do their job. Harold Tweedy arrived several minutes later. His expression was strained.

'You know what to do, Tara,' he said. 'As soon as we get an ID for this poor soul we need to search for a connection between both victims and with Alastair Bailey.'

'Yes, sir.'

'Any leads from your interviews this morning?'

'Nothing so far, but I want to look into the backgrounds of all those we've spoken to, especially those with an interest in the occult.'

'Right. We need to move this on quickly. I don't want to see another victim. Any news on the body of this one?'

'Not yet.'

'I'm sure it's only a matter of time. We'll talk later.' Tweedy bounded off to speak with the senior SOCO. Never had Tara witnessed her boss come so close to losing his cool. He seemed agitated, his voice quivering through his questions and orders to her. She began to realise just how personally he was taking things, and she reckoned it had more to do with the murder of Alastair Bailey twenty-five years ago than these two recent cases. Tweedy's past was coming back to haunt him.

At St Anne Street she instructed Wilson to research the backgrounds of Elsie Greenwood and Carl Sloan, their only links so far to devil worship or whatever these sadistic killings were supposed to be. She decided also to run checks on Greasby's victims, Tina Jeffries and Joanne White. They had told her nothing of any consequence, but that didn't mean they had excluded themselves from the inquiry either. DC Bleasdale had received reports from the probation office regarding Greasby. Tara gleaned little from them except that Greasby had no job, no known associates and confirmation that he had been living at the house in Toxteth that she and Murray had already visited. From Tweedy she got addresses for Alastair Bailey's former wife and one for her son. There was also a daughter, but she was living in London.

* * *

Janet Bailey, now Janet Malcroft, having remarried more than twenty years ago, lived in a modern detached house in Grassendale in the south of the city. It was a road of similar sized houses with neatly paved driveways, conservatories and integral garages. A white Audi was parked in the driveway of the Malcroft home.

When Tara introduced herself and Murray to Janet Malcroft, the fifty-five-year-old ash-blonde widened her eyes in shock. Her first words on being confronted by police officers was to think something bad had happened to a member of her family.

'Is Sandra all right?'

'There's nothing wrong, Mrs Malcroft,' said Tara. 'We wondered if you would mind answering a few questions relating to your former husband, Alastair.'

Despite her make-up it was easy to see the colour drain from the woman's thin face. She looked quite a fit and attractive woman, slim, and didn't look her age. Much taller than Tara, she was dressed in a plain brown jumper, beige jeans and brown shoes. Tara and Murray followed her indoors to a front sitting room. The house was tastefully decorated in neutral colours, cream walls and pine-stained woodwork. It was, however, a little cluttered, warm and stuffy, with quite a few peculiar ornaments of porcelain and brass on the mantelpiece and shelves. Books, magazines, open letters and envelopes were scattered about the sofas and coffee table. Tara spotted a couple of books lying on the floor close to where she sat on a brown leather sofa. One paperback had the title *The Kaballah Unveiled* by S L MacGregor Mathers, but it was the hardback lying beside it which really caught Tara's attention. *The Golden Dawn* by Israel Regardie was by no means a familiar title, but the cover illustration of a pentacle was something that until a few days ago held little significance for her. Now it had a chilling relevance to this case. She made a mental note of both titles, but Janet Malcroft had noticed her inspection of the books.

'They belong to my son, Peter.' She'd perched herself on the arm of a chair waiting for Tara to explain the reason for her visit.

'Interesting cover,' Tara replied. 'I realise it's been a very long time, Mrs Malcroft, but I was wondering if you could tell us a little of what you know regarding the death of Alastair?'

'A very long time ago, Inspector. Have you reopened the case?'

Tara explained the background concerning the murder of Derek Greasby and now, it seemed, a second victim, and how they believed that the cases may be linked to the murder of Janet's first husband. She mentioned also how she got the lead from her boss, Harold Tweedy.

'How is Harold?' said Janet. 'I haven't seen him for years. He and Lorraine were very good to us when Alastair died.'

'He's fine, if not a little perturbed by these recent murders having similarities to Alastair's. Can you tell us anything about the group Alastair became involved with?'

'He never told me much, Inspector. Towards the end of our marriage, he became withdrawn, very secretive about things.'

'Did you meet anyone from the church he had joined?'

'Just once. He talked me into going along with him to a gathering. It wasn't really a church of any kind. It was more like a house party. Plenty of drink and cocaine. It was a shock for me to see Alastair enjoying himself in this company. He'd been teetotal before then, and certainly would not have touched drugs. Later that first evening the whole place descended into a sex free-for-all. I left alone. Alastair refused to come with me. I'd seen him take cocaine; he wasn't himself that night. When he did eventually find his way home, I begged him not to go back to those people, to those parties. I pleaded with him to speak to Harold, but he told me that at last he'd discovered his spiritual freedom, and nothing would change that. He continued to attend their gatherings, and a few months later I could take no more. I asked him to leave us. I couldn't live with a man who was intent on behaving that way. He left us a few days later. I never saw him again.' At that point her voice weakened, and she reached for a tissue from a box on the coffee table.

'Can you recall any names from that first evening? Anyone who held an influence over your husband?'

'They used only first names, at least in front of me.'

'Did you know anyone else, or recognise anyone?'

'Didn't know a soul but there were a couple of celebrities there. That actor Dale Hargreaves, who used to be in those period crime dramas on TV.'

'He's dead, isn't he?' said Murray.

'A few years ago, I believe.'

'Anyone else?' asked Tara.

'I can't remember her name but there was a young TV presenter, on Granada, I think. She read the local news occasionally. She appeared on a few of those celebrity cookery programmes and things like that.'

'Do you think you could find out if she's still around?'

The woman nodded agreement.

'I realise how painful this is for you, Mrs Malcroft, but do you believe that Alastair's death was directly related to the group of people at the church he'd joined?'

'Not so sure that any of those people were directly responsible, Inspector. Having said that I realise that those parties were not the only thing that this group got up to. I can only think that he must have upset some of them quite badly for them to do what they did to him. At the time I was terrified that they would come after me and the children.'

'Can you remember where this gathering took place?'

'Not really. It was out of the city in the countryside. The people who took us there insisted on us wearing blindfolds until we were inside the house. It was a rule of the church, and Alistair was keen to abide by it, even when it came to his wife. But it was a large house, quite old with bay windows, and there were several outbuildings as if it had been a farm at one point. When I left that night, I had no idea where I was. I must have walked for miles before I managed to hitch a lift back to Liverpool.'

'Thank you, Janet. I would like to speak with your son. Do you think he would be at home at this time?'

'Peter? Why do you want to speak to him? He doesn't remember what happened to his father. He was only six at the time.'

'Those books, Janet. I was wondering why Peter has an interest in the occult.'

'I've been clearing out, Inspector. He's had the books for years, long before he left home. He will be at work during the day.'

Janet rose from her seat, lifted a pen and notepaper from the mantelpiece and jotted down an address. She handed it to Tara.

'That's where Peter works if you wish to speak with him. I don't really know how he can be of any help to you.'

They thanked Janet Malcroft for her help and headed back to the station. Tara wanted to have a look through the case files on Alastair Bailey's murder to see what leads had been followed up at the time. Had Dale Hargreaves been questioned? Had anyone identified the female TV presenter that Janet had recognised at the party?

CHAPTER 20

It was a hefty set of files. There was plenty of detail from the crime scene, the post-mortem and interviews with family and friends of Alistair Bailey. Despite mention of the Church of the Crystal Water, no one was identified as having been a member of that particular cult. Tara examined the dozen or so photographs of the crime scene. They were similar to that of Derek Greasby's except that he had been stripped naked only to the waist. Alastair Bailey had been completely naked, and his body was badly decomposed by the time it was discovered. It was likely also that Bailey had been murdered at another location from the place where he was found. There was no mention, however, of a large country house or farm.

Among those interviewed, there was a reference to Dale Hargreaves. Detective Sergeant Tweedy had spoken to Hargreaves at the actor's home in Didsbury near Manchester. He had confirmed that he often attended private parties in the Manchester and Cheshire area, but he said that he was not acquainted with Alastair Bailey and did not recall meeting him at any party. No one else had been identified as being present at the party specifically described by Janet Bailey and no location for such a gathering had been found. Tara noted that a brief list of other possible witnesses had been included, but there was no indication that these had ever been followed up. She lifted the sheet of names from the file and strode across the office to the photocopier. With the original and a single copy in hand, she knocked on Tweedy's door. He nodded for her to come in.

'Sir, can you tell me if any of these people were ever interviewed in connection with Alastair Bailey?' She placed the original sheet on the desk. Tweedy glanced down the list of six names.

'There's nothing in the files?'

'Not that I can see, sir.'

'I was a DS back then; I wasn't the senior investigating officer, so I didn't make all the decisions on who should be questioned. But it does seem like an oversight. Unless, of course, it's in another file somewhere.'

'OK, sir, I'll get Wilson to have a look.'

After speaking to Wilson and leaving him the copy of the list, she returned to her desk and sat ruminating on the names before her. Of the six people listed two were well-known celebrities, she supposed. There was nothing to suggest that they had been present at any party reported by Janet Malcroft. So, what had connected them to this case? Of the four unfamiliar names, three were male and one female. But her eyes returned to the famous. Trudy Mitchell, a stalwart of daytime television, a quiz show host, former newsreader and now also a successful author. Angela Sanders, arguably the country's most famous lesbian, was a journalist and campaigner for gay rights.

CHAPTER 21

I left Collywell's office with a bunch of frigging leaflets. Supposed to help me establish a healthy and active lifestyle. Eat healthy for a healthy heart, go to a gym, or at least twenty minutes brisk walking every day to reduce my chances of stroke or heart attack. Reduce sugar and salt in the diet and go easy on alcohol. Then there's stuff about making friends, volunteering with charities, sports clubs, societies and adult education. Not one thing to tell me how to get my leg over. Not a thing on having the best sex ever or even how to meet the girl of my dreams. I binned the heap.

Hats off to Collywell, though, he's a considerate type of guy. Very dedicated to his job.

'Have you any friends, James, any mates you can go to the pub or to the match with?'

'No,' I said.

'Why is that do you think?'

I shrugged, but he continued to wait for an answer. In the end I gave in, plugged the gap, played his game.

'I suppose I've found it difficult making new friends since I moved to Liverpool.' I could hardly tell him I didn't need people getting too close to me. Wouldn't want them to find out what I get up to in my spare time.

'Well,' he said, 'let's see if we can change that.' I thought he was about to suggest that the pair of us should go out for a night. But that's when he gathered up all those bloody leaflets and gave them to me. 'You know, making friends, maybe through a hobby or by taking the first step, perhaps with a colleague at work, can give you a real lift. Many people who are depressed, for instance, are often lonely or at a loss for things to do, things that will bring them into contact with other people. And quite often as you can testify, crimes are committed by those who have no other outlook on life.'

I hadn't expected the sermon from him, but he does seem genuine. Although, striking up a friendship with my current work colleagues is a non-starter. They're all foreigners and they seem to stick together in their wee ethnic groups. Poles with Poles, Liths with Liths and then there's the Asians. Nowadays, Muslims frighten the life out of me.

By the time I reached my flat, I was feeling horny again. It had only been a week since I did wee Thai. I'd already sold on the van in the usual manner. Took it to an auction in Wigan. I made eighty quid over what I paid for it, but I would have to save up for a while before I bought another one, and I needed a car as well. It's hard to keep an eye on my next girl when I have to walk or get a bus everywhere. That said, I spotted a lovely wee thing when I went to the car auction. She is the tomboy type. Likes cars and lads' stuff. When I saw her, she was climbing all over a souped-up Corsa. She was cute though. Short blonde hair, leather biker jacket, tight jeans and high-heeled boots. She was with a bloke who smoked a lot and kept slipping his hand into the back pocket of her jeans, feeling her arse.

In the end, I had no way of following her. She and her fella drove off in a plumber's van. That was the only lead I would have if I wanted to pursue her. I took a note of the company address and telephone number. With my van sold I had to get a bus back to Liverpool, but the vision of the wee rocker kept me amused on the journey.

It is lonely at times, sitting in my flat, only a TV for company. I know it makes sense not to keep pictures and stuff of all my girls, but it would be nice during the lonely times to get them out and have a browse. Good memories, eh? And that gets me to thinking again about wee Tara. Not so great memories, but I will have to work to fix that.

CHAPTER 22

Friday night and the bar was crowded. It wasn't the most salubrious of nightspots, but its location in the city centre amongst other popular venues and its run-down ambience appealed to those who cared less for the décor and more about the drink. A blues band was setting up its gear on a raised dais in a dark corner of the room. This was his kind of place. Plenty of attractive females, dressed for a night on the tiles, the more refined drinking Prosecco, the less so swilling pints of lager with the lads.

She knew he would be here. She'd tracked him a few times already, wandering the streets, feigning interest in shop windows while casting his eye over every female who passed him by. In the evenings he loitered outside office blocks, following women to the bus stop or train station, lingering by nightclubs as groups of young females, the worse for drink, carried their good time into the damp streets. He was a loner, but he needed to be around them. Tonight, he couldn't help watching as a hefty woman in a tight dress rested her boobs on the bar as she tried to attract the attention of a barman. He couldn't help watching another in a slim-fitting red dress as her boyfriend cradled his arms around her, and she swayed to the music with her back to him. He couldn't help watching the group of six young lasses, squeezed around a table in the corner, having a laugh. They were his type, she thought. Late teens, early twenties, short dresses, tight skirts, skinny jeans and big heels.

She watched him play. A pint of Guinness in his hand, leaning on the bar but his body angled so he could see around him, soaking up their laughter, their scent, their heat, looking for that special one. She could be his tonight, his chosen one or, to be accurate, he could be hers. She knew already that he was aware of her. How could he not have noticed? She pulled men in easily. She turned heads. And tonight? Short leather skirt, tanned legs, low-cut top, shiny black heels, her blonde hair loose around her shoulders – if you were male you would notice. Give it a few minutes, and she would need another drink. She would step to the bar, stand beside him, sense his temperature rising, feel his heart pounding. If she was properly on her game, he would turn his body away from the crowd towards her, and she knew if she were to place her hand at his crotch, he would already be hard.

But tonight, the luck was with him. The luck of the Irish. Two women, happy but not drunk, had taken a shine to her man, and he was delighted to oblige with drinks. They stood either side of him. Bookends. Playful hands touching his arms as they flirted. Not the prettiest, not like her, but his luck was in tonight. She would have to wait for another time. She hoped the two women would be all right. Surely, he didn't act that quickly.

She would get her opportunity soon, and she would make him sorry that he'd ever set foot on this earth.

CHAPTER 23

'Good morning, Tara. Did you have a pleasant weekend?' Harold Tweedy asked.

'Mmm, sir. Yes, sir, thank you. It was nice.'

Tweedy, thankfully, didn't linger, but Murray was the instant replacement.

'Morning, ma'am. We've got an ID on the victim.'

'Morning, Alan.'

'We've found a DNA match to the national database. The name is Maurice Young. Fifty-seven. Address in Toxteth. And he has previous.'

'Oh?'

Murray read from a sheet of paper.

'Yes, released last year after serving four years for sexual assault. Prior to that he did three years for attempted rape, two counts of voyeurism, a fine for drug use and he offended as a juvenile, again sexual assault. Back then he was fourteen, the woman was sixty-two.'

'A coloured past then. So now we must draw comparisons with Derek Greasby, find the common denominator. Any word on finding the body?'

'Nothing, but I'm sure it's only a matter of time.'

'So far we have both victims as convicted sex offenders.'

'You reckon we have a vigilante on our hands? Someone dishing out street justice?'

'We may do, but why such bizarre killings? Has Wilson found anything on those women who were mixed up in the Bailey case?'

'Here he is, ma'am.' Wilson had just come into the office, a smile on his face to counteract Murray's frown. Happy Monday for some. While Liverpool had managed only a draw with Tottenham, much to Murray's chagrin, Everton netted two goals away to Newcastle to win two-one. John Wilson beamed at his sergeant.

'All right, fair enough,' said Murray across the office. 'I suppose a win's a win.'

'Not just a win. Everton move above the Reds in the table.'

'Sorry to interrupt you two football pundits, but dare I ask if there's any news concerning my case?'

'Yes, ma'am,' Wilson replied, lifting some papers from his desk and heading for Tara. Murray took the chance to avoid further teasing concerning his football team and retreated to his desk.

'What have you got, John?'

'Well, ma'am, firstly I did a background check on Tina Jeffries.'

'Find anything?'

'Nothing on Tina as such, but her partner, Don Mason, has a bit of history. One conviction for assault and a caution after an altercation with none other than Derek Greasby.'

'Interesting. I would have said it was worth following up, but with a second victim killed in the same manner I'm not so sure. Find out if there is any link between Jeffries or Mason and Maurice Young.'

'Yes, ma'am. I didn't find anything on Joanne White or her boyfriend.'

'What about these women we found in relation to the Alastair Bailey case?'

'Addresses for both in Manchester.' Wilson handed a sheet of A4 to his DI.

'Thanks, John. It's worth having a chat with them.' She called Murray across the office. 'Alan, let's go to Manchester.' Murray, having just shed his suit jacket, had now to put it back on. He lifted a set of car keys and caught up with Tara on the way downstairs.

Wilson had provided the home and business address for Trudy Mitchell, a once familiar sight on daytime television, but who now worked mostly behind the scenes in production. Tara was already hoping that this was the woman Janet Malcroft had seen at the party she had attended with her husband twenty-five years ago.

At Media City in Salford, they checked in at reception and asked to speak with Trudy Mitchell. Thankfully, it seemed, this would not be a problem, for Trudy was not currently working on a programme which was airing at that time. But still it took nearly thirty minutes before Ms Mitchell made an appearance in reception. She was a shapely woman, but smaller than she looked on TV, Tara thought. Murray beamed as he watched her approach in a slim grey dress and stiletto shoes. Her chestnut-brown hair fell around her shoulders, her face, heavy with make-up, did not indicate a woman of forty-five. Tara introduced herself and Murray, and the three of them sat down around a glass coffee table some way out of earshot of the reception desk.

'We're investigating two murders in Liverpool which we believe may carry the suggestion of ritualistic killings.'

Trudy had positioned herself on the leather sofa in a manner akin to her television interviewing style, legs crossed, hands folded on her lap. It made her seem more interested in the conversation than she may actually have been. Her dark eyes twinkled, and her lips were parted slightly in a forced smile.

'How can I help you, Inspector?'

'Both killings hold similarities to a case of murder that occurred twenty-five years ago. A man named Alastair Bailey was killed in a way that suggested some form of satanic ritual.'

So far there was no indication that Trudy Mitchell was familiar with anything Tara told her. She maintained her pose and fixed smile.

'The killers were never found. We came across your name listed in the case file and wondered if you could tell us why that might be?'

'That is a long time ago, and I have no idea why you would have my name.'

'Were you interviewed by police at that time?'

'I'm afraid not. Sorry I can't be of any help, Inspector.' She acted as though she were drawing the meeting to a close, but Tara had more questions.

'Were you acquainted with the victim, Alastair Bailey?'

'I don't recall the name,' she replied, her smile weakening.

'Did you perhaps meet him at a party back then?' Tara removed a photograph of Bailey from her bag and passed it to Mitchell. Immediately, the woman shook her head.

'He is not familiar to me, sorry. I've been to a lot of parties over the years. I can't remember everyone I've met.' She returned the photo to Tara.

'I understand that but at one particular party a number of celebrities may have been present including Dale Hargreaves.'

'I have socialised with a lot of celebrities, Inspector.'

'I realise that, but we're investigating murder, and I'm interested to know why your name came up in our files.'

'Like I said, Inspector. I can't help you.' The woman rose from her seat. 'If there's nothing further, I really should get back to work.'

Suddenly Murray was on his feet, as if he'd forgotten to say something. 'I was reading somewhere that you once went out with Dale Hargreaves?'

The remark clearly wiped the smile from Trudy Mitchell's face. She fixed a much colder stare at Murray.

'You don't want to believe everything you read in the papers, Sergeant, especially *The Sun*.'

'We don't read that paper in Liverpool, not since Hillsborough. But you were close at one time?'

'Yes, I suppose we were close. I was very young back then, Sergeant. We all do things we may come to regret. Now, if you'll excuse me.'

Murray watched her sidle away, her heels clicking on the floor.

'Phwaw, what a woman.'

'Tetchy, don't you think?'

'I wouldn't kick her out of bed, ma'am.'

'I realise you're not choosy, Alan. But that woman has a tale to tell. If it's not about Alastair Bailey, then it certainly has something to do with her relationship with that actor. When we get back to the station you can dig out the press stories on her and Hargreaves.'

CHAPTER 24

Dinsdale Kirkman liked to go for long walks. Not so much in the beauty of open countryside or by the seashore. He enjoyed the city, the ebb and flow of people rushing about taking little notice of others around them. In the quiet of the countryside or in any lonely place a person stood out. You got noticed by the one or two others you passed on a quiet road or on a path along the beach. But in a city street no one cared a damn who you were, what you were doing or where you were going. He liked the anonymity. He liked it because he knew he stood out from others. People with time to notice would always remember seeing him. It wasn't just his size, six feet, broad, rounded shoulders and a wide girth, or his lack of dress sense, some twenty years or more behind the fashion. Not that he cared much at his age.

What really got him noticed was the mark of port wine, a purple blotch that ran from the top of his right ear, down the side of his face, close to his mouth and tapering to a point below his chin. You would remember seeing his mark if you came across him in the street. His classmates at school always had. Beetroot they'd called him, or Splash or Daz Boy: the only stain that Daz could not get out. Funny, but Fat Dinny didn't offend in the same way. The taunts had left him shy and withdrawn. Only his mum and dad seemed to care about him. He grew up without mates, without girlfriends, and when he came to work in the bank his bosses would never allow him to operate the front desk. Better to keep him from the public view, they said. Despite his woes, he had always remained contented. Not happy, but while his parents loved him, he had company in the evenings, he did what they did, went where they went. Protected. His father passed suddenly from a heart attack, and his mother had another three years before breast cancer took her. She was only sixty-two.

He was left the house, a late-Victorian red-brick in half an acre. A big place for him in which to grow old. But with his loneliness a longing re-emerged. A desire to at last find love with the kind of girls he'd admired from afar as a young boy. His parents used to bring him along to their gatherings, as they called them. He was a teenager then and his attendance had continued until he was in his twenties when his father died. He could do whatever he wanted there. Get drunk, certainly. Drugs even. Women, too. Women who took him to their beds. He was a novelty to them. And then there were young girls, some only five or six years old. Not many but he was allowed, encouraged, to touch them. But he liked teenage girls best. Anything was permitted because he was a member of the church. His father was a high priest and his mother the high priestess. But the parties ceased when his father died, and his mother got sick soon afterwards. She wouldn't let him go to the church alone. But when the parties stopped the urges didn't.

Three-thirty, school's out. His favourite time of day. He could wait a few yards away from the gates as they came out. He watched clusters of girls, laughing, giggling and nowadays tapping stuff into their mobiles as they walked. And then there were the alluring loners, walking hurriedly, eager to get home, no smile, just their long hair swinging behind them as their young asses wiggled by. Most days it was enough just to watch them file out. He chose a different school each day. It saved him from getting noticed. If they caught him, they would send him back inside, and that was one place he never wanted to see again. They did things to you in prison. They played with your head. They made you think you were the lowest of the low. They played with your body too. He didn't like

73

that at all. Men aren't supposed to touch men. Not like that. His mother always told him it was a bad thing. He wouldn't survive jail a second time. So, he had to be careful.

Today he lingered opposite the gates to one of the best schools in the city. It was a private college for girls. It had boarders as well as day students and fancy uniforms. The girls here were very appealing. He liked them about fourteen, nearly women he considered. Someday he would choose one. On a day when he couldn't be caught, couldn't be identified. For now, though, he was content to watch them sidle by. Big expensive cars were parked all around him. Well-off parents came to collect their sweet little darlings. The girls hurried out, tossed their bags in the boot and climbed inside. He spotted one such girl. Very sweet. She was tall but he guessed she was no more than thirteen. She had blonde hair and white skin like those that came from Sweden or Norway. Her mother stood by the tailgate of a Range Rover. She wore a business suit, slim legs, big heels and sunglasses. This girl kissed her mother and set her school bag and hockey stick in the boot.

Dinny took it all in. He was already hard, already fondling himself through his trouser pocket. Then a car drew up beside him obscuring his final view of the young girl. Frustrated, he glared at the black Mercedes. There was a man at the wheel, but a woman, an attractive woman, was sitting in the back. She peered out and smiled at him. He felt confused. Who the hell was she looking at? Still, she smiled. Not his type, way too old and now she was getting out of the car. Had she recognised him? Was it the police? Had they found out what he was doing? They'd come to take him back to jail. The driver looked straight ahead. The woman came towards him. She wore a long black coat and black boots. The coat was open revealing a white blouse, a short black skirt and shapely legs.

'Hello, Dinsdale. How are you? It's been a very long time.'

She knew his name. He should run. He wanted to run. She was police. He had to get away. He'd never been brave. His mother had always protected him.

'You really shouldn't be here, isn't that right, Dinsdale? You're not supposed to watch girls anymore. You know it's bad.'

She'd taken him by the arm, and he lost his grip on his penis.

'Who are you? I don't know you. Leave me alone.'

'Now, now, Dinsdale that's no way to speak to a lady. Why don't you come for a drive, eh? Leave the pretty girls alone.' He pulled his arm away, but with her left hand the woman thrust a knife into his fat side. The wound wasn't deep, but Dinsdale cried out.

'Shush now, Dinsdale. Be a brave boy.' To anyone nearby they looked like a couple embracing. She stroked his port wine mark with the back of her gloved hand, while keeping the knife in his side. Blood dripped onto the pavement. 'Now get in the car. There's a good boy. If you behave, I might let you play with me later. Just like old times.'

He wasn't capable of running now. His side was hurting. Reluctantly, he squeezed his bulky frame into the back seat of the car. The woman climbed in beside him, one hand resting on his knee, the other holding the knife close to his side. As the Mercedes whisked him away, he glimpsed the beautiful schoolgirl climbing into the Range Rover.

CHAPTER 25

Murray had managed to get hold of a telephone number for Angela Sanders and then called to arrange an appointment to see her at home. They parked the car in the driveway of a 1930s white-washed house in Worsley. The gardens were well kept in lawn and shrubs, but the house had suffered badly in recent years with ugly extensions to the side and rear.

Angela Sanders, now in her seventies, didn't exactly welcome the police inside her home but she had evidently decided that she wasn't about to answer questions regarding murder on the doorstep. Tara knew her by reputation only and by the rare appearances of Sanders she had seen on television in recent times. The round woman, wearing a loose black tunic and trousers, who sat opposite her in a dull sitting room of the house, was once an outspoken feminist, civil-rights activist, environmentalist, anti-nuclear protester and campaigner for gay rights in Britain. There had been numerous arrests over the years, mostly involving disorderly behaviour connected to protest gatherings. She kept her silver hair clipped short and she had a ruddy, and now wrinkled, face. She wore a single, gold hoop earring in her left ear.

'So, what's all this about?' she asked curtly.

Tara explained their reasons for being there, but she moved on quickly to her first question and that had more to do with the events of twenty-five years ago. On first impressions of this woman, Tara figured that she would tolerate only straight talking.

'Are you aware or have you ever been aware of a group known as the Church of the Crystal Water?'

Angela Sanders didn't even flinch at the question.

'Yes.'

'In what respect?'

'First came across them back in the sixties. They weren't the only ones, of course, plenty of anarchist groups jumped on the bandwagon.'

Tara wasn't quite following.

'Which bandwagon?'

Sanders glared at Tara and then the realisation appeared to sink in that Tara would have difficulty recalling the eighties, never mind the sixties. The woman's Mancunian tones cut through.

'Sorry, love. You look very young to be a police detective.'

'You think so?'

'Keeping your youthful looks anyway. Where was I?'

Murray couldn't help smirking.

'I know, son. I'm getting on a bit now. Yes, 1965, the Aldermaston March with CND.'

'CND?' said Tara.

'Saints preserve us. The Campaign for Nuclear Disarmament.'

'OK,' said Tara, feeling rather ignorant of things this woman found pivotal to her life.

'Yes, we had devil worshippers, Bible thumpers and all sorts tagging along in those days. Probably thought the end of the world was coming.'

'Can you recall any names from that time?'

'John Lennon but that's no help to you.'

'I meant members of the Church of the Crystal Water.'

'I know you did, love. I'm only pulling your leg. I'll put the kettle on.'

'Not for us, Ms Sanders.'

'It's OK, love. I could do with a cuppa.'

Tara was finding the conversation awkward. She looked at Murray. He shrugged with his usual impish grin.

'Nice place,' he said, gazing about the room. Tara looked around. It was quite a large sitting room, with not much light owing to a cherry blossom tree outside and close to the window. All the furniture looked antique, and there were expensive-looking paintings on every wall.

'Not short of a penny or two, I'd say.'

Angela Sanders returned, shuffling her feet in slippers over the carpet.

'They popped up again at Greenham Common during the protest,' said Angela.

'When was that?'

'I was there from 1982 to '84, so about then.'

'Can you recall any of the members of this church from that time?'

The woman shook her head.

'Sorry, love.'

'Did you have any connections to this church around twenty-five years ago?'

'Not much help am I, Inspector?'

Tara was growing weary of the interview and began to wonder if the woman was playing games with her.

'We have your name on a file relating to the murder of this man.' She handed a photograph to Sanders. 'His name was Alastair Bailey. He was supposedly a member of the Church of the Crystal Water. He was killed at that time. Do you recognise him?'

The woman shook her head and puckered her lips.

'Don't recognise him, and I have no idea why the police should have my name associated with him. Wouldn't be the first time they'd tried to stitch me up.' She left the room once more, leaving Tara feeling quite exasperated.

'We're not getting anything here,' said Murray. 'May as well go.'

A minute later Sanders returned holding a mug of coffee.

'One final question, Ms Sanders,' said Tara. 'Did you ever have an association with the actor Dale Hargreaves or with the newsreader Trudy Mitchell?'

Sanders couldn't help glancing from Tara to Murray and back. It was a hesitation that Tara was happy to note.

'Can't say I wouldn't have minded an association with the lovely Trudy, but no, I never met either one.'

Angela Sanders stood by her front door cradling her mug of coffee in both hands as Tara and Murray's car reversed down her drive. When they'd gone, she wasted no time in lifting her mobile and selecting one of her contacts. When the call was answered, she said, 'They've been.' In answer to a question, she then replied, 'Fed them a story about CND.'

CHAPTER 26

I've got two big problems. Firstly, I've just taken a girl from the Liverpool area, so it wouldn't be such a bright idea to take another one from the same place so soon. It would only help the police draw comparisons and have them deciding that some sort of serial killer is on the loose. Like I've said before, I don't see myself as a serial killer. I take no pleasure in putting an end to the lives of such beautiful wee girls. My thrill is in the taking and having my way with them. They have to die because I don't want to be caught. Simple as that.

My second problem is that I'm skint. I don't have the money to buy another van, kit it out, or to buy drugs. Without the gear I can't go traipsing all round the country looking for my next piece of skirt. So, I'm stuck in Liverpool, bored stiff and growing hornier by the minute.

I started going to a bar on my nights off. The Swallow's Tail is an Irish pub. It's in the city centre and there's plenty of life about the place. My probation officer said I should get out more, said it would help me make friends and steer me away from any bad habits. Bless him, he doesn't know the half of my bad habits. But he is right, though. I need to get out of the flat for an hour or two. My job is a load of crap, but it's all I can get for now. Most of my workmates are foreign and most of the girls aren't that great to look at. So, I found this bar that's lively with a heady supply of pretty arses. It means I can keep my hand in, watching for my type, maybe following them for a bit, saving their details for future use, and I can enjoy the odd pint of Guinness.

I had a bit of a find the other night. I was standing at the bar having a look around and I spotted this wee blonde. In fact, I think she saw me first. She was standing at one of those high tables, you know the type where there aren't any seats, just a place to set your drink? I think we pretended not to be looking at each other. She was cute, though. Reminded me of a certain wee cop, goes by the name of Tara Grogan. She was taller, about five-six I'd say, with long, very light blonde hair and dressed all in black: skimpy top, short skirt and leather jacket. At one point I think she smiled at me, and I was thinking that maybe I could get off with her in the normal way, without the need for white vans and fentanyl. Before I could do anything about it, these two women appeared beside me. They were beyond tipsy, a feed of drink in them already. They stood either side of me trying to attract the attention of a barman. I couldn't help myself.

'Evening girls, how's it going?' They weren't that bad looking. The one to my right was quite tall and wore heels. She had dark brown hair, a nice smile, plenty of lipstick and eyeliner. I guessed she was mid-thirties.

'Great,' she replied. 'Need another drink before I sober up.' The other girl to my left was not so tall, a bit wide at the hips, mousey hair and a face well-used to giggling. That was all she did. Fucking giggle and snigger at everything. Maybe it was just the effect of the drink.

'I'm James, what can I get for you?'

'I'm Kirsty,' said the one to my right.

'I'm Mel,' said the wee one. The pair of them laughed.

'I'll have a Jager and Coke,' said Kirsty.

'What about you, Mel?'

'I'll have the same.'

'You're not twins by any chance?' Mel giggled, and her dark eyes sparkled.

'Not even sisters,' said Kirsty, nudging her body closer to mine. 'He's dead cute, isn't he, Mel?' Her mate giggled, and she put her hand on my arm. I reckoned I was in for a fun night. Strange thing is that while I chatted and flirted with this pair and we bought each other drinks, I noticed the wee blonde and I reckon she was still watching me. Either that or she was looking right through me. It felt great to think a wee cracker like that had eyes for me, but it was also unnerving. Usually, I'm the one who does the looking, the following and the stalking. After a while, with Kirsty nattering away, I noticed the blonde leaving alone. Maybe some bloke had stood her up and she'd been staring at me in desperation. Nice to think that a woman is desperate for you.

By the end of the evening, I had a goodnight snog and a grope of Kirsty and Mel. They promised to meet up with me again. Kirsty gave me her phone number and then Mel did the same. I wondered if they did everything together, and my heart skipped a beat at the thought. Then I saw them safely into a taxi. Aren't I the reformed character? As I wandered home on foot, I couldn't help thinking about the wee blonde. Maybe I would see her again. Great place that pub.

CHAPTER 27

With thick and dark curls cascading around her shoulders and playful dark eyes, Aisling was beautiful. She had no trouble in attracting male admirers, but it was a running joke bordering on a long-established intention that she was holding out for a man not only of good looks but with the means to take care of her in the manner she had always dreamed. Kate, of similar slight build to Tara but with dubious tastes in hair colour, was the most pragmatic of the three friends. She'd established an early career in nursing and found her partner before Tara had even felt settled back in Liverpool after her student days at Oxford. But, like Aisling, Kate had an unquenchable desire for fun and laughter, for girlie nights out and girlie nights in, for clothes and shoes, for Chardonnay and nachos and for the latest gossip, be it focused on celebrities or on their personal lives. That's why, this evening, both girls had invited themselves over to Tara's flat to plan their summer holiday. No sooner had the banter ensued on the topic of past trips to Tenerife when Tara's mobile burst to life with its usual rendition of 'Moves like Jagger'. As she lifted it from the coffee table to answer she saw that it was DC John Wilson.

'Sorry to bother you, ma'am, but we've found a body.'

'Where are you?'

'Wavertree Sports Park.'

'I'll get Murray to pick me up. See you in fifteen minutes.'

After calling Murray, she left her friends to enjoy their wine and hurried downstairs. Murray was there in five minutes and wasted no time in rushing them to an entrance of Wavertree Sports Park. The metal gates were open but manned by two uniformed constables. The detectives were directed to the far side of the park where a line of trees and scrub ran alongside a railway embankment. A cluster of police vehicles were assembled on the grass close to the trees. Wilson approached as Tara got out of the car.

'Is it Young?'

'Don't think so, ma'am.' Tara felt the shock surge through her. If it was not Maurice Young, then they had another murder. The grass already felt soaked with dew as she and Murray followed Wilson into the darkness of trees and thick undergrowth. She felt her jeans snag on some thorns and a thin branch of tree caught her in the face as it flicked off Murray walking ahead of her. SOCOs were in the process of erecting lights around the scene. But with the aid of several torches, Tara saw the now familiar horror of a headless corpse nailed to a circular frame and set upside down against a tree. A thick sludge of mud and blood had gathered where the body had bled out. There was no sign of the victim's head. Shivering at the sight before her, she was thankful that Harold Tweedy was not present for this one.

'Definitely not Maurice Young,' said Murray. 'This one is rather pale.'

'A very big man, don't you think? Must have taken some effort to get him out here.'

Murray sighed his agreement.

'More than one person, surely,' he said.

'When the medical officer arrives, we can get an idea of how long the body has been here,' said Tara.

She noticed the sign hanging from the frame between the legs of the victim. Everything the same as at the scene of Derek Greasby's murder. Still, she had no idea what these inscriptions meant.

'He must be at least twenty stone,' said Murray. 'Don't suppose there's any ID on the body.'

'Not if previous experience is anything to go by.'

'What do these people want? What are they trying to say?'

'I really don't know, Alan, but this can't go on. Three murders in four weeks, and so far, all we have is a resemblance to another killing that happened twenty-five years ago.'

'Last time it was a head and now we have a body. Do you really think this is the work of devil worshippers?'

'Tweedy seems to think so,' she replied. 'But saying it is the work of devil worshippers doesn't mean we have a motive.'

'You mean that it could be made to look like a ritual killing, but the victims have been chosen for other reasons?'

'I'm just finding it difficult to believe that human beings can do this to another human being and then justify it by claiming it as a sacrifice to whatever god they supposedly worship.'

They waited by the cars, away from the crime scene, while forensic investigations continued. She spoke with the man who had discovered the body. A man in his seventies, recently widowed, had been out for a walk with his beloved collie.

'What time did you find the body, Mr Kyle?'

He wasn't tall, with wiry grey hair and a wrinkled face. He trembled from shock and cold. His dog paced on its lead, alert to all the surrounding activity.

'Gone ten, love. I'm usually out here every night at that time.'

'Did you notice anyone around, any vehicles driving through the park?'

'No, love. Couple of kids drove in and out again but didn't stop. What the hell is going on? Is that the same as the others that's been on the news? Poor buggers.'

'Thanks for your help, Mr Kyle. We'll be in touch if we have any further questions. Get yourself off home and a hot drink. You must be freezing standing out here.'

'OK, love, thank you.'

She watched the man stroll away across the grass. Her head ached from the cold night air and from the effects of the wine she'd had earlier in the evening. An evening of relaxation, time spent with her friends, laughter and chat all lost now in the midst of cold-blooded murder. Her dallying was interrupted by Wilson who approached from the scene holding a piece of paper within an evidence bag.

'Thought you might want to see this, ma'am. Another inscription, similar to the last one.' He held the bag out and shone his torch on the wording.

'*It is joy to the just to do judgement, but destruction shall be to the workers of iniquity.* Seems like these words hold a threat. An intention to kill again,' said Tara.

CHAPTER 28

I couldn't wait till I got back to The Swallow's Tail. First time there I had a blast with those two fillies, Kirsty and Mel. I didn't mind if I ran into them again. Sometimes, you know, I think maybe I could settle down with the right girl. But I've never really had the chance. Girls that maybe I've been in love with haven't loved me back. I wonder sometimes if there has ever been a girl who has loved me, and I haven't loved her back. I know for sure that no one has ever told me that they love me. Not even my mother. See what I mean? I always come back to thinking that I'm better off doing what I'm doing. Taking the girl of my choice, no strings.

They were good fun those two girls, although you can only take so much of a giggler. Sooner or later, you feel the need to stick something in her gob to shut her up. But the person I was really hoping to see in The Swallow's Tail was the wee blonde who I think had been watching me. I didn't have much dosh for a night out. The kitchen job was minimum wage, I had rent to pay, and I was trying to save up to buy my next van.

There'd been a few reports on the local news about a woman from St Helens going missing. Hard to tell if the peelers have got much info so far. There was no mention of a van or even details of where the girl may have been seen last. I find that strange because I lifted her not far from the station. There was CCTV there, unless it wasn't bloody working. Anyway, I reckon I'm in the clear with

Thai. Just as well. I'd hate to go down for something that was such a disappointment. Maybe these wee oriental pieces aren't so special, although most of the disappointment was my fault, giving her too much China White.

Ever bloody hopeful, I am. This wee blonde might be worth the effort, although I really shouldn't be doing another girl in Liverpool for a while.

Sure as hell, though, the next time I went to The Swallow's Tail she was there. All alone, sitting at the bar, nibbling on crisps and watching football on the TV. I took a deep breath and dandered right up beside her. I noticed her glance sideways at me then return to the football.

'What can I get for you, mate?' the barman asked.

'Pint of Guinness, please,' I said. I tried to see if she reacted to hearing my accent. Some people in England are put right off when they hear a Belfast voice. Some of them are so fucking stupid though, especially down south, think I'm frigging Scottish. But there was no reaction from the wee lady. When the barman set my pint down in front of me, I noticed that her glass was nearly empty.

'Do you want a refill?' I asked. Coolly she passed her glass to the barman who seemed to know what she was drinking. I was hoping it wasn't one of those bloody cocktails. I wouldn't last long with her if I had to keep her fed with drinks all night. But I was relieved when he returned with a half pint of cider.

'Thanks,' she said with a smile before turning back to the TV. What I saw of her face was pleasing enough. She wasn't an absolute stunner. Used to be a saying when I was a kid that some girls were so pretty you could eat their shite. But this one had a bony nose and freckles, although pretty well disguised with make-up. Lovely powder blue eyes and really blonde hair, the natural blonde. I was fairly certain that her carpet would match the curtains, if you know what I mean?

I must admit that nowadays I know sod all about football. I know the teams certainly but haven't a clue about all these foreign names, these rich kids milking it on the backs of fans loyal to their clubs. Too much money paid for no more excitement. Still, I thought I should make an attempt at conversation. Chelsea was playing Man City.

'You a fan?'

Without turning her head, she replied.

'Love Man City.' After a pause she said, 'How about you?'

'Not of those two.'

'The Reds then?'

'I suppose so. Most people are either red or blue in this city.'

'But you're not from here,' she said. All the bloody while she kept her eyes on the TV.

'True. Where do you think I'm from?' I wouldn't have been surprised to hear her say Glasgow, but I should have given her more credit.

'Belfast, or at least somewhere in Northern Ireland.'

'Well done.'

'What are you doing here?'

'Lived here for nearly seven years.'

'No, I mean what are doing in this pub? Are you meeting someone?'

'All alone tonight. What about you?'

She didn't frigging answer me. Man City had just scored a goal, that wee glipe Agüero. When the replay had finished it was as if we'd never been talking. The match was nearly over, with Man City winning two nil. I was happy to wait and maybe get the conversation going once she'd finished with the football, but all of a sudden, she slipped her wee arse off the stool and lifted her bag from the floor. She'd hardly touched her cider.

'Thanks for the drink,' she said.

'No problem. My name is James by the way. Do you fancy a bite to eat?'

'I'm meeting someone.'

'Another time?'

'Maybe.'

'What's your name?'

'Bye,' she sang with a pouty wee smile.

CHAPTER 29

Harold Tweedy had his Bible open in front of him. He read, from the Book of Proverbs, the words corresponding to those found at the latest murder scene.

'Seems to suggest that the perpetrators are embarked on a campaign of some kind,' said Tara. A silence ensued while Tweedy continued to read. Tara felt compelled to say more. 'The first inscription from the Greasby killing: *Therefore shall they eat of the fruit of their own way, and be filled with their own devices.* It has the same connotation. Less likely to suggest a human sacrifice, more of an execution.' Again, Tweedy did not respond but continued to read. Tara looked at Murray, Wilson and Paula Bleasdale. They too looked bewildered by the super's attitude.

'We hope to have an ID on the victim within the next day or so,' said Murray.

'How so?' Tweedy asked.

A response at last, thought Tara.

'Well, sir,' Murray replied. 'Going by the first two victims, both had history and we had DNA matches on the national computer. Seems probable that the latest guy will be the same.'

'So, you're suggesting that someone is embarked on a spree of killing people with a criminal past? Somebody is administering their version of justice?'

'It's possible, sir,' said Murray.

'Mmm.'

It was back to silence and further reading. Finally, Tweedy set his open Bible on the desk and sat back in his chair.

'I don't disagree with your theory, but in order to move things along we still need to consider a few points. Firstly, why this MO? Why are the killers going to all this trouble? Why not a simple shooting or stabbing? Secondly, why do the killings resemble a murder from years ago, one that so very clearly indicated the work of an occultist group? Answers, folks. We need answers to these questions.'

The group of detectives were dismissed to the operations room. Tara could only sigh as she slumped into her chair. Murray blew air through his lips.

'That went well,' he said sarcastically.

'He's feeling the strain, I think. Three murders and another unsolved from his past. I don't think he can separate them. He's convinced they are linked.'

'And we're the ones who have to find the connection. So, what next?'

Bleasdale's approach was timely. She had a piece of paper in her hand that she passed to Tara.

'Ma'am, the last known address for Maurice Young.'

'Thanks, Paula. We'll get over there and take a look around.'

'Also, ma'am, Maurice Young went to the same school as Don Mason, Tina Jeffries' partner. Might be of interest.'

'Worth having a chat with Mr Mason after all.'

They didn't find much in the flat Maurice Young had occupied prior to his death. It was sparsely furnished with the basics, a sofa, armchair and television in the lounge, a single bed and small battered wardrobe in the only bedroom. There were few provisions in the kitchen, a carton of milk and a nearly empty bottle of The Famous Grouse sat by the sink. A box of cornflakes was found in a cupboard. Murray uncovered a pile of mail and personal paperwork stuffed into a kitchen drawer. It was mostly junk mail, a few forms associated with Young's release from prison and his probation, and some letters from the DHSS dealing with his benefit payments. There was nothing to indicate that Young had any relatives or named next of kin. It seemed that he was a loner. At least they had found the mother of Derek Greasby.

Was there anyone who might care to know that Maurice Young was dead? Was there anyone alive who might have loved him and would mourn his passing? Tara was saddened by the thought of someone going through life so alone, without family or friends. She was struck also by the lack of personal effects in the flat. There was little sign that anyone had really lived in the place, they certainly had not left their mark. It seemed to her that a man had lived a less than happy life, had been murdered, and no one cared. The only item they took with them was a small laptop they'd found on the floor beside the armchair.

'You never know,' said Tara. 'We might find all we need in this little box of tricks.'

Murray drove them from the flat in Toxteth to a builder's yard, off Moss Bank Road, in Widnes. A young secretary in the office directed them to an address in the town where Don Mason was currently working. A few minutes later they pulled into a modern development of houses close to King George's Park. A squad of three men were working on a house extension and the construction of a garage. Murray called out Mason's name, and a man replied from the half-completed roof of the new extension.

'What can I do for you?'

Murray introduced Tara and himself to a broad-shouldered man with spiky grey hair. He wore a red T-shirt and blue jeans.

'We'd like to ask you a few questions,' said Murray.

Mason descended a ladder and approached them, wiping his hands on his jeans.

'Questions about what?' he said in a rather irritated manner. He stared at Tara for a second then proceeded to ignore her as he confronted Murray. Tall and muscular, his eyes were steely blue, his face, in need of a shave, showed signs of becoming leathery in texture from working outdoors. Tara noted also that he appeared much older than his partner, Tina Jeffries.

'Derek Greasby for starters.'

'What about him? I heard he was dead, but you're wasting your time if you think I had anything to do with it.'

'You do have a caution for assaulting him?'

'Yeah, I scared him off, that's all. Walked into our local as if he'd done nothing wrong. Didn't want him getting any ideas on bothering our Tina.'

'And was he scared off?' Tara asked.

Mason looked down at her and grinned.

'What do you mean, love?'

'It's Detective Inspector Grogan, and I mean did he try to contact Tina?'

'Not that I know of. Never set eyes on him after that night he came into our pub.'

'And what about Maurice Young?' said Murray.

'Who?'

'Maurice Young. You both went to the same school.'

Mason took time to think before answering.

'Don't know him. Why, what's he done?'

'He is also dead, Mr Mason. Any ideas on when you last saw him?'

'About 1980, if you're saying we were at the same school.' He smiled sardonically at both Tara and Murray.

'There has been a third victim, Mr Mason,' said Tara. 'As yet he has not been identified, but if I find another link to you, I'll be back with more questions. In the meantime, I suggest you think about these men. If there is anything that you believe can help us find the killer, please call me.'

She handed Mason her card. He stood watching, looking bemused, as Tara and Murray drove away.

CHAPTER 30

I got the chance of another job. Collywell arranged it. I'd been telling him that working in a hotel kitchen was getting me down, and the pay was crap. By our next meeting he'd fixed me up with an interview. It's one of those delivery jobs for a supermarket company. You know the type where some lazy sod does all their shopping online and next day the whole lot is carried right into their kitchen? It would mean I'd be out on the road driving again. Might give me the chance to do some looking around, although I can't really do much in Liverpool for a while. My wee Thai girl's disappearance is still in the news, and you know how I don't like connections being made between one of my girls and another. Besides there's been a lot of police activity round Wavertree in the past few days. Seems they found a dead body in the park. Some rumour too that the poor sod had his head cut off. Who the hell would do the likes of that? Bloody sickos.

'I'm very pleased to see that you're keen to get on with things,' said Collywell. 'Many of my cases just lie back and take all the benefits they can get, and the next thing you know is that they've reoffended or taken to drugs or alcohol. I must say I'm really impressed by your efforts to get on with your life, James.'

'A better job with more money will make things a bit easier for me.'

'I'm sure it will. And before you know it you might be out of that flat and onto the property ladder. Then I can use you as a shining example of how to succeed after prison.'

'Thanks very much, Mr Collywell, for all your help.'

'It's what I'm here for, James.'

So, things are looking up on the job front, and at the moment I'm not causing my supervisor to be suspicious of what I get up to in my spare time. And now I have the chance of a wee girl in the normal way. The wee blonde from The Swallow's Tail can keep me busy until I'm flush enough to buy a new van. At the minute the only way I have of seeing her again is to hang around in the pub, just off Matthew Street, and hope that she wiggles in. I really missed a trick by not following her that last time when we got talking. Still don't know much about her. She's a coy wee thing, but I like that. It's another challenge. Come to think of it, her manner is not so different from my favourite wee policewoman. Playing hard to get, aloof, whatever. In the end they're up for it just like all the rest of them. Takes experience to know how to handle them. Either way, by fair means or foul, I'm hoping to get somewhere with this girl. Would be nice to know her name, though.

CHAPTER 31

Peter Bailey had kept his father's surname rather than change to Malcroft when his mother remarried. At thirty-one he lived alone, didn't bother much with women, and worked five days a week as a mechanic at a car dealership in Speke. Six feet two, short blond hair and athletic build, Tara found him quite handsome. He'd taken an early lunch break from the garage to speak with them at a nearby workers' cafe. She looked on bemusedly as he and Murray tucked into sausages, beans and chips, while she made do with a ham and cheese toasted sandwich and a cup of tea.

'Mum said that you wanted to ask me about Dad,' he said, his voice deep, with the rough edges of Scouse worn off his accent. Tara couldn't help indulging in his pleasant features, a wide smile and beautifully clean teeth.

'Do you remember anything of the time when your dad was killed?'

'Not really. I was only six and Sandra, my sister, was just four. I can remember Dad well enough. He used to play with us all the time, joking and laughing, telling us all about Jesus and Jonah and Moses and other stories from the Bible. He and Mum took us out to lots of places. Chester Zoo, Anfield, kids' shows in the theatre. We had a very happy life until he left us.'

'Do you know why he left home?'

'I didn't understand at the time, but when I was older Mum told me that Dad had got involved with some really bad people and they changed him. Mum said that he became angry all the time; he was drinking and taking drugs. She asked him to leave, and he did. I never saw him after that. I was fourteen before she told me that he'd been murdered.'

'When did you learn that he had become involved with the occult?'

'About the time Mum told me he'd been killed.'

'Is that when you developed an interest in such things?'

Peter stopped eating and stared quizzically at Tara. His eyes seemed to examine her, searching perhaps for a motive in her question. To her it was a less attractive expression.

'What do you mean?'

'I saw some of your books when we spoke with your mum. I am curious to know why you read such material, considering your father lost his life after getting involved in devil worship.'

'But that's just it, don't you see? I was a teenager when I heard about Dad and this church he had joined. I wanted to find out things about why he was killed. About what went on in these churches where someone can end up murdered. I wanted answers.'

'And did you find any?'

'Nothing specific about Dad. I discovered all sorts of things about devil worship, satanic rituals, burnings, sacrifices and people driven to suicide. I tried to find names of people who may have known Dad, but I got nowhere. I asked Mum what she knew, but that didn't amount to much. She didn't really want to discuss it. Didn't want to tell me any more than she already had.'

'What about your sister?'

'Sandra?'

'Has she tried to find out what happened?'

'No,' he snapped. 'And I don't want the police to go bothering her with it. She doesn't need that kind of problem. Besides, she lives down south now. I haven't even told her what's been going on lately.'

'What do you mean?'

'About the killings being like Dad's. That's why you're talking to me, isn't it? Do you think the same people that killed Dad are doing these murders?'

'We have no definite link, but there are similarities with your dad's death.'

'I hope you find them, Inspector.' He smiled at her, and a tiny pang of warmth made her cheeks flush.

'What about your stepdad?' Murray asked.

'What about him?'

'Has he ever mentioned what happened to your father?'

'No, not him. Wouldn't be interested.'

'How do you get along with him?'

'He's OK. Looked after us when we were younger. He's good to Mum, although he works away from home now. But she travels with him sometimes.' He shrugged as if to say there was little more to add.

'Thanks for your time, Peter.' She waited by the door of the cafe while Murray went to pay their bill. Peter Bailey rose from the table and came towards her, smiling. It was as if his face usually did little else but smile. Only her questions had provoked a more serious reaction. She was pleased to see the smile restored.

'Inspector Grogan, there was one thing I forgot to mention. When I was looking into Dad's murder I came across a story. Well, half a story really. Around the time Dad was supposed to have been killed there was a rumour that others had also died. They were apparently mixed up in witchcraft. I don't think their bodies were ever found. At least one of them was a woman. When I checked the newspapers of the time there was no mention of it.'

'How did you hear of it then?'

'Mum told me.'

CHAPTER 32

Bored. Bored and fucking skint. It'll be a while before I get a decent wage from this new driving job. I think Collywell pulled a few strings for them to take me on, though. The guy who interviewed me didn't seem impressed by my career history. Dear knows what he would think if he knew of my real career. But Collywell is a real gem. I wonder what his success rate is in keeping offenders from returning to prison. He certainly couldn't do anymore to help me.

I spent the last week, during my time between jobs, looking around for some talent. Something to fire my enthusiasm. Haven't seen the lovely wee blonde I met in The Swallow's Tail for nearly two weeks. She hasn't been back. I'm not altogether comfortable going to the same pub every night on the off chance that I see her. Too many people to notice me hanging around, and then if she does show up, I'll never be able to do anything more with her than the normal boy-girl thing. I can't ever snatch her because too many people will have seen us together.

I'm going to wear out me frigging shoes with all this dandering about. Last couple of nights I've wandered down by Tara's place. Just walked on by, thinking about her up to her oxters in corpses or out on the town with her wee girlie friends. Bloody cold at night down by the river and not many people about except those going to some boy band concert at the Echo. Plenty of women around there, mostly too young for me. Like I said before, I don't do kids. But even in this day and age there are those parents who aren't so keen to let their wee daughters go to concerts on their own. Either that or the mothers actually get a thrill from watching five wee boys on stage singing a load of shite to a hall full of screaming youngsters. Some of them, though, are what we as kids used to call yummy mummies. Such innocent days they were. Thirty-somethings looking to keep themselves young, looking hotter than their daughters. Nowadays I think the term is MILFs. Too fucking right.

Anyway, I was wondering about down there, taking in the sights as these MILFs were going in to see the show when who comes jogging by? My wee Tara. Running her wee heart out. All clad in the best skin-tight pants and top, hair in a ponytail and the earphones in. Could hardly believe what I was seeing. All those hours I spent waiting for her to come and go from her flat and from that bloody cop shop, and I never saw her out running before. It would have made my life a lot easier if I had. I've taken a few joggers in my time. But now at least I have a whole new aspect to Tara Grogan. Makes me want to get sorted with a new van and some drugs and then I can show young Tara what *I* do to keep fit.

CHAPTER 33

Dinsdale Kirkman. Tara recognised the name. The list of names she'd found in the case files for Alastair Bailey. She retrieved her copy from the filing cabinet beside her desk and looked down the list. There were the two so-called celebrities, Trudy Mitchell, and Angela Sanders. Then the four unfamiliar names, three men and one woman. Dinsdale Kirkman's name was second on the list. Now she had a connection between the death of Alastair Bailey, twenty-five years ago, and the most recent murder. DC Wilson stood by her desk, failing to hide his delight on the DNA test results he'd just brought to Tara's attention.

'Another victim with history,' he said. Tara had yet to tell him of her link to the Bailey murder.

'Alan!' she called across the operations room. When Murray had wandered across to her desk, eating a ham and brie croissant, flakes of pastry spattered on his trousers, she handed him the list of names. 'We might be getting somewhere.'

Murray examined the list, already aware of Wilson's results.

'So, the old man was right,' said Murray. 'Although we still haven't figured out the significance of this list. Why were these names relevant to the death of Alastair Bailey? Angela Sanders and the lovely Trudy Mitchell denied any connection to the case.'

'Both could be lying.'

'Why?'

'Trying to protect their reputations, perhaps,' Tara replied.

'John, what have you got so far on this Dinsdale Kirkman?'

'Forty-eight years old, six feet, twenty stone. He has a large port wine stain on the right side of his face.'

'If we ever find his head,' Murray quipped.

'No known next of kin,' Wilson continued. 'Served four years in Liverpool Prison for attempted rape of a twelve-year-old girl. He was released three years ago on licence and remains on the sex offender register. He lived alone.'

'Where?' asked Murray.

Wilson checked his notes.

'Aigburth Drive.'

'That's out by Sefton Park,' said Tara. 'Let's go take a look.'

She had intended to speak again with Janet Malcroft following on from what Peter Bailey had told her the day before. Other people having disappeared around the time that Alastair Bailey was murdered had rankled with her, not only because of the relevance to this case but lately hearing of a woman disappearing set her thinking on the collection of photographs taken from Terry Lawler's flat. Pictures of more than twenty women who had disappeared without a trace. Now she wondered also why Janet Malcroft had not mentioned these other people when they had first spoken with her. But the matter would have to wait until they'd begun their investigation of this latest issue, the murder of another sex offender.

* * *

Murray pulled off the road into the driveway of the red-brick Victorian house on Aigburth Drive. There was quite a garden surrounding the house which was well hidden from the road by trees and shrubs. The expansive lawn had a thick covering of fallen leaves. Tara inspected the three-storey building which appeared to have a basement with a separate entrance. The place seemed as gloomy as she was now feeling, after three recent murders and no real leads.

A biting wind rustled the bushes as she stepped from the car, instantly regretting the choice of skirt, tights, shoes and leather jacket. She would have been warmer in a long coat, boots and trousers. Murray had come prepared with a jemmy to force the lock on the front door. She waited at the bottom of the three steps leading to the porch as he fiddled with the lock. The information they had so far on Dinsdale Kirkman left her with little expectation of what lay inside. If Greasby and Young were anything to go by, then not much. Hearing the splintering of wood, she turned to see Murray finally kick the door open. When she stepped inside behind him, she was surprised by the elegance and cleanliness of the surroundings. She gazed upon a polished parquet floor in the hall with dark oak panelling on the walls, several photographs and vases of artificial flowers on three slender tables. The place smelled of wood polish and despite the house having been unoccupied for at least several days, she guessed, she could not find a speck of dust.

There was a single door to the left of the staircase, while to the right and straight on she noticed three more. Murray had already proceeded along the hallway toward what she assumed to be the kitchen. She left him to it and tried the knob of the door to her left. It was solid, wood-panelled, heavy and creaked as she pushed it open. She felt a slight drop in the air temperature, and the odour of wood polish faded as she entered the square room. It benefited greatly in terms of light by having two windows, one at the front of the house and the other to the right-hand side. Each item of furniture looked to be old, 1950s or 1940s perhaps, but in good condition. Fine wood occasional tables, a tall and heavy bookcase filled with old and some fairly new looking volumes. She ran her eyes across the titles: Shakespeare, Hardy, Trollope, Churchill, Dickens, Encyclopaedia Britannica, Edgar Allan Poe, Brontë,

Austin, all leather-bound editions. There were also more recent works in hardback with glossy covers: Stephen King, Le Carré, Fleming, James Herbert, Dennis Wheatley, Jilly Cooper and James Patterson. She didn't really know what to expect or what to make of the collection. Should there be works on the occult or should the shelves be adorned with pornographic magazines as was the case for the storage box belonging to Derek Greasby? Before leaving the room, she noticed that not even the cushions on the sofa and armchairs were out of place. The black-leaded fireplace was set with coal and logs. The room was comfortable and well maintained despite the chilliness.

She heard Murray whistling as he poked around in the kitchen. It wouldn't surprise her if he was looking for something to eat. Across the hall she opened another solid door to reveal a sitting room equally as charming as the first. It contained similar furniture, had a flowery patterned wallpaper in pinks, greens and cream, but also a large flat-screen television.

She emerged from the room at the same time as Murray appeared from the kitchen.

'Find anything?'

'Nothing much,' she replied. She made it to the last door before him and turned the knob. She pushed open the door to a darkened room, and saw that internal shutters were closed over the windows. When Murray found the light switch, two wall lamps came on. Tara toppled backwards at the vision before her. Murray caught her before she hit the floor.

CHAPTER 34

They stood in the dining room, dimly lit by the two lamps. A long solid table sat in the middle of the room surrounded by six ornate dining chairs. But what had stolen the breath from Tara, and sent her reeling, was the sight of what someone had presented on the table. Several sprays of fresh flowers, now beginning to wilt, were arranged on the centre of the table as if for a formal dinner setting. The centrepiece was an intricately shaped silver tray and placed upon it was a human head.

Murray was already on his phone calling for a full incident team of SOCOs. Her initial shock having subsided, Tara forced herself to look closely at the macabre table setting. She stepped closer to read a small rectangular card that sat on the silver tray in front of the head of a man. She could only assume at this stage it was the head of Dinsdale Kirkman.

'*I will mock you when your fear cometh,*' she read.

'They'll be here in a few minutes,' said Murray.

'We'll wait outside. Best not to contaminate the scene any further.'

She was grateful for the fresh air, despite the cold wind.

'I could easily get back on the fags, right now,' said Murray.

'What the hell is going on, Alan? If what's in there is not Kirkman then we have another victim.'

'It's him all right. I saw the birthmark. The dark red blotch on the right side of the face. Didn't Wilson say that Kirkman had a port wine stain?'

She wasn't thinking straight. Murray was right. It had to be Kirkman. And this time the killer had placed the victim's head in his own home, his dining room. Although they now had a link between the murder of Alastair Bailey and the present spate of murders, she had no idea of what it meant. Kirkman's name had appeared on a list that was in some way associated with the inquiry into Bailey's death, but she didn't know why. She didn't know the significance of the list. Had those people named been considered as suspects or had they been noted as potential victims? Certainly Dinsdale Kirkman, twenty-five years later, had met his end in similar fashion to Alastair Bailey.

Within an hour the house had been cordoned off and designated a crime scene. A team of forensics and SOCOs were moving about inside, going through each room. Tara and Murray remained outside awaiting developments of any interesting finds but also on the arrival of Superintendent Tweedy.

When he stepped from the car, driven by Paula Bleasdale, Tara thought he seemed brighter than she had seen him in a while. Wearing a dark suit, white shirt and college tie, he looked healthier than of late.

'Well, Tara, looks like progress is being made?'

'Sir. It is at least a connection to Alastair Bailey.'

'Yes indeed. I was thinking that we should set up a meeting with Rosemary Black. She was the senior investigating officer on the Alastair Bailey case.'

'Could be very useful, sir.'

'She's retired now, but hopefully she might recall why she had that list of people and perhaps we can get something on this Dinsdale Kirkman.'

They were interrupted by the crime scene manager, a man as tall as Tweedy but at least twenty years younger, with dark hair greying at the temples. His name was Trevor Scott.

'You guys can have a wander through the house now. We're about to enter the basement flat, so if you can stay out of there until I give you the nod.'

'Many thanks, Trevor,' said Tweedy.

Tara firstly directed her boss to the dining room where she had discovered the gruesome scene of the head set upon the table. She and Murray proceeded upstairs, where a couple of forensic officers were still at work lifting prints from doors and the wall panels. This time the pair remained together although Tara hoped that there should be nothing more shocking to be uncovered. Once again, she found the three bedrooms and bathroom on the first landing to be immaculately kept. The beds were made, albeit with dated quilts; there were expensive carpets on the floors and antique dressers and bedside tables in each room. If Dinsdale had been living here, she couldn't tell in which room he had slept. Quite a few photographs were displayed, some of an age where black-and-white photography was the norm. She guessed they were all shots of family and a few probably dated back at least a hundred years, judging by how the women in some of the pictures were dressed.

A narrow staircase led to an upper floor and a small landing with two doors. Again, instinctively, Tara and Murray stayed together. The paintwork and décor were less enchanting, the woodwork and panelling, rather than stained, were painted a dull cream. When Murray pushed open the door to the room at the front of the house they were met by a scene of disorder. Pieces of old furniture, chairs, small tables, curtains, lamps, paintings in heavy frames and books were strewn about the attic room.

'Bit surprising,' said Murray, 'considering how tidy the other rooms are.'

'Leave it for now.' Tara went immediately to the second door and pushed it open. 'Wow!' She remained at the threshold gazing about the bright and airy room. 'Come and see this, Alan.'

Murray followed her inside a room set out as a boy's bedroom. A single divan bed with a *Superman* duvet was set amongst a scene coming down in boyhood wonders. There was a train set laid out on a table to one side of the bed, posters on the walls of Liverpool teams of the 60s, 70s and 80s, one of The Beatles from the film *A Hard Day's Night*, another of Bowie as Aladdin Sane and one of the Sex Pistols. A bookcase held all manner of football annuals, comics and stories of history: Nelson, Captain Cook and Alexander the Great. Surely, Dinsdale, a man of forty-eight, had not continued sleeping here? Then she heard a male voice calling her from the ground floor. It was Tweedy.

When she reached the hall, the superintendent and Scott awaited her.

'Something you need to see, Tara,' said Tweedy. She followed her colleagues outside, and Scott led the way down a short flight of steps to the basement flat. He held the door open for Tara, Tweedy and Murray to enter. Stepping from a hallway, they entered a room that extended all the way to the rear of the house. Every window of the basement was shuttered from the inside. At that moment they had only a single circular fluorescent light on the ceiling to illuminate the entire room. But it was sufficient for her to see what lay within.

CHAPTER 35

Harold Tweedy wasted no time in using the camera on his mobile phone to capture the images adorning the walls of the room. But for these symbols in a shimmering gold, the walls were dark, either of black or a very deep purple. Tara couldn't decide which. Each pattern was about two feet in size, positioned halfway between the floor and the ceiling which also displayed several different patterns.

Tara recognised some of them from what she had already learned from Tweedy. Pentacles, hexagrams, the ankh, she had seen before, but what was their significance and why were they on the walls of this house? She felt uneasy in here. There was a chill and a peculiar silence. Yes, there was the noise of officers moving about in the large room, but their voices seemed muffled as if the sound died in mid-air. She saw Murray disappear through a doorway at the top right-hand corner, and she followed.

'Very cosy,' he said when Tara joined him. It was a smaller room, carpeted and with the walls painted a deep red and emblazoned with more symbols of gold. A huge bed, quite low to the ground, occupied most of the space. It was covered by a leopard print blanket, and several large cushions were propped against the brass bedstead. But what caught Tara's attention was the image on the wall above the bed. Painted in black, silver and gold was the head of a goat within two concentric circles, the eyes of the beast clearly peering down onto the centre of the bed.

'Nice bed,' said Murray.

'Rather you than me.'

She rejoined the others in the main room as Tweedy was taking a photograph of a large rug on the floor. Scott emerged from yet another room, the door of which was well disguised as part of the décor of the walls.

'Small kitchen in there,' he said. 'And a storeroom.'

Tara went alone to inspect the rooms. The kitchen seemed quite normal, a stainless-steel sink unit, an electric cooker and wall cupboards with Formica doors. She found some crockery and a supply of various glasses: for wine, champagne and beer. A further search showed little indication that the kitchen was still in use. There was no food or drink to be found in the cupboards or in the small storeroom off the kitchen which was separated by a sliding door. Instead, she found a collection of books with unfamiliar yet sinister titles: *The Magus* by Francis Barrett, *The Book of Pleasure* by Austin Osman Spare, *The Six and Seventh Books of Moses*, *The Occult Roots of Nazism* by Nicholas Goodrick Clarke, *Magick* by Aleister Crowley, *The*

Book of Lies, also by Crowley and *Agrippa's Occult Philosophy* by Heinrich Cornelius Agrippa. There were at least a dozen more titles set on three shelves above two wooden trunks on the floor. These were painted black and labelled with a solitary symbol she recognised from Tweedy's tutelage as Nero's Cross, a much-used symbol in the 1960s and 1970s to represent peace and the fight for nuclear disarmament. But she had also learned that it was an anti-Christian sign and was referred to as the Rune of Death. She lifted the hinged lid of one trunk by the metal latch to find a collection of bright clothing. Raising one garment in the air, she saw it was a gown made of white satin. She lifted out another in green and purple, and noticed at least two more in black. There was a collection of cloth hoods also in black satin. The second trunk contained a supply of what appeared to be items used for BDSM: harnesses of leather, heavy studded belts, a couple of whips, handcuffs, several leather masks and some plastic bottles of sex lubricants.

She was thankful now for the cool breeze when at last she made it outside. Murray and Wilson were comparing notes, and Tweedy was in conversation with Trevor Scott. Seldom had she seen her boss so animated at a crime scene. He must have taken at least twenty photographs of the basement flat. Suddenly, she felt so alone, so helpless, so at a loss to make sense of what she had just witnessed. A house, which at first seemed a home but for the gory remains of its tenant, and then, in the basement, a den of mystery. A place of witchcraft, devil worship, hedonism, she had no other words to describe it. Right now, she'd give anything to have the job of her friend, Aisling, rather than have to think on this case. She needed joyful thoughts, laughter, an arm around her, telling her all would be fine.

* * *

A meeting took place in Tweedy's office when the detectives arrived back at St Anne Street station.

'The symbol on the floor rug,' said Tweedy, examining the image on his phone, 'I haven't seen that before. Three stars set above a black sun.' Murray retrieved prints of the image from the printer and passed them to Tara and Tweedy.

'Could that circle be connected to the pentacle?' Tara asked.

'I can't say for sure,' said Tweedy. 'It's definitely the symbol of the Black Sun, Renaissance German and nowadays associated with neo-Nazi occultism.'

'And the three stars?'

'Could be Stars of David. It's anyone's guess.'

Tara studied the image. The black sun looked more like a wheel with intricate spokes rather than anything indicative of the celestial body. And what was the significance of the three stars, Stars of David as Tweedy had suggested?

'Well at least we have established a link between these present deaths and the work of occultist groups,' said Tweedy. 'Hopefully, with that list of names that you uncovered, Tara, we will have a connection to the murder of Alastair Bailey.'

CHAPTER 36

First week on my new job, and it's been OK. Glad to see the back of that stinking hotel kitchen and that arse of a head chef. Before I left, I added a cupful of salt to his lobster bisque. Serves the bugger right for being up himself.

It's been tricky getting used to finding addresses around the city, but I just have to pay more attention to my satnav. I didn't realise before I started that apart from driving all over the place, having a look around me for talent, I would also meet quite a few possibilities when I carry groceries into their kitchens. I didn't realise that so many MILFs do their shopping online and have it delivered by people like me. It's opened up a whole new world. Having said that I've never taken a mother before. Always been careful about that. But my need is greater than some snotty kid in a pram or an attention-seeking brat in a strop because Mummy won't buy them a new phone or the latest designer shoes. And delivering groceries gets me into the homes of these women.

It surprises me how MILFs go about their house. Some of them are all dressed up in business suits, busy career women, grudgingly taking a moment to receive their delivery before rushing off to the office. They seem to be frantic, as if they're juggling several things at once. Some of them don't even get off their phones when they let me in, and if I'm lucky I'll get a shout of thanks as I walk out their door. Then you get the ones who really piss me off, checking every detail, tearing strips off me if something's wrong with their order. Most of them are ugly anyway and wouldn't deserve the likes of me showing them a good time. Although that's probably what's wrong with them. They're coiled up like a spring, not getting enough from their hubby. Even on my first week I've met a couple who seem to enjoy the experience of having their groceries carried into their kitchen by a man. Hardly wearing a stitch, some of them, claiming it's very warm in the house and they must turn the heating down or that they've just got up from having a nap. A nice lady gave me a peck on the cheek to say thanks when I helped her to empty one of my trays. I'm telling you, give me a few weeks and I'll have one of them, no worries. And another thing surprises me, the number of people who seem to live alone nowadays.

There are lots of men, bachelors, divorced or merely sad loners. But loads of women too. Could make my job very easy indeed.

A couple of nights ago I'd just left the van back at the store and was coming out of the shop when I ran into someone I knew. It was that blonde bird from the pub, and she looked to be heading into the store. Pity she wasn't on my delivery round, I thought.

'Hi there,' she said. She stopped right in front of me, obviously wanting to chat or else she would have strolled on by.

'Hi. Fancy seeing you here.' I nearly asked her what she was doing here then realised it was a daft question. Anyway, she answered it without my asking.

'Just popping in to get a few things.'

'Is this not a bit out of your way?' I hadn't a baldy notion where she lived, but I thought it might prompt her to tell me.

'Just passing.' How wonderfully evasive. With such tact this girl could be in my line of business.

'Haven't seen you in the pub lately,' I said.

'I've been busy. Lots of work on at the moment. But I'm free on Thursday night if you're going to be there.' She smiled, and her eyes twinkled under the lights of the car park.

'I'll make sure I am.'

She smiled again, and I smiled back.

'Well then I'll look forward to it. Bye,' she said in a singing voice.

I watched her strut into the store, high heels, short skirt and one of them poncho things. Sweet. Couldn't help myself wondering, though, that it was a bit strange to have run into her like that.

CHAPTER 37

It was Harold Tweedy who drove her out of the city to the village of Aughton, about ten miles north. On the way he filled her in on a little of his career history, particularly around the time of Alastair Bailey's murder.

'So, you didn't work full-time for DCI Black?'

'Not at all. In fact, I worked in a different division at the time. I attended the scene of the murder, but the case was allocated to Rosemary. When I heard that it was Alastair who had been killed, I offered my services, in light of my association with him through my church. Rosemary was grateful for my help, but she remained professional, recognising that as a friend of Alastair's I was rather too close to the investigation. That's why I think it's best for us to meet with Rosemary. I don't have an insight to all that went on at the time. I'm just very disappointed that we never tracked down the killer.'

'What is she like?'

'Affable, businesslike and a workaholic best describes her. If I had to criticise her work at the time, I would say she had a tendency to chase after every lead like a raging bull, but then when it didn't appear to be going anywhere, she quickly dropped it and went charging after another. In my opinion, Tara, I think some things were missed. Maybe we can figure out what they were, and it will shed some light on our current predicament.'

He drew up in a road running through the centre of the village outside a stone cottage with a gravel driveway and a small green sports car parked at the side of the house. Dogs began barking at the sounds of their footsteps on the drive. Rosemary Black evidently had been expecting them.

The seventy-year-old woman, slim with fair hair, styled in a tight bob, hugged Tweedy, kissing him on both cheeks.

'Lovely to see you again, Harold,' she said in a loud, cheerful voice. She was dressed in blue jeans, a teal-coloured tunic and brown boots. Tara decided immediately that the woman looked and acted much younger than her age. Stylish and vibrant, she thought of the former detective.

'And you, Rosemary. You're looking well. Retirement obviously agrees with you.'

'Retired from policing, yes, but my days are as hectic as ever. If it's not working in the Oxfam shop, I'm doing something on the parish council, or I'm at church choir practice. When the weather is behaving then it's tennis or golf or a good stroll on the moors.' Rosemary smiled at Tara. Tweedy realised he hadn't introduced them.

'Rosemary, this is my greatly valued colleague DI Tara Grogan. She's taking charge of this case.'

'Very pleased to meet you, Tara. Harold obviously holds you in high regard. I hope I can be of some help this morning.'

'I'm sure you can. Thanks for sparing the time.'

Rosemary led them through a narrow hallway with a stone-tiled floor to a sunroom at the rear of the cottage, bright and cool despite the late autumn sunshine. There was nothing to indicate that the woman shared her home with anyone. Everything was tidy and in its place. When they'd finished here Tara would ask Tweedy if Rosemary was married. The former police detective had tea and coffee at the ready, with buttered scones and chocolate biscuits. They sat down around an old dining table, the surface cup-stained and scratched.

'So, Alastair Bailey, how can I help you? I take it that his murder has some bearing on these present killings?'

Tweedy outlined their findings so far on the murders of Derek Greasby, Maurice Young and Dinsdale Kirkman.

'All three have a similar MO to Bailey. We didn't have a definite connection to the old case until we found that Dinsdale Kirkman's name appeared on a list of names in the Bailey case files. When we searched Kirkman's home we found evidence of a connection to occult practices.'

Tara retrieved a paper from her bag and showed it to Rosemary.

'We were wondering if you could tell us the reason for this list,' said Tara.

The wrinkles on the woman's face became more evident as she read down the list of names.

'My, my,' she said with a chuckle. A silence ensued as she continued to examine the list of names. 'It was a long time ago; I can't believe it's been twenty-five years. Alastair Bailey had been a friend of yours, isn't that correct, Harold?'

'Yes. We were members of the same church until he became involved with a satanic group.'

'Mmm.' Rosemary seemed to be digging into her memory. She remained in thought, still peering at the names. Tara wondered if they would get anywhere at all. At last, the woman spoke, albeit with a question. 'You say this list was in the case files?'

'Yes,' Tara replied. 'Can you recall interviewing any of these people at that time?'

Rosemary Black seemed to glare at her young visitor, and Tara sensed that she may have sounded impatient.

'I don't think you should draw any significance from these names as a collection. It's certainly my handwriting, but if I remember correctly, they weren't all suspects or witnesses at the time. Let's start with the easiest. Lawrence Williams. I don't recall him being relevant to this case, but he was already known to us around that time. I think he was a suspect in a case of attempted murder. You can check back in the files for that. Simeon Jones had some connection to either Bailey or Trudy Mitchell; I can't remember who. Mitchell was investigated because she had an association with that actor Dale Hargreaves. It was well known that he followed some form of satanic religion.'

'Was she questioned at the time?' Tara asked.

'Yes, I think so. Don't ask me what the outcome was. Anyway, it's bound to be in the files. There was definitely something odd in the relationship between her and Hargreaves.'

'What do you mean?'

'It was all over the papers at the time. Apparently, Mitchell moved into the home that Hargreaves still shared with his wife. All three were linked to occult activities at the house. I think the kids had to be taken away by social services.'

Tara thought about her meeting with Trudy Mitchell. She hadn't been forthcoming on her relationship with Hargreaves and, if Rosemary Black was right, then she'd lied about having been interviewed by police at the time of Alastair Bailey's murder.

'Angela Sanders, now there's a case in itself,' said Rosemary. 'She was mixed up in all sorts. Not necessarily illegal, of course. Greenham Common protests, gay rights, legalise cannabis, free the Birmingham Six, the miners' strike, the war in Iraq. Stuck her oar in every issue of the day. Again, though, I don't know why she came to our attention in relation to Bailey. If she was relevant, it should be in the files.'

Tara got the feeling that Black was hinting that she should have done her own research before coming to see her. She was sure, though, that the only time these names had cropped up in the Bailey case files was on the list she'd brought to Rosemary Black. So far, the retired officer had not given a reason for the origin of such a list. But she had compiled it and had separated the celebrities from the unknown. She was willing to guess that Rosemary Black had merely committed some of her own thoughts on the case to paper. Now, having met the woman, Tara didn't think she was likely to admit it.

'OK, now the last two names I certainly recall well. Dinsdale Kirkman, I remember putting him away for sexual assault of a young girl, but that wasn't long before I retired, about twelve years ago. Again, check the files. But Dinsdale had a strange upbringing. He was an only child, was doted on by his mother and tolerated by his father is the best way to describe it. Charles Kirkman was, for a time, our prime suspect for Bailey's murder. We knew he was deeply involved in devil worship. For goodness' sake, he'd published hundreds of pamphlets on the occult. And when the name you gave us, Harold…'

'The Church of the Crystal Water?'

'That's it. When this Crystal Water thing was mentioned to potential suspects or witnesses, Charles Kirkman's name would come up. Of course, we could never find anyone prepared to admit to being a member of this church, and when we questioned Kirkman he flatly denied its existence.'

'Did you search his home at Aigburth Drive?' Tara asked.

Rosemary glared at Tweedy and then Tara.

'Of course, we did. The place was as clean as a whistle.'

'What about the basement flat?' said Tara. 'We have found a lot of material to suggest that some form of satanic ritual was practised there.' Rosemary once again looked coldly at Tara.

'As I said, it was no secret that Kirkman had an interest in the occult. The entire house was clean. There was no evidence of involvement in Bailey's murder. Investigations into Kirkman came to a dead end. In any case, a year or so later he died.' Rosemary took a final glance at the list and handed it back to Tara.

'Why is Dinsdale's name and not his father's on this list?'

Rosemary Black shrugged.

'As I've said earlier, I can't remember why I compiled this list, so I can't tell you why Dinsdale's name is there.'

'And Kelly Pritchard?' Tweedy asked. He'd taken the list from Tara and scanned down the names.

'Again, I can't say exactly why her name is grouped with the others.'

'But you remember her?' said Tweedy.

'Oh yes, absolutely, but it may be that she was separate from the Bailey case entirely.'

'How do you mean separate?' Tara asked.

'Around the same time as Bailey died, Kelly Pritchard disappeared. She was thirty years old. Her parents reported her missing to us. They said she had joined a religious cult and they were worried about her. No one heard from her again. We never found her body.'

'Do you believe she was killed by this cult?' Tara asked.

Rosemary Black shook her head.

'Maybe, but the reason Kelly was never seen again was that at the time she left home she was terminally ill. She only had a few weeks to live.'

CHAPTER 38

I knew it wouldn't take me long to hang my hat on one of these lovely women who do their shopping online. She lives way out by Tarbock Green in a lovely red-brick cottage with a big garden and set back from the road through the village. She is a bit bigger than the women I would usually go for, more of a size ten or twelve than an eight. But I can't resist a cracker like her. I'd guess she is close to forty, a good figure, and looks bloody brilliant in a skirt and blouse. She has dark hair styled around her face, dark eyes, long lashes and a cute wee button nose. So far, I've delivered stuff to her house twice. She's the type that tells you her life story without prompting. Naturally chatty.

I don't think I could stick living with her, she would probably drive me nuts, but then I'm only planning on having her for one night.

So, from two calls at her house, I've seen her kitchen, carried groceries down her hall and caught a peek of a cosy sitting room: low beams, wood-burning stove, lots of bookcases. I gave her the name Vicki. She's divorced, has no children and works in a law firm in Liverpool. Her parents are dead. She likes to holiday in the Caribbean with her sister, loves cooking, goes to the theatre with her girlfriends, drinks wine (mostly French) and doesn't have a man on the go at the moment. When her mouth isn't working, she will listen to the answer you give to her questions. Of course, I didn't tell her an ounce of truth. I'm just a hard-working delivery man who minds his own business.

This driving job is going to be the best job in the world. Vicki doesn't stand a chance. Sure, I've a little more research to do. I just have to choose the time and place and chatty Vicki will be having the time of her life. Hopefully, she will shut up long enough to enjoy it.

CHAPTER 39

She picked up Murray back at the station, but before setting off to see Janet Malcroft she issued Wilson and Bleasdale with another list of tasks. Not wanting to be seen as ineffectual, she thought it best to have another check through the case files for the information that Rosemary Black had suggested would be there. She wanted more on the Kirkmans, more on Sanders and more on Trudy Mitchell and her peculiar relationship with Dale Hargreaves.

She sat once again in the lounge of Janet Malcroft's home, marginally tidier than on her previous visit. Whether it was the effect of colder weather outside with a strong wind blowing but the house felt cooler and less stuffy.

'Mrs Malcroft, Peter told us that at the time Alastair was killed there was talk of others, including a woman, having gone missing.' Tara sat on the sofa, while Murray, remaining on his feet, took the opportunity to browse the living room, examining framed photos and glancing over paperwork that was still in abundance on the coffee table.

'I wish he hadn't told you that, Inspector.'

'Why is that?'

'It was only a rumour, never confirmed.'

'How did you come to hear the rumour?'

Janet Malcroft jumped to her feet and concocted a sudden interest in the mail scattered over the coffee table that Murray had been trying to study. She began tidying, stuffing sheets of paper into envelopes.

'I really can't remember. There was so much going on with Alastair's death, the inquest, the funeral and the press taking an interest. For all I know it might have been the police who mentioned it.'

'The woman who disappeared, was her name Kelly Pritchard?'

'I've just told you; I can't remember.'

It seemed probable to Tara that Janet Malcroft might well have learned about Kelly Pritchard from the police, but why was she so nervous all of a sudden? Her next question to the woman was unlikely to improve matters.

'What do you know of the Kirkman family, particularly Charles Kirkman?'

Malcroft stared, her eyes widening, looking worried now at Tara. Again, she hesitated before resuming her seat and answering the question.

'I've never heard that name before, Inspector.' She glanced at Murray as if she thought she were being closely scrutinised.

'Really? It never came up? The police didn't mention the name at the time of your husband's murder?'

She shook her head.

'I'm afraid not.'

'You don't recall meeting Kirkman on the night Alastair took you along to the party you told us about?'

'I may have done. I am sorry, but I can't remember. Now if you don't mind, I've some shopping to do.'

'One last question,' said Tara. 'The woman you said you remembered from the party, the TV personality, was it Trudy Mitchell?'

Malcroft closed her eyes and shook her head several times. 'I really can't remember any more. This is all too much. Now please leave.'

Tara blew air through her lips when she got back in the car with Murray.

'Do you think I hit a nerve?'

'I don't understand why she became so defensive,' said Murray. 'She was the one who told her son about the people who went missing at the time of Bailey's murder.'

'Maybe she's not too happy about her late husband's case being reopened. It's been twenty-five years and she has moved on. She probably doesn't need the hassle.'

'Where to next?'

'Home, I think. I need to get my feet up for a while.'

'I do a good foot massage, ma'am.'

'Yes, Alan, I'm sure you do but I can manage on my own, thank you.'

'Just saying. The offer's there.'

'Yes, thank you, enough familiarity for one day.' He sat grinning like a man up to mischief with his girlfriend. She was his boss, for goodness' sake. 'Tomorrow we'll have another chat with Trudy Mitchell, find out why she lied to us about being interviewed by police. Hopefully, Wilson will have found something on the Kirkmans and these other mysterious people.'

On the way home she planned her evening: a long shower, a curry from the freezer zapped in the microwave and then catch up on some television, avoiding, of course, any police dramas. Murray dropped her off at the entrance to her complex at Wapping Dock, but as she walked through the gate, she was startled by a car roaring by from behind her. She turned to see a white van making the corner and speeding away. For a second, she wondered about James Guy, the man who'd forced her into his van, drugged her but thankfully was caught before he could rape her. She shivered, and as she did so visions of recent crime scenes flashed by. She shivered again.

CHAPTER 40

Now I know I haven't lost it. Thai was me just having a bad day. Vicki was pure magic and so easy. I took her from her own driveway. Simple. There's no bloody CCTV out in these parts. She lived on a dark country lane, with plenty of space between one house and the next. All I had to do was wait until she was reversing her lovely white BMW 4 Series Convertible out of her drive, and then I blocked her in with my latest white van. I just sat there waiting. Eventually, she climbed out of her car and came towards the van. I jumped out to greet her. She was already asking me to move out of the way when she realised who I was. When she smiled, I shoved my hand under her throat, slid open the door of the van and pushed her inside. Once I got her all comfy, I went to her car, switched off the engine, locked the door and we were off to the seaside.

Honestly, a woman like Vicki only comes along once in a millennium. She was everything I'd hoped she would be. What a fabulous body. Such a shame to have to put it to sleep forever. Maybe I could find a way of keeping a woman like Vicki for longer. If I found a place to keep her hidden, I could revisit the same gorgeous body over and over. When I grew bored with her then I could dump her at sea. It's a bit late for Vicki, though. The thought only occurred to me as I sailed *Mother Freedom* into a berth at Conwy. I wonder though if that's what I should do when I get around to snatching Tara Grogan. I suppose that once a police officer goes missing the whole country would be turned over in searching for her. I might attract too much attention. If Tara were to go missing, I'd be the first one they'd call on since I have history with the wee cop. But there's no way I'm giving up on her. I spent eighteen months in jail because of the wee detective. I owe her big time.

CHAPTER 41

At St Anne Street Murray was at his desk, his head down, reading. Paula Bleasdale beckoned Tara as she walked through the door.

'Morning, ma'am. I've just given DS Murray some info on the Kirkmans. And I found an address for the parents of the girl you mentioned yesterday.'

'Her parents are still living?'

'Seems so, assuming I've got the right people.' She handed her a Post-it with an address in Bootle scribbled on it.

'Thanks, Paula.'

'No problem. DS Murray has something else to show you.'

Tara made her way to Murray's desk. He looked up and smiled as though he'd just picked a winner at Aintree.

'Have a look at this, ma'am,' he said, rising from his seat and indicating that she should read what he had on his screen. 'A couple of stories on the Mitchell-Hargreaves affair. Old newspapers from twenty years ago.'

She took Murray's seat, clicked the mouse, and began to read the story on the screen. It was taken from a daily tabloid and dated nearly twenty-two years ago, approximately three years after the death of Alastair Bailey. The headline read: *Is this the end for Dale and Trudy?*

A photograph below showed a dishevelled looking Hargreaves leaving a London nightclub with an unidentified girl hanging on his arm. There followed a speculative report on the private, or not so private life, of the Shakespearean and television actor Dale Hargreaves. At the time of the story Hargreaves was forty-seven, he'd been married twice, and the second marriage had been in the spotlight because Trudy Mitchell, a pretty twenty-year-old, had been brought into the marital home. Since Hargreaves had children, there was speculation that she may have been employed as a nanny. That seemed unlikely, the report read, since Mitchell already had a blossoming career on television.

The report continued in the same vein, highlighting the occasions when all three, Hargreaves, his wife Amy and Mitchell, stepped out at celebrity functions, and the time when Hargreaves spoke of his interest in the occult and how his beliefs allowed such a *ménage à trois*.

Tara was already bored by the story. Apart from confirming that Hargreaves was involved in devil worship of some kind, there was nothing to be had from the piece. The purpose of the story, however, was to hint that the relationship between Mitchell and Hargreaves was at an end. Tara scrolled on to another report, similar in content, although it suggested that all three people in the relationship were involved with occult practices. A photograph of Trudy Mitchell wearing only bikini briefs with her arms covering her breasts, showed her to be a beautiful young woman. There were several shorter pieces on Mitchell, or on Hargreaves and his wife. Tara scrolled through them searching for something that would link Hargreaves to Alastair Bailey or perhaps to an association with the Kirkmans. She wondered if the name Kirkman lay at the centre of all that had occurred twenty-five years ago.

Eventually, she found a story reporting that Hargreaves had been interviewed by Merseyside police in connection with the murder of Alastair Bailey. He had been questioned, the report said, because Hargreaves and Bailey had been involved, allegedly, with black masses. He was released without charge. She couldn't find anything on whether Trudy Mitchell had been questioned at the time. The final stories of interest were from less than twenty years ago and dealt with the death of Dale Hargreaves. He died of natural causes, a massive heart attack while on the set in Hampshire of a new TV period drama. The mystery came afterwards. No one ever attended a funeral and no one, including his wife, seemed to know, or at least was not prepared to reveal, what had happened to his body.

CHAPTER 42

Vicki's disappearance caused a bit of a stir. It seems she was a well-known and popular woman around Liverpool. She certainly had lots of friends, all of them mystified by her vanishing off the face of the earth. Her ex-husband has been questioned by police, and the papers mentioned that Vicki's marriage had been stormy, both husband and wife having affairs before the final split. I love this kind of thing, suspicion falling on the husband. It draws the police away from the likes of me. No one has come up with any reason why an attractive thirty-eight-year-old woman would simply disappear unless she had been abducted. If the husband doesn't have an alibi for the time when Vicki was supposed to have disappeared, he's fucked. The police have appealed for witnesses to any suspicious activities in and around Vicki's home. In other words, they haven't got a baldy notion what happened to her. At this rate my work will be featured once again on *Crimewatch*. And while they waste taxpayers' money searching for her, Vicki is safe and sound at the bottom of the Irish Sea. I reckon one more girl and I'll be ready for another crack at Tara Grogan.

I went down to The Swallow's Tail for a celebratory pint. My tasty blonde friend said she would be there, but she was a no show. I waited a couple of hours for nothing. This one seems a bit scatty. I really should check her out. I should follow her and get an idea of her routine if she has one. I know nothing about her, and she knows nothing about me. We've hardly spoken and yet she keeps popping up on my radar. I can't help thinking that there is something very strange about her.

CHAPTER 43

Trudy Mitchell appeared less relaxed than she had been on their first meeting. It was surprising, considering that she was seated in her apartment in the Salford Quays, a place she used when working at the studios, a short walk away. Her home nowadays was a cottage in Oxfordshire, where she retreated at every opportunity. This morning she was less well dressed, a pair of blue leggings, a pink vest and long navy cardigan, her feet in a pair of slippers. With less make-up and untidy hair, she looked older. She sat, looking perturbed, on the edge of her sofa as Tara explained the reasons for her second visit.

'I wanted to ask you about your relationship with Dale Hargreaves.'

'And how is that relevant to your inquiry, Inspector?'

'As you told us, there was much information to be found in the press from the time you and Hargreaves were together. It was also reported that Hargreaves admitted having an interest in the occult. I would like to know how far that interest extended and your involvement, please.'

Mitchell looked from Tara to Murray, both seated opposite her on a sofa. It was as if she were considering whether or not to reply at all. But Tara already had a wealth of experience with these kinds of people and their reluctance to assist the police. She was happy to wait. Before she left St Anne Street she'd learned from Paula, who'd been studying the Bailey case files, that Mitchell had indeed been interviewed by police at the time of Bailey's murder but had denied any association with the victim.

'There's very little to tell,' she said at last. 'When I lived with Dale he would go off, sometimes for three or four days. When he came back, he was always cagey about where he'd been. I used to pester him with questions, and eventually, one weekend, he and Amy took me along to one of his gatherings.'

'Where did you go?'

'I really can't remember, but it was out in the countryside. It was late at night and very dark. A farmhouse, perhaps.'

'Can you remember any of the people you met there?' Mitchell shook her head. Tara noticed a pack of cigarettes on the coffee table. The woman looked as though she needed one, but probably didn't smoke indoors.

'Last time we met you told us that you had not been interviewed by the police when they were investigating the death of Alastair Bailey.'

'Did I? You know, Inspector I still can't recall.'

'We now know that you were questioned, and you claimed not to have known the murdered man.'

'Then I suppose that's correct if you say it is.' Mitchell seemed visibly relieved by her own reply. But Tara had a notion that Trudy Mitchell still knew more of those times than she had admitted and, if so, Tara was willing to bet that she would not appreciate her next question.

'Did you meet the Kirkmans at this gathering you spoke of? Dinsdale or Charles?'

Mitchell turned pale, she glanced again from Tara to Murray. Tara, as before, was happy to wait for an answer.

'Yes, I think I remember that name, but I can't say for sure that I ever met either one.'

Murray weighed in with a question.

'Do you know what happened to Dale Hargreaves' remains?'

Trudy Mitchell looked directly at Murray with a forced smile bordering on a sneer. 'Our relationship ended long before Dale's passing.'

'But do you know what happened to his body?'

The smile slipped from her face, replaced by a look of contempt. 'And I've just told you that we were not together at the time he died.'

'What about Amy?' asked Tara. 'Does she know what happened to her husband's remains?'

'She may well have done, Inspector, but she died three years ago.'

Murray had another go at the woman.

'Strange set up you had going back then. You in a relationship with Dale and yet you lived with him and his wife.'

'Bizarre as it may seem, Sergeant, all three of us were happy with the arrangement. Now I think this meeting is over. I'm not prepared to answer any further questions as you seem determined to delve into my private life. I can't see how any of it is relevant to your investigation.' She rose from the sofa, suggesting that Tara and Murray should head to the door.

They stepped into the hallway of the apartment block, but Tara wasn't quite finished with Trudy Mitchell.

'You know, Ms Mitchell, three people have been murdered. The latest victim was Dinsdale Kirkman, and he is in some way linked to whatever occurred twenty-five years ago. I will come back again if I find that you have not been forthcoming with information.'

The woman smiled weakly.

'I'm sure you will, Inspector. Goodbye.'

They waited in the corridor for the lift to ascend.

'Infuriating woman,' said Tara. 'What is she hiding that prevents her helping in a murder investigation?'

'Still, a fine-looking specimen.' Murray pressed the button in the lift for the ground floor.

'Oh, Alan, for goodness' sake, let's leave your fantasies out of it for now. Did you notice when I told her Dinsdale Kirkman had been murdered?'

'No.'

'Her eyes lit up. Just for a second, but she definitely felt something on hearing that news.'

'She and Malcroft are the closest we've got to whatever happened all those years ago. Is Trudy holding back because she was involved in some way along with Hargreaves in Bailey's murder, or is she merely holding back on her private relationship?'

'Whatever, but her motive is in protecting herself – be it staying out of jail or simply preserving her celebrity reputation.'

CHAPTER 44

The Pritchards were now in their eighties. Tara had made an appointment by telephone to see them. She didn't want to shock the couple by turning up unannounced on their doorstep.

Norman Pritchard, not a tall man but agile for his age with thin silver hair and sagging flesh on his face, answered the door. He led them into a back sitting room where Molly Pritchard, a tiny woman with permed silver hair, was seated on a reclining chair in the corner watching television.

'Turn down the sound, Molly. Police are here.'

'Good morning, Mrs Pritchard,' said Tara.

There was little response from the frail woman, who merely smiled at her visitors and mumbled something. Norman seized the remote and muted the sound on the TV.

'Our Molly has Alzheimer's, likes the antiques shows on telly.'

Tara smiled at the woman, and she and Murray were invited to sit. The room was clean and tidy with comfortable furniture and homely décor, a flowery print wallpaper, several family photographs hanging on the walls and three displayed on a mahogany unit. A collection of delicate porcelain figurines was lined along the tiled mantelpiece. A gas fire pumped out heat that Tara already found stifling.

'We wanted to ask you about your late daughter, Kelly, Mr Pritchard. Was she your only child?'

'Goodness no. Three lads and two daughters. Kelly was the second youngest.'

'So, you have plenty of family around you?'

'Yes, except for our Mark. He's a doctor in New Zealand now. Doing ever so well.'

'Would you mind telling us about what happened to Kelly all those years ago?'

Tara noticed Molly stirring on her chair, and again the woman attempted to speak, but there was only a jumble of half-spoken words.

'Must be twenty-five years ago, I think. Kelly was about thirty at the time. No, let me think. Started before then. I think she was about twenty-seven.'

'What started?'

'Got herself involved with a strange bunch of people. Her and her boyfriend at the time. Strange lad. Didn't seem to have a job but never looked short of money either. Anyway, they started going to this church. That's what they called it, but it didn't seem like no church to me. Not like Christian. Might have been Buddhist or some other mumbo jumbo. Broke our Molly's heart. You read stories all the time about young people going to join these weird cults and that's the last you hear of them. Remember that place in America where all those people died? Waco, I think it was called. That was down to some strange cult.'

'Was it called the Church of the Crystal Water?' Tara asked.

Norman Pritchard thought for a moment then shook his head.

'No, love. I can't remember the name, but I don't think it was called that.'

Tara looked at Murray, her confusion deepening. At every turn they found something else new and then were struggling to find true verification.

'It was a while before they left home,' Norman continued. 'First time they went to America. Took little Corey with them, and when they came back, they had our little granddaughter, Aeron.'

'Kelly had two children?'

'Yes, lovely kids they were.'

'Were? What happened to them?'

'When Kelly got sick with the brain tumour, they stayed with their dad, Keron, the weird boyfriend. Kelly spent more time here with us. But once she found out from the hospital that she didn't have long, she said that she wanted to be with her family. When she got back with Keron they decided to go to their church community so that Kelly could spend her last days there.'

'Is that when you reported her missing to police?'

'We only did that so we could find out where this church community was based. We wanted to see Kelly before she died. In the end we were too late. Keron contacted us and said that Kelly's spirit had moved on. They were holding whatever kind of funeral those sort of people do. It was better if we did not attend.'

'What about the children?'

'Keron said they were staying with him in the church community. He told us he was soon going back to America. Never heard from him after that.'

'Do you know where this community was located?'

'We found an address among Kelly's things that Keron sent to us. We thought it might be the place where Kelly died. One day we drove out there, but it was just a big country house with a couple of people living in it. Certainly, weren't no church. The lady of the house told us it was a family home and that it used to be a farm. She didn't know anything about a church community.'

'Do you think you could take us there?'

'It's been twenty-odd years, love, but I suppose I might remember once I get my bearings. Only thing is that I can't leave our Molly on her own.'

'How about if you go with DS Murray, and I'll keep Molly company?'

'Do you hear that, Molly? This young policewoman is going to look after you while I'm out.'

Molly looked at her husband and smiled.

'Now you behave yourself, I won't be long.' There was some mumbling as Norman kissed his wife on the forehead and turned up the sound on the television.

Tara sat with Molly and endured several daytime programmes, from air sea rescue to a show on cowboy builders. She was relieved when the lunchtime news came on. An hour and a half later, her phone burst to life with its pop tune. It was Murray.

'Found the place, ma'am, no problem. Norman brought us to it straight away.'

'That's good. Where are you exactly?'

'A lovely spot close to Delamere Country Park. Between Chester and Northwich. It's a big old farmhouse. The outbuildings don't look to be in use, and no one is answering at the house.'

'OK, take a note of the address and have someone at the station check it out for the owner, then get back here.'

'Hold on, there's a car coming up the lane. I'll call you back, ma'am.'

Less than a minute elapsed before Tara's phone rang again.

'Well?'

'They did a quick about-turn when they saw us.'

'Did you get a note of the car reg?'

'Better than that I saw the driver.'

'Anyone we know?'

'Oh yes. That woman from the Goth clothes shop.'

'Elsie Greenwood?'

CHAPTER 45

She drove fast down the lane. She didn't bother to stop at the junction with the road, fortunately clear of traffic. Elsie drove so much faster than she was used to doing. Eventually, close to Birkenhead, she pulled into a lay-by, stopped the engine and reached for her mobile. With hands shaking and breathing heavily, she managed to select the name from her contacts.

'It's me,' she said, her voice quivering. 'They were at the house, waiting for me. I don't know how they found it.'

'Calm down, Elsie. Who was at the house?'

'The police, the detective who came to the shop asking questions.'

'What did they want this time?'

'I don't know. I didn't stay around to speak with them.'

'Did they see you?'

'I'm sure they saw the car, but I don't know if they recognised me. It was that big guy, the detective sergeant, but I didn't see the woman. There was an old man standing with him. What do I do? I can't go back there.'

'It's all right, Elsie. You haven't done anything wrong. Just relax, take a few deep breaths.'

'But what if they start tearing the place apart?'

'You haven't done anything wrong. Stay calm. Where are you now?'

'On my way back to the shop. I left Katrina in charge. I have to close up.'

'That's fine. Just behave normally. If the police have recognised you or got your car registration they'll come calling. But you need to stay calm. Don't tell them anything; don't agree to anything. I'll get a solicitor if you need one.'

'Oh my God. What about our things? We need to move them, get them out of the house. You need to help me. Get some of the others to help me.'

'Elsie, listen to me. The police may not be interested in the house or what's inside there. They may have simply wanted to speak with you again.'

'Then why didn't they come to the shop? I shouldn't have run off, but I panicked. I didn't know what to do. And how do they know I'm connected with the house? We should have done something after they first came to see me. How are we going to explain? We'll have to tell them what goes on there.'

'Don't worry, just go back to the shop and carry on as normal. I will contact the others and cancel our next gathering.'

'But I live there. Where am I supposed to go now?'

'I told you, go about things as if nothing has happened. Relax, Elsie, we'll get through this.' She ended the call. She couldn't relax. Her head was pounding, her temples pulsing. She lit a cigarette and took several long drags. Suddenly, she had the feeling that everyone was looking for her, everyone was after her. She locked her doors and checked the mirror. The urge to keep running was holding sway over staying to face them. After smoking another cigarette, she felt a little more relaxed about facing them. She started the car and headed to her shop.

CHAPTER 46

Elsie Greenwood didn't have long to wait before the police came to see her. An hour after returning to her shop, Tara and Murray's car stopped outside.

'Afternoon, Ms Greenwood,' said Murray with a glib smile as he came into the shop. 'Sorry we didn't have time for a chat earlier. We'd like to ask you a few questions if that's all right?'

She looked nervous, flitting about, tidying a rack of dresses then retreating behind her counter.

'Katrina, can you leave us for now?'

Her young assistant scanned the faces of the visitors but obediently retired to the back room of the shop.

Tara got straight to the point. 'Can you tell us what you were doing earlier today at that house?'

'I live there, Inspector. It's my home, and I don't take kindly to seeing police officers standing in my drive without invitation.'

'Just doing my job, Ms Greenwood,' said Murray.

'What is it you think I can help you with?'

'How long have you lived there?' Tara asked.

'About twelve years.'

'Are you the owner?'

'No, just a tenant. What is this about, Inspector? Have I done something wrong?'

'We have recently learned that your house was associated with a cult community about twenty-five years ago.'

'Before my time. I am the only one who lives there now.'

'A woman went missing. She was a member of this cult, and it is thought that she died at the house. Her body has never been found.'

'The man you saw with me,' said Murray. 'He was the father of the woman. Her name was Kelly Pritchard.'

Greenwood shook her head and seemed to relax.

'I don't know that name, and I'm not aware of anyone dying at the house.'

'We also believe that a man named Alastair Bailey may have been murdered there.'

'I can't help you, Inspector. I know very little of the history of the place. As far as I know it was a working farm before I moved in.'

'You've never heard of Alastair Bailey?'

'No, I'm afraid not.'

'What about Charles Kirkman?' Murray asked.

Tara didn't think the woman's face could become any paler, but somehow, she turned white.

'No,' she replied hesitantly.

'If you don't mind, we would like to look around your home. We'd prefer to do so with your co-operation, but if not, we can get a warrant?'

'Then you'll have to get a warrant. I've done nothing wrong, Inspector, and I don't see why you are harassing me. I've answered your questions, none of which have any relevance to me.'

'Let's hope that is the case, Ms Greenwood. We'll be in touch.'

Their next call was to Abercromby Square. Wilson had already come through with details on the landlord of the house near Delamere Park where Elsie Greenwood lived. It was Dr Carl Sloan.

CHAPTER 47

She pulled into a side street, off Picton Road, did a three-point turn and parked so that she was looking across the road facing a mini-market. He lived in the flat above, his entrance just to the right of the shop. There were no lights showing in the first-floor windows. It was late, past ten o'clock already. Where could he be? What was he up to? Already she had decided that he was responsible for the disappearance of the legal secretary who'd gone missing from her home in Tarbock Green. It was all over the news. James Guy, she'd decided, was the kind of man who would have no qualms about doing such a thing. Snatching a woman off the street, or from her own home, doing as he pleased with her and dumping her when he'd finished. And yesterday he'd had the nerve to turn up at The Swallow's Tail in the hope of seeing her. Given the chance, he would claim her as his next victim. She'd watched him sidle into the pub, not a care in the world. She enjoyed the effect she'd had on him. She would string him along for a few more days.

Five young lads strolled by her car but not without taking a good look at the woman seated behind the wheel. Her heart raced as she prayed that they would walk on by. One of them, a boy of around sixteen, with short hair, and dressed in baggy jeans and a dark zip-up sweatshirt, thumbed the keys on his mobile as he texted. His mates stopped to wait for him. Two of them plonked their bottoms against the bonnet of her car, unconcerned about the owner within. What should she do? She couldn't afford to rile these youths, nor did she want to draw attention to herself, not when James Guy could return home at any minute. The youths didn't seem particularly threatening, but she should drive away now, to hell with James Guy. She didn't want to confront these kids. Then suddenly there he was on the other side of the road striding towards the door of his flat and dressed in dark trousers and a combat-style jacket. As he pulled his key from his pocket, he glanced around him. She lost sight of him; her view obscured through the windscreen by the two lads leaning on the bonnet.

The next thing she saw was the light going on in the room on the first floor. An agonising wait for very little. The irony of her situation hit home when the boys, as quickly as they had arrived, hurried down the road. She remained for several minutes, watching the light behind a pale curtain in the flat. She didn't like James Guy; of that she was certain. But he did look handsome. She would continue to keep an eye on him and find out what he got up to when not working. Something evil, she was sure of it. She was certain also that James Guy must soon come to an end.

CHAPTER 48

Cheshire police were responsible for conducting a search of the house near Delamere Park. Tara, Murray and Tweedy were in attendance along with Carl Sloan and Elsie Greenwood. Both houseowner and tenant remained passive as six uniformed officers went through each room of the stone building. They had been briefed by Tara on what to look out for: evidence to suggest that occult worship or practices took place on the premises; anything connected to one or more of the recent murder victims: Greasby, Young and Kirkman; or clues relating to the events of twenty-five years ago when Alastair Bailey and Kelly Pritchard both died.

It was early morning, damp and cold, but Sloan and Greenwood remained outside with Harold Tweedy. No one spoke. A police guard had been placed at the entrance to the lane the night before to prevent anything from being removed from the property prior to the search. When Tara and Murray had arrived at the house, Carl Sloan was already present. Neither he nor Greenwood made any protest. Both had said little and complied with each request made of them.

Indoors, Tara and Murray moved through the house watching the uniforms searching cupboards, drawers, cabinets and bookcases. The house was tidy but suffered from a lack of daylight through small windows, and was furnished with a jumble of dated rather than genuine antique furniture. A sitting room at the front of the house was clearly well-used by Greenwood. It contained a television, a sixties-style teak drinks cabinet and sideboard, a self-assembly-type desk littered with paperwork and a green and cream striped cushioned sofa, rife with cat hair. The kitchen to the rear was mostly clean and tidy save for the morning's breakfast dishes, a meal for two abandoned when the police had arrived. Two further rooms on the ground floor were laid out, it seemed, as meeting rooms, a variety of chairs set around the walls of the front room and a table set with eight chairs in what was presumably a dining room. As with the Kirkman house, Tara noted the many books about the occult, the mystic and several political and religious writings, including a copy of *Mein Kampf*, and several about Islam. There were, however, just as many paperbacks of popular fiction: Jilly Cooper, Agatha Christie, Jackie Collins and Maeve Binchy.

A book collection was not enough to prove any connection to recent or historic murders; Greenwood had already admitted being a witch. Whatever that meant, Tara thought. There were five bedrooms upstairs, two appeared to have been used the night before, so presumably Carl Sloan had stayed over. The white veneered wardrobes, in what was clearly Elsie's room, held a peculiar variety of clothing, mostly black, in leather, latex and PVC. Folded jeans, T-shirts and jumpers sat neatly in a chest of drawers. Shoes, mainly black, were arranged on a stand at the bottom of the wardrobe. Tara noticed, on a dressing table, a collection of jewellery, neatly placed in a box with necklaces hanging from a brass stand. Some of the necklace fobs were peculiar looking objects, symbols she assumed to be associated with the occult or pagan in origin. The walls in the room were decorated in what Tara guessed were astrological symbols, stencilled onto a painted background. Beyond the clothes, décor and books that displayed an interest in the occult, they found nothing in the house to suggest any connection to murder. Tara reported back to Harold Tweedy.

'Nothing of any real significance, sir.'

Tweedy nodded his understanding, but Tara glimpsed Sloan looking sombrely at Greenwood.

'We're starting on the buildings out the back,' said Tara. 'Ms Greenwood, can you provide keys to any of the sheds?' The woman opened her handbag and produced a lanyard that held at least a dozen keys of varying shapes and sizes. Without a word she handed them to Tara.

To the rear of the house was a farmyard measuring approximately forty yards by thirty and enclosed by outbuildings, sheds, stables and a hay barn. At the farthest end from the house there were gated openings on both sides to the left and right. These gave onto lanes, largely overgrown through lack of use. Beyond the lane to the south were open fields and pastures although there were no animals grazing. To the north, the lane disappeared into woodland. The yard had a concrete base, and outside one of the sheds sat three wooden picnic tables. Tara passed the bunch of keys to Murray who went off to supervise the uniforms already waiting by the first of the sheds.

While the search was taking place, Tara ambled to the centre of the yard. Here there was a circle marked into the ground and judging by the black patches on the concrete, it was a place where fires had been lit. Set around the circle were heavy logs laid out as seating. Tara noted familiar symbols roughly carved into the bark, and through the blackened patches on the ground she noticed that a large pentacle, a five-pointed star within a circle, had been etched into the concrete. She didn't need much more to tell her that this place was used for gatherings of some kind. If there had been a place, a church of the occult, in existence twenty-five years ago where people may have been murdered or sacrificed then surely, they had found it. Before leaving the station for home the night before, Wilson had established that the previous owner of the house prior to Carl Sloan had been none other than Mary Kirkman. Had they now found the base for the Church of the Crystal Water?

She turned around to see Murray and a couple of uniforms emerge from the first single-storey shed.

'A workshop, ma'am,' he called. 'Old tools, wooden boards and planks, a few logs and a couple of axes.' She acknowledged his report and watched as he proceeded to the next doorway, one leading into a two-storey building. She wandered to the opposite side of the yard, where two uniforms had undone a heavy padlock and were sliding open a sturdy wooden door. When she reached the entrance, she saw a bare room inside with concrete walls and floor. There was a cold damp smell but nothing to see. To the right-hand side, however, she noticed that the two officers had unlocked and passed through another doorway that led to a flight of steps. There were no obvious lights or switches to be found, but she followed them down the thirteen concrete steps into the darkness of yet another empty room without windows. The light from a torch illuminated the entrance to a second room, where both constables were standing, frozen, it seemed, to the spot. Neither one dared move. Only their heavy intake of breath signalled they were still alive. Guided by the dim light, she stepped into the room and stood beside them. In less than a second, she wished she hadn't.

The two constables, both in their early twenties, stood open-mouthed, neither daring to speak. Tara remained at the doorway looking at each object as it was illuminated by the constable's torch. The room was cold, a coldness that seemed to enter her body at her toes and snake its way up and through her slim frame. Her hand was clasped over her mouth. It had been a long time since she'd come so close to retching.

A wooden shelf, about six feet off the floor, ran the entire way around the walls of the room. There were various objects and shapes set upon this shelf: wooden models of pyramids, oddly shaped crystals, ugly stone sculptures of cherubs and angels, demons and gargoyles. But on the wall, above an open fireplace, where the torchlight had come to rest, sat a row of large glass jars. Cylinders. In each was contained a head – a human head.

She counted eight jars, eight heads. Then she grabbed the torch from the constable and scanned the room. There were no more. Forcing herself to do it, she drew close to the jars and shone the light. There was nothing to identify any of them, but they seemed well preserved. The first on the left was a male, the surrounding liquid was discoloured, but she could make out what had once been a heavy face, strong features, a large nose, thick ears and dark hair. The second looked female, smaller, with long dark hair having settled around the bottom of the jar. The next two were males, younger than the first, then another female, two males and finally a female. Tara shuddered. What was she looking at? A set of trophies? A laboratory?

'Go fetch Superintendent Tweedy,' she barked at one of the uniforms. 'And get a forensic team out here.' The young constable bolted for the door, his footsteps echoing off the walls of the adjacent room.

'What is this, ma'am?' the other uniform asked.

'I wish I knew, Constable. Go upstairs and make sure we don't get everyone stampeding down here to have a look. Superintendent Tweedy and DS Murray only.'

'Yes, ma'am.'

Left alone with only the torch, she examined the room. The walls seemed black and as with the basement flat at the Kirkman house there was a display of various symbols painted in gold. Many of them were now familiar to her, but some were not. In particular, she was drawn to one that Tweedy had failed to identify. The image took up most of the wall at the back of the room, some twenty feet from the fireplace. Three stars over a black sun as Tweedy had described it. But he hadn't known the significance of it. When she lowered the torch, the beam lit up a portion of the concrete floor. There, too, was the same image, three stars over a black sun painted in black and gold. Had she now found the place where Greasby, Young and Kirkman had been murdered? If so, why had their heads and bodies been placed where they could be discovered?

She heard footsteps on the stairs, and within a few seconds, she had Tweedy and Murray for company. Once again, she illuminated the row of jars with the torch.

'Oh my God,' said Murray when he saw the first one. Tweedy wasn't quite so vocal.

'Eight of them, sir,' said Tara, panning the beam of light along the shelf. No one spoke for a few moments then Tweedy stepped forward and stood before the fourth jar from the left. It stood directly above the wide fireplace. He peered closely at the head immersed in a fluid, while Tara kept the torch fixed in one place.

'What is it, sir? Have you noticed something?'

'I'm fairly sure I'm looking at the head of Alastair Bailey.'

CHAPTER 49

Dr Carl Sloan sat uneasily on a plastic chair in a ground-floor interview room at St Anne Street station. He didn't seem happy at having first been arrested and then kept waiting for Tara to arrive to conduct the interview. Murray had been assigned the task of interviewing a nervy Elsie Greenwood in the room next door.

Tara had deliberately taken her time in getting to work, and she'd instructed Murray to do the same. Superintendent Tweedy had suggested they took some time to relax and gather their thoughts before resuming work on this case. At times they needed to draw breath and find a way to deal with the traumatic aspects of their jobs. The discovery of a collection of human heads would not be an easy image to erase from one's mind. So, Tara had spent the latter part of her evening in the company of her friends, Kate and Aisling, drinking wine, having a chat and watching telly. Both friends knew how to behave around her when Tara had mentioned having a horrific day. In her situation horrific didn't simply mean busy, hectic, things not going to plan. No, Kate and Aisling were used now to horrific meaning a death, a grisly murder, a disturbing crime scene. The three girls had a laugh, relaxing in each other's company.

She'd taken her time over breakfast, a rarity most days, a long shower and a leisurely pace when getting dressed. By the time she arrived at the station, gathered her files and entered the interview room, Carl Sloan looked ready to explode.

Once the preliminaries had been carried out, she wasted no further time in getting straight to the point.

'Dr Sloan, why was there a collection of human heads on your property?'

'They've been there for years,' he said dryly.

'Why is that?'

Sloan had requested his solicitor be present. A burly man in his late forties with little hair and wearing a grey suit, nodded once to indicate that Sloan should reply to the question.

'They were left there by the previous owner.'

Despite the interview being recorded, Tara was making her own notes.

'How long have you been the owner of the house?'

'Thirteen years.'

'And in that time, you have never thought it necessary to deal with this collection?'

'No. They weren't doing any harm down there. I have done nothing wrong, Inspector, and I would like to go now.' When Tara didn't respond or even look up from her notetaking, Sloan turned to his solicitor.

'Really, Inspector,' said Michael Coombes. 'My client has answered your questions and can offer nothing further. I think it's time he was released.'

Tara raised her head, trying her damnedest not to fume.

'Gentlemen, we're not dealing with a find of naughty pictures, or even a stash of drugs. We're talking about the discovery of human remains on your property, Dr Sloan. You will not be going anywhere for a while.' Coombes pulled a face that showed his distaste at being admonished, but he made no reply.

'The name of the previous owner of the house, please?'

'Can't remember.'

'Was it Kirkman?' Tara already knew the answer. They'd established such details, but she wanted to be sure she was getting Sloan's co-operation.

'Yes, that was the name. Mary Kirkman.'

'Do you know why the previous owner had these remains on her property?' Sloan looked at Coombes for guidance. The solicitor intimated that his client should respond.

'As far as I know the farm was used for the practice of satanic rituals.'

'And were these remains used in such rituals?'

'I really don't know. I was never there. It was before my time.'

'Yet you continued to maintain the room with the jars in place and symbols of the occult on the walls and floor? Do you practise satanic rituals in this room?'

'I don't live there, Inspector.'

'I didn't ask you if you lived there, I asked if you practise satanic rituals in that room. I will be asking Ms Greenwood the same question.'

Sloan rubbed his face with both hands and sighed deeply.

'There are certain pagan rituals performed there. Not satanic as you suggest.'

'Do you use the human heads in your rituals?'

'No. We left them in place in response to a request from some of our members. They do not comprise any part of our worship.'

'And what exactly do you worship?'

'We embrace the rituals of our pagan ancestors, Inspector. Some of these practices are druidic in nature. We celebrate ancient festivals such as Samhain and Beltane, we dance the maypole, we investigate ancient teachings such as Cerridwen's Cauldron of Wisdom.'

'Human sacrifice?' Tara interrupted.

Sloan took his time in answering, and he did so with a smirk.

'Not in recent times, Inspector.'

'How about twenty-five years ago and the murder of Alastair Bailey?'

'As I have said, that's before my time.'

'Do you know the names of the people whose heads you have stored on your property?'

'I'm afraid not.'

'I will need a list of the names of members of your church.'

'I'm afraid I can't do that either.'

'Can't or won't, Dr Sloan?'

CHAPTER 50

Murray had a more abrupt interviewing technique. He had less patience than Tara in trying to extract information. It didn't matter whether the suspect was male or female, nervous or confident, frightened or bold.

'Ms Greenwood, what were the heads of eight people doing on a shelf in your home?'

'They've been there longer than I have lived in that house.'

'Who put them there?'

'I believe it was done by members of the church who met there at one time.'

'The Church of the Crystal Water?'

Elsie Greenwood's face widened in surprise at the question. She almost smiled, something she hadn't managed since her arrest.

'I would hardly think so, Sergeant.'

'Why is that?'

'The people who used to meet there would not have been associated with the Church of the Crystal Water.'

'Can you identify any of the heads that were found?'

'I know only two of them. Charles and Mary Kirkman.'

'The parents of Dinsdale Kirkman?'

'Yes. They were the high priest and priestess of the group who used my house before I lived there. The Kirkmans owned the place before Carl bought it for our group. The reason for my living there is to look after the place and to prepare for our meetings.'

'So, despite your denial when we first met, you are a member of the Church of the Crystal Water?'

'Don't be ridiculous.'

'I thought it a sensible question, Ms Greenwood. But tell me why the heads of the Kirkmans are preserved in jars in your home?'

'Both Kirkmans died of natural causes, I believe. It was supposedly part of their belief that the soul remains within the mind after death and not in the body. While the remainder of the body can be discarded the head should be saved.'

'Strange.'

'Unconventional, perhaps.'

'Where did the bodies end up?'

'Hard to say. Usually the remainder of the body is cremated and the ashes are scattered.'

* * *

Tara and Murray met over coffee in the canteen. Neither one was pleased with the information they had so far drawn from Sloan and Greenwood.

'Do you believe what you're hearing, Alan?' He was halfway through a fruit scone, dropping crumbs on his trousers and trying to sweep them onto the floor.

'I'm surprised at how blasé they are in talking about this stuff. They don't seem to understand how bad it looks. It's like we've found a couple of stuffed animals in a cupboard. They're behaving as if they've done nothing wrong.'

'Makes me wonder how much they're covering up.'

'It won't be hard to confirm how long Sloan has owned the house and how long Greenwood has lived there. The trouble comes in trying to find out exactly what goes on in the place. What the hell do they do with eight human heads in glass jars?'

'My problem with the whole situation is why do they keep such secrets regarding their rituals and at the same time go public with these brutal murders?'

'You really think they are killers?'

'Someone in their group must be. My guess is that it's one of their so-called older members. And so far, Sloan is reluctant to identify any of them. Somebody put those heads on that shelf. If one of the heads is confirmed as Alastair Bailey and another as Kelly Pritchard, then I'd say the murderer lies within this group.'

'So far, ma'am, there has been no evidence found in the place to suggest a link to any of the recent deaths.'

'I know. We need to get names out of Sloan or Greenwood. What happened twenty-five years ago at that farm is connected to the deaths of Greasby, Young and Kirkman. I'm certain of it.'

CHAPTER 51

When Tara entered the room, she found Elsie Greenwood sipping tea and chatting quietly with her solicitor. Carol Sherman, a woman in her mid-thirties, slim, well-groomed but not such a friendly face, was first to speak.

'Detective Inspector Grogan, my client feels that she can be of no further help in this situation and would like to go now.'

Tara smiled weakly at both women. She sat down opposite them, setting some files upon the table. She usually preferred to address the person being questioned and not the accompanying brief.

'Ms Greenwood, I appreciate that you have willingly answered our questions thus far, but I have some more questions to ask you.'

'I really don't think my client can offer anything more, Inspector.'

'Let's see, shall we?' said Tara with a curt smile. 'How did you come to be living at the farmhouse, Ms Greenwood?'

'I moved up north from Essex and opened my shop. I already knew Carl from years back. I was looking for somewhere to rent and he offered me the farmhouse. He had just taken it on as somewhere to hold our gatherings, and I was happy to look after preparations for our meetings.'

'So, it was very convenient for you both?'

'Yes, it was.'

'What was your reaction on finding those heads in the outbuilding?'

'It was a shock at first, but then both Carl and I have an interest in the occult, the macabre, so I got used to them being there.'

'Who insisted that they remain in place?'

'Carl did.'

'Didn't you wonder why they should be there? Weren't you curious as to who those people had been?'

'Sometimes, Inspector, in our circles it is better not to ask such questions.'

'Oh? Why is that?'

'There are many secrets within the circles of the modern order. What you are entitled to know depends on your status.'

Tara began to feel that she might be getting somewhere with Elsie Greenwood, that hopefully she could tease out of her the information she really needed. The names of those involved in the activities of twenty-five years ago.

'But you did know about the Kirkmans. Tell me what you know of them. How did they die?'

Greenwood shrugged. 'Natural causes, I believe.'

'Did you ever meet their son, Dinsdale?'

'No.'

'Did he not attend your meetings?'

'No.'

'Are there any of your present members who would have been members of the Kirkmans' group?'

Greenwood looked sideways at her solicitor. Sherman whispered something.

'I can't answer that, Inspector.'

Here they go again, thought Tara.

'Can't or won't, Ms Greenwood?'

The woman did not reply and did a good job of looking determinedly at Tara. But the young detective was not about to be put off by some middle-aged woman claiming to live and be ruled by a secret code of ethics. People had died at the hands of brutal killers. The quest for justice surely must outweigh the need for the protection of a religious secret.

'Ms Greenwood, we found the remains of eight people at your home, three men have also been murdered in this city recently and I believe there is a connection. We could be looking at eleven murders. Do you understand the seriousness of the situation? Are you aware that I can charge you right now, along with Sloan, with conspiracy to pervert the course of justice? That is not a slap on the wrist offence. You will go to prison if you are found guilty.'

'I don't appreciate you trying to intimidate my client,' said Sherman harshly.

'I'm stating the situation as I see it, Ms Sherman. What jury will not convict when they learn that human remains were kept at your client's home and yet she refuses to discuss the matter?'

Pushing back her auburn hair from her ear, Sherman whispered to Greenwood. A discussion ensued between the pair, Greenwood looking increasingly worried. Eventually, Sherman spoke.

'Please put your question to my client once again.'

At last, thought Tara.

'Ms Greenwood, can you please give me the names of those members of your church who may have been associated with the group led by the Kirkmans?'

'I can't do that, Inspector. The names of our members remains a private matter. Only Carl Sloan can take the decision to reveal that information.'

Tara could do little else but glare at the two women. Snatching her files from the table she rose from her chair.

'Depending on what Sloan has to say, you will be charged with perverting the course of justice, if not murder.' She walked from the room and went next door to Carl Sloan.

Murray had got nowhere with the history academic. But Tara was not prepared to circle the issues any longer. She barged into the room and issued the same warning to Sloan that she'd delivered to Elsie Greenwood. Sloan's brief took it in the same manner as Carol Sherman had.

'That's intimidation, Inspector Grogan,' said Coombes.

'Call it what you like, Mr Coombes, but if I don't get a list of names associated with Dr Sloan's organisation he will be charged. I have enough evidence to get a conviction, but his assistance in finding whoever killed these people may just help with a reduced sentence. I'll leave you to consider your options.' Tara and Murray left them alone.

While the two detectives drank coffee in the corridor nearby, Coombes left the interview room in a hurry. Not long after, Carol Sherman followed suit, and Tara ordered that both suspects be returned to their holding cells. If she was right, Tara guessed that Coombes had been instructed by Sloan to contact all members of his flock to make them aware of the situation and to prepare them that very soon their names would be given over to the police.

CHAPTER 52

Tara arrived home and flopped gratefully onto her sofa without removing her coat or dropping her handbag. For a while she lay still, hearing only the odd creak as her heating came on, or a thud as a door slammed further along her floor of the building. Eventually, she kicked off her shoes, but continued to clutch her bag across her stomach. Her mind wondered, and soon she was gazing at cheerful scenes of her childhood with her parents and brothers holidaying in France, then of outings to town with Kate and Aisling.

She thought then of Simon, her first real love, and of their time spent at Oxford and inevitably to the pain of their break-up. And this pain led to thoughts of the next, the death of Callum, she, pregnant with his child. Tears filled her eyes at the vision of her cradling her tiny son for a few brief moments before they took his lifeless body from her. Then fear at what may have happened at the hands of James Guy when he bundled her into his van and drove away. She had no memory of this, just a gnawing within that made her nervous of men, of getting close to any man. She fell asleep with swirling thoughts of Tweedy reading his Bible, and Murray stuffing a sandwich into his mouth.

She awoke in darkness, still holding her bag, her feet cold and her shoulders stiff. It was an effort to prise herself from the sofa, but slowly she made it to her feet, gazing about the room as if she were a stranger here. It was her home and yet she had this irksome feeling that maybe she would never know real comfort. Not when her life remained in such turmoil. Traipsing to the fridge, she removed a carton of apple juice and poured a glassful. She'd finished by the time she reached her bed. Her watch read 4:20. It was hardly worth going to bed now and yet she was far from rested. The compromise was to remain clothed but to slip under the duvet.

At seven she was wide awake and businesslike. Negative thoughts were gone like the tide. A shower, fresh clothes and a bowl of cornflakes with breakfast news on the TV and she was feeling more confident of facing the day ahead. After tidying her kitchen, she grabbed her keys and bag and headed downstairs to her car. But her day got a whole lot worse much sooner than she'd envisaged. A man in his mid-thirties, her neighbour from one floor below, stood in the centre of the forecourt with his briefcase in one hand, the other in his trouser pocket. He was staring intently at a car. It was a blue car but was drenched in a dirty red liquid that had begun to dry on the windscreen and bonnet. It took a few seconds for it to register with Tara that he was looking at her Ford Focus. Much of the liquid had run off the bodywork and had seeped onto the ground.

'Is that blood, do you think?' said the man. Tara nodded once, but she was already on her mobile. 'Bit of a sick joke. Is it yours?'

Again, Tara nodded, and the man smiled his sympathy then strolled along the row of vehicles until he reached his BMW.

'Alan, can you pick me up this morning? Someone has splashed what looks like blood all over my car.'

'I've just called Wilson to hitch a lift. Looks like acid all over mine.'

Wilson obliged by picking up both of his colleagues and driving them to St Anne Street. Tara ordered Sloan to an interview room straight away.

* * *

'Dr Sloan, I do not think that having your people threaten police officers by daubing their cars in blood and acid will do much to improve your situation.'

'I'm sorry, Inspector, I have no idea what you're talking about, and I don't appreciate false accusations. My solicitor will be here soon, I hope, so you can prepare for my release.'

'We'll see.' Tara slammed the door on her way out. She'd love to wipe that smirk off Sloan's face. On the one hand she hoped she was close to solving the murder of Alastair Bailey from so long ago, yet frustratingly, she felt no closer to unravelling the mystery of the recent deaths. She waited by her desk for news of the solicitor's arrival. Murray and Wilson chatted about cars and football, while she perused a few emails and dealt with a couple of texts from her friend, Kate. When Michael Coombes turned up at the station reception it was well after eleven. Tara was less than pleased until she realised that the person most inconvenienced by Coombes' late show was his client, Carl Sloan. It transpired also that Carol Sherman was of the same firm of solicitors. Apparently, she had not found it necessary to turn up to represent Elsie Greenwood.

'Do you have something for me, Mr Coombes?' Tara asked before the solicitor had joined his client in the interview room.

'Very eager, I see, Inspector. If you don't mind, I would like a word with Dr Sloan first.'

She gave them ten minutes and had a coffee with Murray, using the break to discuss their next move should Sloan provide the requested information.

'Could be time consuming if it's a long list,' said Murray.

'I know, but I'm hoping there might be one or two familiar names on it.'

'You're thinking of Trudy Mitchell?'

'Seems the most likely. She admitted an involvement at the time, and there was her relationship with Hargreaves who was closely associated with occult worship.'

'You know, we should get Mitchell out to the farm to see if it was the place she had visited at the time.'

'For that matter we should do the same with Janet Malcroft.'

They were interrupted by a call from a sergeant at the desk downstairs to say that Sloan and his brief were ready to see them. Tara waited another ten minutes before she and Murray entered the room.

'Your list of those associated with Dr Sloan's group,' said Coombes with a conceited look on his face.

He slid a piece of lined A4 across the desk. Sloan remained silent, avoiding eye contact with her. Tara studied the sheet containing handwritten names. She counted twenty-nine.

'Is this a complete list of your membership?'

Coombes glanced at Sloan, who merely shrugged.

'As complete as you're going to get, Inspector,' Coombes replied.

Tara sat back from the table and examined the names. None of them were familiar. She did a second take searching specifically for Mitchell, but she wasn't there. Sloan sat with arms folded, a smug grin on his face.

'I take it that my client is now free to leave?'

'Dr Sloan, you and I both know that this list is of no help to our enquiry.'

'It is what you asked for, Inspector,' said Coombes.

Tara ignored the solicitor and addressed Sloan directly.

'Someone in your church requested or insisted that those heads remained on your property. That person, I am assuming, was a member of the group who met there at the time of Alastair Bailey's murder. I want to know their name, please.'

Again, Sloan looked at his solicitor.

'I need to know what went on at the farmhouse twenty-five years ago, Dr Sloan. As I have already said, you will be charged with perverting the course of justice before you leave here today.'

'Three people have been murdered recently,' Murray added. 'Your helping us now might prevent any further deaths.'

Still Carl Sloan remained silent, but his smug expression had disappeared, replaced by a grave look of doubt or even fear. Eventually, Coombes asked for some time alone with his client. Tara and Murray obliged, spending the time to arrange to have their cars collected, Tara's cleaned and Murray's to be repaired. When they returned, Sloan was on his feet, pacing the room, hands in his pockets.

'The name we believe that you require,' said Coombes, 'is Janet Malcroft.'

CHAPTER 53

They wasted no time in requisitioning a car and getting out to the Malcroft home in Grassendale. Tara recalled seeing a white Audi parked in the driveway when they were last at the house. Instead, this morning she saw a small red van with the name *Dobson Car Sales & Servicing* displayed in white lettering on the side. The doorbell was answered by Peter Bailey, looking shocked and anxious.

'She's gone.'

'Where?'

'She's getting a flight to Malaga.'

'How long has she been gone?'

'She wasn't here when I arrived, but it can't be long.' Murray was already on his mobile to arrange for police at the airport to stop the woman from boarding a plane. 'I don't understand,' Bailey continued. 'She called me at work, said she had to leave urgently, that she would explain all later. Why are you here? What has she done?'

'We need to speak with her, that's all,' said Tara, ushering Peter back into the house.

'Then why did she run?'

Tara briefly explained the situation, but when Murray came off his phone the pair of them hurried to their car, leaving a confused Peter Bailey looking on from the doorway of his mother's home. With the aid of a siren, they soon reached John Lennon Airport in Speke. They dashed through security and into departures and, on the assumption that Peter Bailey was correct, they found the gate for the forthcoming flight to Malaga. Just as they reached it, they saw the EasyJet plane pushing off from its stand. Tara sighed in frustration, but Murray gave her a nudge. Re-entering the lounge was a harried looking Janet Malcroft, in blue jeans, white blouse and flat shoes, flanked on each side by a uniformed police officer. Murray showed his ID, and they accompanied the uniforms and Malcroft to a security office.

'Some questions for you, Janet. Sorry to spoil your holiday,' said Tara. 'It was a holiday you were taking?'

'I'm saying nothing until I see my solicitor.'

After Malcroft was cautioned, Tara and Murray drove her to St Anne Street. Before Tara began the interview, she arranged for Sloan and Greenwood to be charged with conspiracy to pervert the course of justice.

Murray had ensured that Malcroft's solicitor was present before they entered the interview room. An hour later, Tara and Murray stepped into the room to face a pale-looking Janet Malcroft, who was seated beside none other than Michael Coombes.

'I see that representing members of an occult church is a bit of a speciality, Mr Coombes?'

The solicitor grinned sardonically at Tara but made no reply.

Tara outlined the reason why they wished to speak with Janet Malcroft. The woman lowered her head as Tara spoke.

'We believe you are associated with the activities that take place at the farmhouse owned by Dr Carl Sloan. Is that correct?'

'Yes.'

'We also believe that the human remains found on the property were retained at your insistence. Is that correct?' The woman nodded as tears began to flow. 'We need a verbal answer, Mrs Malcroft.'

'Yes,' she replied, wiping at her eyes with a crumpled tissue.

'Can you tell us why?'

'The soul remains in the head when the body dies.'

Tara already knew that answer. She wasn't interested in their beliefs; she wanted hard facts.

'Your former husband's head, we believe but have yet to confirm, was one of those found on the property. Can you tell us what happened to him?'

'I didn't kill him.'

'Tell us what happened, Janet. Why was he killed?'

'He was killed because he was discovered to be an activist of the Church of the Crystal Water.'

'I don't understand. Weren't all of the people who attended meetings at the farmhouse members of this church?'

'I don't think you understand exactly what the Church of the Crystal Water is, Inspector?'

'Then perhaps you should explain.'

'The Church of the Crystal Water is not an occult or devil-worshipping group. It is a Christian organisation.'

'I'm sorry, Janet, but I thought Alastair had become a member of an occult church and that was the cause of your marriage breaking up and eventually Alastair's death. That's what you told us when we first spoke with you.'

The woman broke down in tears, crying into her lap. She tried to speak but the words were lost in her sobs.

'Why don't you take a few minutes, Janet? Have a chat with Mr Coombes, and I'll arrange some tea.'

Tara looked forlornly at Murray when they stepped out of the room.

'I can't take much more of these bombshells. Tell me, how are we any closer to finding our killer?'

CHAPTER 54

'When Alastair first brought me along to Vera Deitate, the Kirkmans' church, I was frightened.'

'Vera Deitate?'

'It is short for *de Ecclesia in Vera Divinitate*. Church of the True Deity. The farm was called Vera Deitate. I'd realised that Alastair was getting involved in some very strange things, but he kept telling me that everything was fine. And he was right, I told myself. Charles and Mary were wonderful, so friendly and welcoming that I really felt at home. The other members were the same, just ordinary people like us. And everyone seemed to have a great time. I looked forward to going each Saturday and getting more involved. You see, it was the social aspect I took to more than any of the rituals. With two young children, it was difficult at times to get out for an evening. Most of it seemed like a load of nonsense, although I could see that Alastair was very keen on learning what it was all about. After a few visits the gatherings became a little strange. I was aware that drugs were available, and some people stayed overnight. I just wanted to get involved. I'd already made several friends. Alastair was very wary of becoming embroiled in the after-show as it was called, but one night I pleaded with him to stay and reluctantly he agreed.

'I can only describe what happened as a sex orgy fuelled by drink and drugs. But I enjoyed every minute, and I couldn't wait for the next week. That's when things began to go wrong. Alastair did not want anything to do with the after-show, and he certainly did not want me staying there without him. We had a furious row which resulted in neither of us attending any meetings for a couple of weeks. Eventually, I persuaded him to come back with me, but he didn't want to stay overnight. We had another row. I stayed, and he left in a sulk. I thought that's all it was, Inspector. Alastair sulking. When I got home, he pleaded with me not to go back, but I was hooked on the experience. I took cocaine, and I loved the sex with other men and women, too. So, I started going to the gatherings on my own and Alastair stayed at home with the children. That's what ended our marriage. It wasn't him; it was me. A few months later we separated.'

It wasn't the story that Tara had expected to hear. From what Tweedy had told her, and Malcroft on their first meeting, it seemed that Alastair Bailey was the person who'd got too involved with this so-called church. Then, of course, both she and Tweedy were under the impression that the occult group was called the Church of the Crystal Water.

'What happened to Alastair? Did he return to the group?' Tara asked.

Janet Malcroft had regained some composure at this point, but tears began to seep from her eyes once again.

'It was all my fault. Before we separated Alastair begged me to stop going to Vera Deitate. I had continued to attend our own Christian church, and he said everything would be fine as long as I kept my eyes on Jesus. I told him Jesus was dead and that Vera Deitate was the right path. That's when he told me he had become a member of the Church of the Crystal Water. I didn't understand. I knew nothing of this church. He told me that they maintain great secrecy, their objective is to disrupt the work of subversive, extremist, satanic and occult organisations throughout the country. His only reason for attending Vera Deitate was to discover what went on there and then to find a way to break up the group and bring souls to Jesus. I was so angry with him. I mocked his beliefs and threw him out.'

The woman broke down in tears again, but Tara needed the remainder of the story. At least she might be getting close to the truth of what happened to Alastair Bailey, although she couldn't see how it had any bearing on the recent murders.

'You've done very well, Janet, thank you. But I really need to know what happened to Alastair.'

Used tissues were piling up in front of Malcroft as she fought to hold back her tears. Bags had developed below her reddened eyes, and each time she dabbed at them with a tissue her hands trembled.

'I didn't kill him, Inspector. You must believe me. I couldn't; I wouldn't. I still loved him.'

'Tell me what happened, Janet.'

'After we separated, I kept going to Vera Deitate. My friends there were so understanding. They helped me to cope with the children, suggested I brought them along to meetings. There were several other young children who came. They just seemed to play happily in one of the rooms while the adults did other things. You must believe me; I didn't know that anyone did things with the kids. I thought they played under supervision. But it was the drugs. I suppose I was never aware of what really went on.'

'What happened to Alastair?' Tara sensed that other issues were flooding the woman's mind, and she was drifting away from the subject.

'I told my friends that Alastair and I had separated. And I told them that Alastair was a Christian and he'd begged me to come back to God. Then I mentioned the Church of the Crystal Water. At first, I wasn't concerned by what I'd told them. They were my friends. They wouldn't do anything to hurt me. But then Charles Kirkman came to see me at home one day. He asked a lot of questions about Alastair and about one of our close friends, Simeon Jones, who was also a member of Vera Deitate. He said he wanted to help us with our marriage and reassured me that whatever happened I could always turn to him and Mary. They would take care of us.

'A couple of months later, while we were in the middle of one of our rituals in the backyard at Vera Deitate, Alastair and Simeon were brought before us. Most of us were high on coke, and everyone was laughing and cheering. I really didn't understand what was going on. Then Charles appeared in his robes, as usual, but he began the ritual by first replacing his silver hood with a black one. Suddenly everyone cheered. And I can remember all the children coming out of the hay barn to watch, including Peter and Sandra.

'The next thing I saw was Alastair and Simeon being stripped by some of the other guys and tied to old cartwheels lying on the ground. Both men were screaming, everyone was going crazy, cheering and laughing and throwing their drinks over the two of them. Simeon began reciting scripture. Revelation, Chapter twenty-one. Strange that I can remember that. Charles retorted with his own words and then mocked them by reciting from Proverbs. The whole farmyard erupted. People were drinking, smoking dope, dancing. Some people were having sex, and a couple, a man and a woman, urinated over Alastair and Simeon. Then a woman stepped forward with a hammer. Charles handed her nails, and she hammered them into Simeon's and then Alastair's hands. Please believe me, Inspector, I didn't want any harm to come to my husband or Simeon, but I was crazy, everyone was crazy. It just happened. I'll never get the sound of their screams out of my head as the nails went in. Alastair called out to me. And I did nothing. I should have stopped it. I should have saved them, but it was the drugs, I was so high on coke none of it seemed real. It was just play. Then they hammered nails into their feet.

'Mary Kirkman was our high priestess. She removed her robes and stood dressed in a black leotard and mask. The woman who'd hammered the nails presented Mary with an axe. It was like an ancient weapon, a huge shining blade. Everyone cheered, rising to a crescendo as Mary raised the axe above her head. It only took one blow and Simeon's head came off. With Alastair it took three. It was viewed as failure because with sacrifice the head is supposed to be removed with a single blow. There was blood everywhere.'

The image, shown to her by Tweedy, of the goddess Baphomet holding a human head, flashed into Tara's mind. She felt strange. Cold. And yet, horrifying as it was, all she wanted was to know what happened next.

'A fire had already been lit and Simeon's body, still nailed to the wheel, was set on top of the flames. Some of the guys brought a van into the yard and Alastair's body was lifted inside. Charles told us that he wanted to send a message to members of the Crystal Water of what would happen if they ever again tried to disrupt Vera Deitate. They drove away.

'That night I slept with Charles and Mary. I never heard anything more of Alastair until the police told me they had found his body in Croxteth Woods. A few months later, at one of our meetings, Charles concocted a ceremony of placing the heads of Alastair and Simeon, already in glass jars, onto our altar. I threw up when I saw them.'

Tara could do little but stare into the eyes of this woman. She was always shocked to hear the details of a murder retold by a witness or by the killer, but this tale had plumbed the depths of depravity. It was the stuff of horror movies designed to thrill and excite. Surely such a story could not be true. This could not have happened in this country, never mind on Merseyside. How could this woman have kept it hidden for so long? She was talking about a man she'd been married to, a man who she'd loved, had borne his children, and yet she'd looked on as he was gruesomely put to death in the name of some bizarre and fiendish belief. Tara tried her best to hold her anger, and her disgust, at the woman sitting before her.

'But you continued to attend the meetings at Vera Deitate?'

'Yes. Charles and Mary kept their promise and looked after me. Despite what you must think, Inspector, they were very loving people.'

Tara had dropped her gaze momentarily but looked again in horror as Malcroft continued to sanctify the actions of her friends. The glare from Tara was enough to stop the woman from saying more. But Tara wanted to hear it all. Maybe the link to the recent killings was still to be found in Janet Malcroft.

'Please continue, Janet.'

'Things are different nowadays. When Charles, then Mary, passed, their heads were removed and placed beside the others. At least their souls remain with us. Carl is not so keen on having them there, but the older members insist upon it.'

Tara fought the urge to slap the woman. How could she now speak so callously, so lacking in guilt about her association with this group of people?

Murray had remained unusually quiet during the telling of the story. Tara supposed he had also never heard anything like it before. They now had their killers identified for the murder of Alastair Bailey, but they had no further clues as to who was responsible for the deaths of Greasby, Young and Kirkman. Someone, perhaps, who may hold a grudge against this mystifying church. But Murray had an insightful question to ask of Janet Malcroft.

'You mentioned a woman who hammered nails into the hands and feet of the victims and who gave the axe to Mary Kirkman. Is she still connected to your church?'

Malcroft bit down on her lip.

'No.'

'Her name, please?'

Malcroft glanced sideways at Michael Coombes. His expression remained passive. Tara doubted if he, too, had ever heard such a debauched tale, although she had begun to suspect that he may also be a member of this group. Janet Malcroft dropped her gaze as she, reluctantly it seemed, answered Murray's question.

'Angela Sanders,' she muttered.

CHAPTER 55

I've already sussed out my next wee girl. I just have to organise a new van, but I might have to wait until payday. All I can do for the time being is keep tabs on her. I'm telling you, without this delivery job I'd be bloody stuck right now. And I'd be horny too, a pressure cooker about to blow. Dropping off groceries really gets me to the centre of things, right where I want to be. I've got my eye on this yummy mummy or what's the modern term again? MILF. Definitely a MILF. She lives in a big house in a quiet cul-de-sac in Woolton. I know that's not so far from where I found Vicki in Tarbock Green, but this will be the last for a while in Liverpool. After I've finally taken the sultry cop, Tara, I'll probably move on. London, I think. You can lose yourself there; it's like a country all of its own. Too many people. No one is going to notice the likes of me. I'm too quiet, too careful in what I do.

Anyway, this MILF in Woolton, my name for her is Ella, has three kids, teenagers I'd say. In fact, give them a couple more years and Ella's daughters might be worth a look. For now, though, the ever-youthful looking Ella, forty-something, friendly, neat wee body, nice pins, reddish brown hair flowing down her back and wears the style of clothes her daughters would wear, is the woman for me. I've delivered groceries to the house every week since I've been in the job. I've walked through her hallway into her spacious kitchen, all mod cons, a big conservatory stretching into a lovely garden, beautiful lawn and flower beds. It's dead nice, I think. The sort of place I once dreamed of having but, of course, my life turned out differently.

'Where's Colin today?' she asked the first time I called. She was texting on her phone and trying to check her delivery at the same time.

'On holiday for two weeks. Sunny Lanzarote, lucky for some.'

'Mmm, I'd love to get away at this time of year.' Suddenly, I pictured her lithe body sprawled on a sun lounger.

'And why not?' I said.

'You must be joking. Too much to do round here. Sonia has tennis three days a week after school. Cherie has piano and Becky has a social life that I have to drive her to and from. Then there's evenings with Guides, homework, and refereeing all the arguments between my lovely daughters.'

'What about your husband? He could do all that and let you have a break.'

She laughed out loud. LOL.

'Have you got time for a coffee?'

'Sure, thank you,' I replied, and on we went chatting. A very friendly lady. After that first meeting I decided she was chosen, and I gave her one of my names. Next time I delivered it almost seemed like she had been waiting for me, but I suppose it was her shopping she was actually waiting for. We still had time for a chat and a bit of a flirt. She was dressed for going out, I reckoned, and so I commented on it.

'You clean up well.'

'Thank you for noticing.' She did a bit of a twirl. 'Not too bad for a mother of three teenagers.' She wore a black dress, off her shoulders with a lace trim and a pair of black stiletto shoes with gold studs and buckles. Plenty of make-up, eyeshadow and eyeliner. 'Out with the girls from the office this evening.'

'Anywhere nice?'

'Dinner in town and then we might let our hair down at a club.'

'Lovely.'

'Clubbing's not really for me. I'm getting on a bit. Most of the girls are in their twenties.'

'You can't be much older,' I mischievously suggested.

'Aw bless! I'm forty-three.'

'Never. And what about that winter break?'

'Huh, no chance.'

'You could always come along with me.'

Her eyes looked on me in a reproachful manner.

'Thanks for the offer,' she replied, shaking her left hand and wedding ring at me.

I told myself that if Ella didn't have a hubby, I would be well in there. I reckoned she sort of fancied me. I reckoned she needed more than what her husband was giving her. So, I decided it would be my job to give her the time of her life.

CHAPTER 56

Tara was convinced that each member of Carl Sloan's church had been tipped off through the solicitor Michael Coombes that the police were intending to speak with them. Janet Malcroft certainly had made a run for it, and when they went to speak with Angela Sanders, she also had fled. If Malcroft was telling the truth, then Sanders had been an accessory to murder. But what Tara needed now from these people was information that would lead her to find the person responsible for the present murderous campaign. Was there someone within that group, perhaps associated with Sanders or Malcroft, going around crucifying then decapitating their victims? She needed the truth; she needed information before someone else met the same fate.

Tara was saddened by the reaction of Harold Tweedy when he listened to the recorded account of what had happened to Alastair Bailey. He looked crestfallen. He seemed devastated by the revelation that Janet Malcroft was closely involved with her husband's murder and shocked to learn that Alastair, rather than succumbing to a church of the occult, had actually been fighting against it. When the recording had finished Tweedy asked Tara for some privacy. As she left his office, she saw him reaching for the Bible at the corner of his desk.

* * *

She went to her fridge for a second glass of wine. Tonight, she thought, she could be well into a second bottle. Having turned down Aisling and Kate for a night at the cinema, she felt that her loneliness was the best therapy to deal with the memory of a harrowing day. She may have become accustomed, or at least desensitised, to gruesome discoveries of what one human being can do to another, but this case had raised the bar. She hoped she would never reach the point where she wasn't shocked by the reasons that some people commit murder. If that day ever came it was surely time to get out of this way of life.

* * *

Next morning, with no Angela Sanders to interview for the time being, she and Murray drove out to the supposed *Church of the* Vera Deitate. Still designated a crime scene, she stood outside the house gazing around her at the fields on every side, except at one corner where a lane disappeared into the woods. From where she stood, she noticed that there were no other houses or farms within sight. It was quite an isolated place, well chosen to accommodate the activities that occurred here.

Although they now had a story from Janet Malcroft to explain the murder of her husband, Tara hoped to find something that would indicate that the recent victims of this horrific method of killing were also connected to this place. She took the ground floor, while Murray went through the upstairs of the house. But there was little of interest beyond the books that she leafed through. They contained strange symbols, descriptions of rituals and rites, but nothing to give a clue to murder. It was surprising also, Tara thought, that there were so few personal belongings of Elsie Greenwood in the house. She'd lived here for twelve years yet, apart from her clothing and the books, there was nothing to indicate any person called the place home. Murray, to his childish delight, had opened a drawer in a bedroom to find a selection of sex toys. He'd also discovered a drawer containing paperwork, utility bills and personal finances, but he was less interested in those.

Without the knowledge of the macabre discovery in the outbuildings, it would be hard to find anything sinister about Vera Deitate. Together with Murray, she paid another visit to the basement room where the heads had been discovered. They'd been removed now for forensic examination, and hopefully she would soon have the identities for all the remains they had found. She knew of the Kirkmans, Charles and Mary, of Alastair Bailey and, according to Janet Malcroft, Alastair's friend Simeon Jones. Of the others to be identified she hoped that one of the females was Kelly Pritchard, and one of the males, she guessed, would be the actor, Dale Hargreaves, if this was the place he had attended.

If that were so, then she reckoned another chat with the alluring Trudy Mitchell would be appropriate. Something about the woman rankled with Tara. She didn't like her much, but that wasn't the reason. Was there a possibility that she was also present when Alastair Bailey had been killed? Her name did not appear on Sloan's list of current church members, but having stated that she didn't like what she saw when she attended gatherings with Hargreaves, was she a candidate for holding a grievance against these people? Did she have motive to kill? Tara recalled the expression on the woman's face when she heard that Dinsdale Kirkman was dead. And what of the Kirkmans? They seemed to have wallowed in such decadent behaviour and revelled in sadistic killings. Tara found it difficult to imagine either person with any endearing qualities, and yet they'd been the leaders of a church with a sizeable congregation. She could never relate to a belief system that condoned such barbaric activities.

'Creepy place, even with those heads gone,' said Murray.

'I know. It's hard to believe there are people who enjoy these kinds of surroundings. I wonder what they get from their worship.'

'A one-way ticket to hell? What do all these symbols mean, anyway?'

Suddenly, there was a loud bang as a door slammed. Murray bolted for the stairs. At the top he found the door to the upper room closed. Tara quickly joined him as he tried the handle.

'It's not locked.' They stepped outside, looking around the farmyard.

'Do you think someone deliberately slammed it?' Tara asked.

'Maybe.' A shiver passed through her. Murray left the door ajar to examine whether it moved freely on its hinges. There was little movement at all. 'Let's look through the rest of the place,' he said.

She left Murray to poke around in the other sheds, opened a gate and strolled into the lane that led into the woods. A stiff gust of wind lifted her hair, and she thought immediately of the slammed door, thinking now that it had merely been caught in a brief draught. She didn't breathe any easier.

There were a couple of pieces of old farm machinery discarded on the grass verge, a plough and a roller, rusted and probably beyond use. Within a few minutes, walking slowly, she was in amongst the trees, first a border of pine, then birch and ash, and further along much older trees, oak, beech, horse chestnut and sycamore dominated. The lane appeared seldom used, becoming less defined the further she walked. Glancing behind, she'd lost sight of the farmhouse. All was quiet but for some bird calls, crows high up in the branches increasingly bare of leaves. Something caught her eye. Something to her right, off the lane, in among the trees. At first, she thought it was someone moving, and she called out a hello. Stepping off the lane onto a carpet of dead leaves, she peered into the depths of the woods, trying hard to distinguish between tree trunks and perhaps a human form. Finally, she focused on something. She watched for movement, hardly daring to breathe. A few more paces forward and she realised. She recognised a shape, the image before her. She took several more paces, her feet making no sound upon the damp earth. Close enough now to be certain, she pulled her phone from her pocket and called Murray.

CHAPTER 57

A team of police and forensics officers were once again required at Vera Deitate. They were soon at work on the site where another headless body, fixed to a circular frame by nails at the hands and feet, had been placed upside down against the trunk of an oak tree. Tara had already seen all that she needed to see. She hoped she was right in that she had stumbled upon the body of Maurice Young. If not, then they had yet another victim. This time, of course, the body had been placed on the doorstep of this satanic organisation known as *de Ecclesia in Vera Divinitate*, Church of the True Deity.

Before the forensics team arrived, and once Murray had joined her, she'd stepped close enough to the decaying body, awash with insect life, to read and note the sign posted between the open legs of the victim. Another piece of scripture.

> *For her house inclineth unto death and her paths unto the dead.*

* * *

Tara and Murray spent the afternoon in discussion with Harold Tweedy in his office.

'Yes, it's another verse taken from Proverbs,' said Tara, 'but to me it's been deliberately chosen to infer a threat. A threat against this so-called Church of the True Deity.'

'I agree, Tara,' said Tweedy. 'It's very unlikely that members of this group would leave a body on their own property.'

'But what motive is there for killing any of these people?' Murray asked. 'We know that Dinsdale Kirkman had a connection to this house through his parents, but we don't know for sure if he was ever a member. Even if he was it still doesn't tell us why he was murdered. Then there's Greasby and Young. Both were sex offenders, but were they into devil worship?'

Tara couldn't disagree with Murray's reasoning. They may have solved a murder which occurred twenty-five years ago, but where was the link to the present day?

'Why the same MO?' Tara asked. 'Surely the present killers are trying to show that there is a connection with the past.'

'Could be someone associated with Bailey or his friend, Simeon Jones,' said Murray.

'Family?' said Tweedy. 'Someone out for revenge?'

'Against who?' said Tara. 'The present-day church is not the same organisation that existed twenty-five years ago. The name is the same, but Sloan and Greenwood were not around back then.'

'But Janet Malcroft and Angela Sanders were,' said Murray. 'Either one of those women could be the key to this whole affair.'

They didn't get the chance to finish their discussions. Tweedy's phone rang, and when he'd finished the call with his counterpart in the Cheshire police, he suggested that they all return to the Vera Deitate farmhouse.

Light was fading by the time they reached the woods and the site where the body had been discovered. Now a much larger area had been cordoned off by tape. It stretched from the tree where the body was positioned, out to the right and left then back towards the lane. Tara now realised that where she had first stood looking at the body was a natural clearing within the woods. A place perhaps for people to gather. But when they were met by the crime scene manager, DI Stephen Balmer, a jolly man in his forties, short and pot-bellied, she soon learned that the area had been used for an entirely different purpose. None of them were permitted by Balmer to enter the clearing.

'Bones,' he said. 'Lots of them.'

'Human?' asked Tweedy.

'Some are, definitely, but I'd say there are some animal remains also.' Balmer indicated the area they'd sealed off. 'Not sure yet if we are looking at a mass grave or a place where ashes have been scattered.'

'Whoever placed the body here knew exactly the significance of this spot,' said Tara. 'It's been done to draw attention to the place. We need to speak with Sloan again.'

'And we need to track down that Sanders woman,' said Murray.

As they made their way back to the car Tara wondered if Sanders had really taken flight, or had she been found by the killer and was now the next victim.

CHAPTER 58

I need to get myself a car as well as a van. It's a pain in the arse having to get a bus out to Woolton, while I'm trying to build a picture of Ella's routine. It makes for a long, slow process. And the other night I got seriously spooked. I was wandering about, close to the cul-de-sac where Ella lives, trying my best not to look conspicuous, when I suddenly got the feeling that somebody was watching me. As I was dandering along I heard a car approaching from behind me. Usually I don't bother looking, just keep my eyes straight ahead, but then this car slowed down. I thought maybe it was someone about to stop and ask for directions to somewhere, but as I turned to look it speeded up again and roared away. It was a big old thing, a dark coloured Mercedes. I didn't recognise the driver; couldn't even tell if it was male or female. But it got me thinking that maybe I'd seen that car before. I know that I'd joked with the girl from The Swallow's Tail about her stalking me, but was there really someone taking notice of what I got up to?

Thinking about it, I realised that I couldn't afford a car *and* a van, so the next day when I was out on my delivery round, I stopped off at a car auctions place near St Helens, one I hadn't used before, and had a look for a van. I needed some cover while I was watching Ella. By now, though, I'd decided, like many of my snatches, that Ella would have to be taken from a spot away from the family roost. She wouldn't be so easily lifted as Vicki. Not with three daughters and a useless husband hanging around the house.

I managed to buy a well-used Renault Trafic for less than two grand. That was nearly all I had, so I would have to wait for a while before I had enough dosh to buy some China White from Janek. At least I was mobile.

The first night out in her and I swore somebody was following me. I couldn't make out the vehicle in the dark, but I reckon it was that big Mercedes. I drove around for a while, with no particular place to go, just keeping an eye for any signs that a car was tailing me. Within a couple of miles there was nothing behind me, and I began to think that I was doting.

A day later I made another delivery to the Ella household. This time I found her busy, once again flitting about the house trying to gather up things to take to her girls when she picked them up after school.

'Sorry the place is such a mess, James. Haven't even had time to tidy the kitchen.'

'No problem, love. How was your night out?'

'Mmm?'

'Your night with the girls from work.'

'Oh that. Damp squib really. I was home by half ten. Didn't bother with the club.'

She looked a bit forlorn, and at that moment I felt the urge to give her a hug, a bit of comfort. Instead, she noticed me staring at her. I think she was embarrassed.

'Thanks, James. I'd better let you get on your way.'

No offer of coffee this time, I thought, as she held her front door open for me to carry out one of my food crates. Next time you see me, I thought, will be your last.

CHAPTER 59

It was Friday morning, but she had no enthusiasm for work. The office was buzzing with information on the identities of those found at the Vera Deitate farmhouse. She tried to remain isolated from the chatter, staring at her screen but absorbing little of the information displayed.

'You were right, ma'am,' said John Wilson, standing at her desk with yet another file in his hand. 'Dale Hargreaves is confirmed as one of the heads found at the farm.'

'Yes, but it feels strange that as far as we know there was no foul play in his case.'

'And Kelly Pritchard, too?' Wilson asked.

'Quite possibly nothing criminal there, either. Her father told us that she had a terminal illness when she went to live at the farm.'

'Just bizarre ways of holding a funeral.' Wilson set the files on her desk and moved away to banter with Murray over the current fortunes of the Liverpool team. Tara left the folders untouched. She had other things to occupy her thoughts.

What had they uncovered at the farm? The remains of how many people were scattered in that clearing? It could take months to figure out. And how many murder investigations would ensue? But as she scrolled through the alerts on her screen, the issues of daily policing on Merseyside, the robberies, stabbings, car thefts and assaults, one item suddenly leapt out at her.

A young woman from St Helens was still missing. She read the details. Marni Evans, a nineteen-year-old administrative assistant, last seen leaving work in Renshaw Street in Liverpool. Dressed in grey trousers and jacket, white blouse and brown mid-heeled shoes. Tara stared at the picture of the woman. She looked Asian or perhaps of mixed race, with a bright smiling face. Tara hoped for her safe return. Just thinking of the possibility that she was another victim of a serial killer that she believed was out there filled her with dread.

Was Marni another one to add to the list of unknowns? Someone who might never be found, alive or dead? Had the journalist, Terry Lawler, really been onto something when he'd gathered those pictures of women who had disappeared without trace? She could scarcely believe the next bulletin. It concerned a woman who'd been reported missing from her home in Tarbock Green. There might, of course, be quite logical and personal reasons for someone to disappear for a short period of time. Most people reported missing turn up within two or three days, but Tara had learned to decipher the sinister from the more inert cases. In a way she hoped that a case like this would someday land on her desk. It would give her good reason to revisit the files of those women identified by the deceased journalist, Terry Lawler.

CHAPTER 60

Before she left work it was confirmed that the body found in the woods at Vera Deitate was a match for the head impaled on the railings of the Anglican cathedral and therefore was that of Maurice Young. He had been a sex offender and not long released from prison at the time of his murder. Janet Malcroft had voluntarily identified the heads of Charles and Mary Kirkman, Alastair Bailey, Simeon Jones, Dale Hargreaves and Kelly Pritchard. So far, they had no clues as to the identity of the two remaining heads, one male and one female. Both may have been members of the church and died, as the Kirkmans and Hargreaves had, of natural causes, or they may have been victims of the ritual murders that had taken place at this isolated farm.

Janet Malcroft was unable to assist with the identity of the woman or the man. It brought Tara round to thinking again of Tweedy's theory on ritual human sacrifice. That many victims are chosen because they are regarded as low life, people of little value and therefore dispensable. With Young's body having been placed in a significant area within the woods and displaying such chilling words that seemed to be the issue of a warning, Tara was convinced now that someone had a grievance against Vera Deitate or against one or more people connected to the organisation. Did it have anything at all to do with the killings of twenty-five years ago, or was it entirely separate and aimed instead at the present incumbents? Apart from Dinsdale Kirkman's connection, through his parents, to Vera Deitate, she had no reason to believe that the other recent victims, Maurice Young or Derek Greasby, were linked to the church. Only Dinsdale's name had appeared on the list of names in the file from the original investigation. She still did not know why. And although Sloan and then Malcroft had filled in much of the detail, she felt that something was being held back. Or perhaps there were others who could fill the gaps. She needed to speak again with Trudy Mitchell, and she had to find Angela Sanders.

* * *

The ever-diligent John Wilson was first to greet her on Monday morning. Right away he had something for her to think about.

'Ma'am, a report came back on the check of Maurice Young's computer.'

For a second, she had to think on who Maurice Young was, never mind recall the occasion when she and Murray had searched his flat and brought back a laptop.

'You all right, ma'am?'

She glared at the young detective constable, who looked as though he was regretting having asked.

'You look pale,' he said.

'I'm fine, John. No make-up this morning. Didn't have time. Thanks for asking.'

'No problem. I'll leave this with you.' He placed a folder on her desk and seemed relieved to be on his way. She puffed air through her lips and wearily opened the file. Every part of her body ached. Her late-night run on Friday had done her little good. She should have followed it up with another on Saturday and Sunday. Instead, she'd spent all of Saturday in bed. Sunday was no better, but after turning down lunch at her parents, she started into a bottle of wine. By evening she was gorging on chocolate biscuits and ice cream. This morning her reckless behaviour was coming back to haunt her. A hangover didn't make reading easy. Within a few minutes, though, she realised exactly what lay before her.

'Wilson? Wilson?'

There was a ripple of laughter around the office.

'What's so funny?'

'You sound like Tom Hanks, ma'am,' said Murray. She looked blankly at her sergeant.

'What do you mean?'

'*Castaway*, the movie?'

Tara waited for the rest. Not having seen the film, she had no clue what Murray was talking about.

'His mate was called Wilson.'

She nodded once.

'Right.'

'Wilson was a basketball,' said Wilson.

All of it was lost on Tara, and she was in no mood for light-hearted banter. With both Wilson and Murray now at her desk she was able to comment on the report she'd just read.

'According to his browsing history, it appears that Maurice Young was interested in some very strange sites on the internet.'

'They call it the dark web, ma'am,' said Wilson. 'Not your normal subjects in there. Even the porn is very different.'

'Thanks, John. Anyway, it seems he made contact through one of the sites he visited. And he'd arranged through his email to meet someone. That someone may just be the person who killed him. We need to track them down.'

CHAPTER 61

Angela Sanders peered through the curtain, her garden wet with rain, the single wooden gate securely closed. She had always been thankful for this place. It was hers and hers only. No one had ever shared it. Now it was her refuge. It was a charming cottage in a quiet picturesque village. She was known here; she'd had the place for more than thirty years, but no one ever bothered her. She'd always come when she'd wanted to be alone, to write, to think about life, her career and her relationships. Even Lottie, her partner of twelve years, had never set foot in the house. Lottie was aware that her lover went off on her own at times, but she never questioned her; happy, it seemed, to remain at their home in Worsley. Besides, Lottie also had a bolthole up north in Scotland to stay with her aged mother in Aberdeen.

On this visit to her cottage, however, Angela was afraid. She had the tranquillity of her beloved cottage, but this time it was not enough. She'd never thought it would come to this. After twenty-five years, she'd never thought it would come to anything. It was ancient history. Who was around now to care about what happened back then? But everything had suddenly changed. When poor Dinsdale had been killed, everything changed. Something had gone terribly wrong. There was someone out there who knew, someone who remembered. Poor Dinsdale had been a simple lad, a mummy's boy way back then. He'd been allowed to do as he pleased under the rule of his father. Anything was allowed at Vera Deitate under the rule of Charles Kirkman. Dinsdale had been given girls to play with, to keep him amused while the adults drank wine, snorted coke and fucked.

That scar, the stain on his face, was the mark of the devil himself. That's what he'd been told. And as he grew older, he believed he could do as he pleased because the devil was in him. The older girls, women like her, had taken a shine to him. They'd all taken him to their beds. He was a novelty. But despite his opportunities with the older females, he would always go back to the young girls. That's what got him into trouble. How he had survived prison was a miracle. He was a lost soul when his parents had passed. No one took an interest in him. Except the beast who'd killed him.

She turned up the heating in her lounge. Angela hadn't felt this cold since her days on Greenham Common when the dampness seeped into your bones and all you could do was stand around a campfire warming your hands. But at least she'd felt safe back then. She had friends, many friends. And she was protesting for a better world. Now the missiles were gone, but the world seemed no better for it. Her disillusionment had led her into other things, new thinking, strange beliefs, and then she'd met Dale Hargreaves and through him Charles and Mary. They had revealed a whole new vision to her, a belief that there is another route through this mortal life. And she'd embraced all of it, the rituals, the sex, the belief in mother earth and the celebration of life. But when Charles and then Mary had passed, she lost interest in Vera Deitate. She had not been near the place in years.

Janet had been good to her recently, keeping her informed of what was going on. They were both afraid now, but she had more to fear than Janet. Everything seemed to point back to the night Alastair Bailey was put to death. What else could it be? Someone looking for revenge for their human sacrifice. But who was present on that night all those years ago, and now had decided to hit back? She had wracked her brain trying to picture a face, a face of someone who hadn't approved of their sacrifice. She could scarcely remember Maurice Young, and certainly could not say for sure that he was present on that night. As for this Derek Greasby, she'd never heard of him before his name appeared on the news after he'd been murdered. Janet had been out of her head the night Bailey was killed, stoned and more interested in having the hands of Dale Hargreaves slipping inside her trousers than doing anything to put an end to her husband. Angela was the one who'd taken pleasure in nailing his hands to the wheel, taken delight in the screams of pain while her comrades jeered. She'd relished handing the axe to Mary to cleave his head, and she loved the sex with her high priestess when it was over. Now the police were looking for her because these recent killings resembled their execution of an infidel. Janet had pleaded with her to give herself up. She'd been worried for her.

'What if the killer comes after you?' she had said when they had last spoken by phone. 'At least the police can protect you, Angela.'

But it was all right for Janet, who'd only been a witness to the killing of her husband. She was in much greater trouble. She had participated in the killing. She had ordered that the body of Simeon Jones be thrown into the fire and that the body of Alastair Bailey be put on display as a warning to those bastards in the Church of the Crystal Water. She could never go to the police. She would stay put and hope that no one would find her. Already, she regretted not fleeing the country. She wondered if Janet had managed to get away.

Standing again by her window, Angela peered once again through her lace curtains. A car pulled up outside her gate. Fear swept through her; she felt a tightening in her chest. They had found her.

CHAPTER 62

It took me longer than I'd hoped to set my plan in motion. Ella worked three days a week in an office in the university, John Moore's, in a building not far from the Metropolitan Cathedral. She usually parked her people carrier a few streets away. I decided that the best time to take her was as she walked from her office back to her car in the evening. The only trouble was she didn't always manage to park in the same street each day. But I hoped for a wet evening with few people about, and I would simply have to work fast.

And it went like a dream. Ella was one of the easiest snatches I ever had. I took the whole day off work. I set up a meeting with Janek at Lime Street station and bought as much China White as I could afford. It would certainly be sufficient to see off Ella. By early afternoon, I had the van prepared with a mattress, a large wheelie sports bag, gaffer tape, cable ties and syringes: the tools of my trade. Just before five o'clock, I found a parking space in a quiet street that I reckoned Ella would have to walk down to reach her car in the street beyond. I was lucky to find a space beside a high garden wall. At least on that side of the street no one was likely to see me shoving a woman into the back of the van.

The whole operation was as slick as oil on a hooker's ass. With little effort from me, Ella practically stepped through the side door into the van. A funny thing this time, and I can't really explain why, but I didn't want her to recognise me at that point. Before jumping out of the van to grab her, I slipped on a dark balaclava. With her all dosed up with China White and secure I drove her out to Leasowe Lighthouse, the scene of my disaster with Tara Grogan when yon big git DS Murray rudely interrupted proceedings. I thought that choosing this spot might help re-energise my intentions towards the pretty wee detective.

Again, it all went like a dream. Ella was great, not as great as Vicki, but it wasn't bad from the oldest woman I'd ever had and my first ever MILF. You should have seen the surprise on her face when I pulled off the balaclava. It was precious. Afterwards, however, things got a bit scary.

I had Ella all packed away in the sports bag, and I headed for Conwy where I'd moored *Mother Freedom*. It was late by then, nearly two in the morning, because I'd really taken my time over Ella. I hadn't expected to see many cars on the road. But a mile or so after leaving the lighthouse car park I noticed headlights in my mirror. I didn't worry too much at that point, but by the time I was into Wales and on the road to Conwy those same lights were behind me. What the fuck?

CHAPTER 63

He'd been parked in his van for more than eight hours. What the hell was he doing? She was frozen and had at times to switch on the engine to get the heater going. Her back ached from sitting behind the wheel, and her eyes were growing weary from constantly watching the exit of the car park at the lighthouse. She had a little food with her – a bag of crisps, a chocolate bar and a bottle of water. But her fear now was falling asleep and missing him drive away.

She'd been watching him from late afternoon. From the time he'd made his contact with the drug supplier at the railway station to when he'd parked up near the cathedral. There was no way she could have witnessed what he did while parked there, but she was fairly certain he'd abducted someone. She guessed that it was the woman he'd been stalking who lived in the nice house in Woolton. She couldn't know for sure. And now, sitting opposite the entrance to the Leasowe Lighthouse car park, she couldn't know for sure what he was doing with her. Maybe, strange as it may seem, his meeting with the woman was consensual. A couple having an affair. It wasn't difficult to talk herself out of the notion. But if he was raping or killing her, what was taking him so bloody long?

Her car was partially hidden beside another so she hoped he wouldn't notice it when eventually he did emerge from the car park. She had to discover what he would do next. If he had killed the woman, she wanted to know what he did with the body.

Close to two o'clock, as she fought off sleep, she saw lights appear in the distance, some way down the lane to the car park at the lighthouse. It was the haunt for many lovers in their cars, so she didn't get too excited as the lights drew nearer. But then they veered to the side as the vehicle pulled onto the road, and she saw it was the van. She let it go for a few seconds then drove off in the same direction.

CHAPTER 64

After three in the morning and this bloody car was still tailing me. I was nearing Conwy, and I hadn't made up my mind. Should I head for the boat and hope that the car wasn't really following? That it was just coincidence? Or should I lead the bastards a merry dance through Wales? What the hell did they want from me? Was it undercover police? Or some bloody sicko? I was getting seriously spooked. It's no joke driving about the countryside in the middle of the night with a dead body in your van.

Rather than making for the quayside car park, I stayed on the Expressway, went through the tunnel and headed out along the coast. All the while I kept a check on my mirror. Those same lights were a hundred yards or so behind. I put my foot down, and for a time the car dropped away. A few moments later it had restored the distance between us. I considered pulling over to let it pass by, but what if it stopped and the police wanted a word? I'd be in deep shit.

Then I thought that if I drove into Bangor, I could lose them. I knew the streets pretty well. Many of them are narrow and one-way or pedestrianised. I could draw the car into the town centre, speed up and try to confuse the driver.

When I reached the town centre, I made for High Street and was intending to go as far as the cathedral. I sank the boot. Suddenly the car behind me was out of sight as I rounded a corner. Then a stroke of luck. I came upon an entrance to a modern development of apartments. There was a short tunnel underneath the building that opened onto a square, forming a parking area for the residents. Quickly, I made the turn and sped through the entrance. I killed my lights and pulled to the right. Now I was out of sight of the street and hopefully my pursuer would drive on by. In a few minutes I guessed that the car had passed, the driver probably cursing himself that he'd lost me.

I sat for another half an hour, trying to relax, hoping the black Mercedes was gone for good. Cautiously, I pulled onto the street, got my bearings, and soon was back on the road to Conwy. I saw no more of the car, and by the time I reached the quayside at Conwy I felt safe enough to stop and organise the transport of poor Ella from the van to *Mother Freedom*. If anyone was watching me, I saw no sign of them. As the dawn broke, I motored *Mother Freedom* from her berth and out to sea. When I'd finished despatching Ella, I put in at Caernarfon. Finally, I made sure there was no one about when I returned by bus to Conwy, picked up the van and headed for home. Somehow, I would have to find out who had been driving that bloody car.

CHAPTER 65

She had followed the van all the way into Wales. Finally, she lost sight of him in the centre of Bangor. She realised that he knew he was being followed. He had deliberately tried to lose her. She wondered if he knew that it was her. Was he playing a game? What the hell was he doing driving through Wales in the middle of the night? The only answer she had was that he was intending to dump the body, assuming he had killed the woman he'd taken. Since she'd lost him, she was never going to find out where he had deposited the body. Disappointed, she headed back to

Liverpool. She'd have to work out a strategy to stop this man from ever taking another woman. He deserved the fate that was coming his way.

CHAPTER 66

It was a simple though chilling question, and Sloan was not being helpful.

'I don't know,' he said for a second time. 'I've never been in those woods.'

'It is your property, Dr Sloan. Doesn't your group hold meetings down there?'

Tara already had the answer to her question. She'd spoken with Elsie Greenwood earlier in the day. The woman had admitted to performing rituals in the clearing where Maurice Young's body had been found. Sloan was the leader of this church, surely, he should know the reason why they had chosen to hold meetings there.

'All right, we do,' he conceded at last. 'It holds a significance for the older members of the church.'

'You mean the likes of Janet Malcroft and Angela Sanders?'

'Janet, yes. Angela Sanders is not a member of our congregation.'

'And why is it a significant place?'

'Some believe there is a concentration of energy there. A place where the spirits gather. Years ago, in the time of the Kirkmans, it was customary to scatter the ashes of the departed members there.'

'Only the members?'

'Yes, as far as I know.'

'Not the victims of ritual sacrifice?'

Carl Sloan scratched at his forehead and sighed. He looked tired and weary from the interrogation. He'd been released on bail and this morning had returned voluntarily to answer more of Tara's questions. So many more questions had surfaced after the finding of Maurice Young's headless body in the woods at Vera Deitate. A clearing in the woods that harboured the remains of, so far, countless others. It was Tara's hope that none of them had got there through being murdered or sacrificed. That all were as a result of a ritual burial following death by natural causes, a strange practice though it was.

'We do not perform human sacrifice, Inspector. Among the remains of our departed you may find the bones of our animal sacrifice, lambs and goats. That is all.'

'Why do you think the body of Maurice Young was placed there?'

'I have no idea.'

'Was he a member of your church?'

'Not of my congregation.'

'But in the past?'

'I believe he may have been a member in the Kirkmans' time.'

'Do you think that someone is out to discredit your church, or is seeking revenge for something your church has done?'

'Ridiculous.'

'Is it really? What about the Church of the Crystal Water?'

'Surely it no longer exists?'

From the look on Sloan's face, Tara was thinking that this man was not quite so well informed as she had first thought. Either that or he was a supreme master at hiding the truth.

'Three people have been murdered recently, two of them were likely to have been past members of whatever group used to meet at Vera Deitate. The nature of their deaths indicates a connection to a murder twenty-five years ago which is directly associated with one of your current members, Janet Malcroft. All the murder scenes had a passage of scripture taken from the Book of Proverbs. Alastair Bailey was said to have been a member of the Church of the Crystal Water, a Christian group supposedly dedicated to the disruption of satanic worship. The latest find of a body was on your property in a place significant to your rituals. And you cannot see that someone is trying to get at your church?'

Sloan could do little but stare at Tara. Her analysis of the case had stunned the academic to silence.

'Can you think of anyone who is likely to hold a grudge against you, your church, or another member of your group?'

'I'm afraid I can't, Inspector.' Any lingering traces of arrogance from the university lecturer had evaporated. His voice weak, the man was now resigned to a horror he had not previously contemplated.

Tara looked frustratingly at Murray. They'd taken themselves to the station canteen for coffee, although it was lunchtime for the detective sergeant.

'What do we do now, Alan?'

'Sloan's been no help at all, and yet we keep finding more to connect his church with the whole affair.'

'But if he and Elsie Greenwood were the killers, surely, they would not have brought their victim so close to home? Someone has a score to settle, and if it's not with Sloan or Greenwood then it's someone else within this organisation, church or whatever you wish to call it.'

'I'd put my money on the Malcroft woman. She's admitted seeing her first husband murdered. Despite his death she's remained involved with this cult, and she's insisted upon keeping those heads on display…'

'Yes, I know, but as a member of this cult why would she want to attract attention?'

Sally, a cheery woman in her fifties, and the canteen supervisor, set a plate of sausages, chips and beans in front of Murray. She smiled at Tara who'd made do with a fruit scone.

'Thanks, Sally,' said Murray. 'I'm starving.'

The woman laughed. 'Long way to go before you're starving, Alan love.'

Tara smirked as Sally, humming an unfamiliar tune, sidled back to her kitchen.

'I'm thinking more of her children,' Murray continued. 'If Peter Bailey and his sister have discovered that Janet was responsible for their father's death, then maybe they are exacting revenge on that church and their mother.'

'Do you think that all of the recent victims, Kirkman, Greasby and Young, were involved with killing Alastair Bailey?' Murray couldn't reply, his mouth full of chips. 'If you're right about exacting revenge then there will be more killings. Janet told us that Angela Sanders hammered the nails into Bailey's hands. If that's true, then her life is also in danger.'

To Tara's amazement, Murray set down his knife and fork.

'What if the Bailey children are the modern-day Church of the Crystal Water?'

CHAPTER 67

Tara and Murray continued their discussions into the evening at a city centre pub. They covered every aspect of the case, pondered every angle, each suspect and victim. The conversation left both convinced that someone connected to the murder of Alastair Bailey was now embarked on a campaign of revenge for his death. Several pints into the discussion, the chat moved to wider issues of their jobs, their views about Superintendent Tweedy, his

Christian faith, and how he coped with the depressing nature of murder investigation. Soon they were comparing their failures in personal relationships. In her years of working with Alan Murray it was the most open conversation they had shared. She would always feel a special bond with him, indebted to him for rescuing her from the hands of James Guy. Tonight had been a good remedy for her hangover. All she felt now was tiredness. She needed a good night's sleep. As they parted for home, she gave him a peck goodnight on the cheek. His eyes lit up.

'Goodnight, Alan. See you in the morning.'

* * *

While they had spent the previous day questioning Carl Sloan followed by their evening at the pub, Angela Sanders had been arrested at her cottage by officers from Devon and Cornwall police. She was quickly transferred by car to Merseyside and St Anne Street for questioning in relation to the murder of Alastair Bailey.

The woman looked no different from when Tara had last seen her: plain dark clothing, little make-up, the single hoop earring, but now a more nervous countenance.

'Well, Ms Sanders,' Tara began, Murray sitting beside her. 'When we last met you denied knowing Alastair Bailey. Is there anything you'd like to say about that?'

'No.'

'We have a witness who was present at Vera Deitate when Alastair was killed. This witness claims to have watched as you hammered nails into the hands and feet of Alastair Bailey and Simeon Jones.'

'Not me. Your witness is mistaken.'

'This witness also claims to have seen you present an axe to Mary Kirkman who then used it to behead both men.'

Sanders shook her head and glared directly at Tara. She didn't seem as bemused by the sight of the young detective as she had on their first meeting.

'Not me,' she replied. 'How did you find me?'

Tara realised that she had only Janet Malcroft's word to go by, but she was surprised that Sanders seemed more concerned about how she was found by police in Cornwall, rather than by the accusations put to her.

'Your house in Worsley was searched. An address for a cottage in Cornwall was found. We simply had the police down there check it out for us.'

The woman frowned but didn't respond.

'Were you acquainted with Derek Greasby, Maurice Young and Dinsdale Kirkman at the time of Alastair Bailey's death?'

'Never heard of them.'

'Were you a member of the Vera Deitate church at the time of Alastair Bailey's death?'

'No.'

'When did you leave the Church of the True Deity?'

Sanders glared again at Tara, but it was met with a thin smile.

'Who told you all these lies about me? They're making it up. I didn't kill anyone. I wasn't there. I don't know what you're talking about, love.'

This time Tara glared at Sanders. She was disappointed by the woman's attitude but realised that she wasn't about to implicate herself in a murder. She'd probably guessed the identity of the witness. And Tara was well aware that Malcroft's version of events was all she had. It was the word of a woman who had lied previously and who at the time of her husband's murder was high on cocaine.

'Ms Sanders, I'm sorry that you have decided not to co-operate with our enquiry, but the matter is not finished. Derek Greasby, Maurice Young and Dinsdale Kirkman have been murdered, and we believe it is connected to Vera Deitate. Someone has taken issue with that organisation, and we think it's related to the killing of Alastair Bailey. If you are linked in some way to his death, then your life also may be in danger. It would make sense for you to share with us anything you know about Alastair Bailey or the activities of Vera Deitate.'

'Can I go now, Inspector?'

CHAPTER 68

Superintendent Tweedy was keen to get a measure of the latest developments in the case, especially since the arrest of Angela Sanders which had heightened the interest of the media. Sanders had always been a controversial figure, and she was well known in Britain for her radical views. Her arrest had made national news bulletins. It was irritating and yet a relief to the detectives at St Anne Street that she had been released pending further investigation. As matters stood they had only the word of Janet Malcroft as to how her first husband had perished, and at the time she'd been high on cocaine. She was hardly a reliable witness. Convicting Angela Sanders as an accessory to murder would be difficult based only on Malcroft's version of events.

'John mentioned that you have some more leads to follow,' said Tweedy to both Tara and Murray. They were seated in his office, Tara having just brought her boss up to date on the interview with Sanders.

'Yes, sir. John has managed to trace a brother of Simeon Jones who may be able to explain Simeon's involvement with the Church of the Crystal Water.'

'I've tried asking around some of my friends who were in our congregation back then,' said Tweedy. 'The name Simeon Jones rang a bell with one or two of them. He was definitely a close friend of Alastair's, although I certainly do not remember him.'

'Also, sir, we have to follow up on the person who was in contact online with Maurice Young. They had arranged to meet. Could be the last person to have seen him alive, or it could be the person responsible for his death. And, sir, I want to speak again with Peter Bailey and his sister.'

'Why is that?'

'If these murders are a case of revenge for the killing of Alastair Bailey, then his children have motive,' said Murray.

'Could just as easily be someone related to Simeon Jones out for revenge,' said Tweedy.

'Or to someone related to the other unidentified victims found at the farmhouse,' said Tara.

'I agree,' Murray replied. 'But we don't have any names except for the Baileys.'

Tweedy looked grave. Tara could see that he still felt a personal hurt or guilt regarding Alastair Bailey. It would suit him more, she thought, if it turned out that the recent killings had nothing whatsoever to do with his old friend or his family.

* * *

Trevor Jones was a hefty-framed man of sixty-three, with bushy grey hair and a ruddy face. A sheep farmer and Welsh speaker, he sat on a kitchen chair listening intently as Tara explained the reason for her visit. She and Murray, after the long drive into North Wales, were grateful for the piping hot tea and freshly baked bread with butter and strawberry jam. Trevor's wife, Nerys, had been very welcoming.

'Simeon told me everything that went on in his life, up to a point,' said Trevor Jones, his elbows on the table and his thick hands clasped together. His green eyes, in watery and reddened sockets, darted from Tara to Murray. 'Then one day he said that he had met some wonderful people.

Good Christian people, he said. And he told me that they had a job to do for the Lord.'

'Did he mention the Church of the Crystal Water?' Tara asked.

The farmer shook his head and grunted a no.

'Did he mention the names of any of his friends?'

'Used only Christian names, but I can't remember them now.'

'What job was he doing for the Lord?'

'Very cagey, was our Simeon, but we prayed several times for the work he was doing. Trying to rid the place of very evil practices, he told me. He and his friends were helping people who had fallen into depravity.'

'Did he say where he was doing this work or what it involved?'

'No. He didn't say much about it, although he seemed very concerned for some children, and we prayed a lot for them. He said they were exposed to some very unsavoury goings on. Drugs and sex parties. Nerys and I still wonder what happened to them.'

'Any names?'

The man shook his head. The news that Tara had brought him would not be easy to absorb. She'd explained about the finding of human heads at Vera Deitate and her belief that one of them was Simeon, based on what Janet Malcroft had told her and her subsequent identification.

'When was the last time you saw your brother?' she asked.

Trevor Jones rubbed the tears into his face and sighed deeply.

'I suppose I never thought anything was wrong for about five or six weeks after I last saw him. I knew if he hadn't been in contact with me, he would certainly have spoken to Mother. When I realised that he hadn't been to see her, I knew something was wrong. He would never have gone more than a week without checking on her. I went to the police, and he was listed as missing. Heard nothing until you turned up this morning. Mother has passed on now and never knew what happened to her youngest.'

Tara couldn't help her tears as she looked at the strong farmer grieving for his brother. She hated bringing such tragic news to a relative of a murder victim. She hated more those who inflicted such pain on the innocent. She was saddened always by the spread of sorrow through a family or through a community at the tragic loss of life. But as she had learned, almost from her first day on the job, look at the victims and you won't stop until you've caught the killer.

She had gained little from Trevor Jones except that her gut feeling was growing that someone who was around at the time Alastair Bailey and Simeon Jones were murdered, now had reason to kill Derek Greasby, Maurice Young and Dinsdale Kirkman.

CHAPTER 69

'What do you know of the Church of the Crystal Water?'

Peter Bailey stood at the door of the garage workshop, a heavy spanner in his hand. He didn't look pleased to see Tara and Murray. She'd thought him quite affable on their first meeting and certainly well mannered. Today he seemed angry and irritated.

'Never heard of it.'

'Has your mother ever mentioned it in connection to your father?'

'No. And I don't want you bothering my mother again. She's been through enough.'

'And what about you, Peter? How are you feeling right now?'

'What do you mean?'

'Your father's remains being found, and your mother knowing of them all this time since he was killed.'

'That was her business, part of her belief.'

'What about your belief? Don't you want the people who killed your father brought to justice?'

'But it was the Kirkmans who killed Dad, and they're both dead.'

'There were others involved. Don't you want to see them pay for what they've done?'

'You mean my mother? I've told you to leave her alone.'

'What about Derek Greasby or Maurice Young or Dinsdale Kirkman? Did you want them to pay for their crimes?'

'What are you talking about? Are you suggesting that I had something to do with these murders?'

'Did you, Peter?'

'No way. You people are nuts if you think me or my family had anything to do with murder.' He pointed his spanner at Tara. 'Leave me alone and stay away from my mother.' He turned and walked back into the garage.

'I wonder what Janet has told her son,' said Tara. 'He's certainly angry about something.'

'Depends on what he already knew of his father's death,' said Murray. 'Must have been a shock to learn that his parents were on opposite sides when it came to this devil worship nonsense. That it was Janet who got involved against her husband's wishes.'

'But is Peter aware that Janet is still a member of Vera Deitate?'

They climbed back into the car, and Tara checked her notebook for the address of their next call.

'Do you think devil worship is just nonsense?'

'A load of old tosh,' replied Murray.

'Some people say the same thing nowadays about Christianity.'

'Maybe, but you don't see many human heads in glass jars in the Church of England.'

As they were moving off from the small forecourt of the garage a red van emerged from the rear of the building and sped onto the main road. Peter Bailey was at the wheel, a mobile phone clasped to his ear.

'Where's he off to?' said Murray, immediately taking to the road in pursuit of the van. Tara wasn't quite so keen.

'Never mind, Alan. Just as likely to be job-related than him running off to speak with Mum.'

'There's something we haven't considered. Mother and son working together to get their revenge on those who murdered Bailey.'

'But why would Janet Malcroft have waited twenty-five years if she wanted to avenge her husband's death? The Kirkmans were already dead. Ultimately, those two were responsible for his murder.'

'Maybe she'd discovered that her son had only recently taken up the crusade.'

'That would suggest that he carried out the murders without the knowledge that his mother was a witness to the killing of her husband, and that she has continued to be a member of the Vera Deitate.'

'Reason then for both to be shocked and angry with each other.'

CHAPTER 70

Tara thought it a rather unlikely spot for a trace on an email of this nature to lead. Then again, the person who had been in contact with Maurice Young may simply have used a computer in their workplace. Murray parked outside the shuttered entrance to Oak-bespoke, a furniture-making enterprise set within a modern business park close to the river and a little over a mile from Tara's apartment at Wapping Dock. When Murray rang the bell, within a few seconds, the green metal shutter began to rise, and before them stood a young woman with dark hair, wearing denim dungarees and a royal blue T-shirt.

'Hiya,' she said with a cheery smile, as if she already knew Tara and Murray well.

'Hello, love,' said Murray. 'I'm Detective Sergeant Murray and this is Detective Inspector Grogan…'

'Hiya,' she said again to Tara. 'I'm Sharon.'

'We'd like to speak to whoever is in charge please, Sharon.'

'That'll be Jemima. Follow me.' She led the way through a workshop, where a middle-aged man with a bald head and glasses was applying a dark polish to a beautiful circular dining table. The smell of wood, polish and varnish hung in the air, while Radio Two blared as Tara and Murray were shown into a partitioned office to the rear of the workshop. There, seated at a computer, was a woman of around thirty in a dark green jumper, with blonde hair in a ponytail, fresh-faced, wearing little make-up and a pair of glasses resting on a bony nose.

'Jemima, these police officers want to speak to you.'

With a smile the woman looked up from her computer.

'Hiya,' she said in similar tone to how Sharon had first greeted them. 'How can I help you?' Sharon left them and returned to a bench where a long dowel was held in a vice and proceeded to apply a stain with a small brush.

Tara explained the trace of the IP address linked to emails exchanged with Maurice Young.

'Has anyone who has access to your computer been in contact with this man?' Tara asked.

'Don't recall that name, but it may be one of our customers. Is there a problem?'

'Who has access to your computer?'

'We have two. This one is for office work and another in the workshop is for CAD.'

'CAD?'

'Computer Aided Design. We use it for drawing plans of our furniture. I use it mostly, but Sharon is learning. So why do the police want to know if we've been in contact with this man?'

Tara didn't reply to the woman's question, allowing Murray to take over.

'Someone using this IP address was in email contact with Maurice Young. He had attempted to make arrangements to meet.'

'Is there something wrong in that?'

'A week after the last email was sent, Maurice Young was murdered.'

'Oh, my goodness. And you think I may be in danger?'

'If you're the person who was in contact with him then you may have been the last person to see him alive.'

'He did ask me to meet him, but I didn't reply.'

At least that tallied with what was found on Young's computer, thought Tara.

Tara stood impassively as Murray continued to question the woman. Why on earth hadn't she admitted to knowing Young from the outset, instead of the pretence that he may have been a customer or that her young assistant may have been the one who'd used the computer? Awkward, Tara thought. Toying with them. But why?

'Why did he want to meet you?' Murray asked.

The girl smiled, and her eyes widened.

'Business. He wanted to discuss a design for a coffee table.'

'Why didn't he come to the workshop?'

'Between you and me, I think it was just an excuse to meet me for a drink.'

'And are you in the habit of meeting up with total strangers you've encountered on the internet?'

'I've done it a couple of times. I'm single, Sergeant. I've not had much success with men so far.' She smiled at him, and Tara could see Murray flush with embarrassment or most likely a lurid thought. 'My photograph is on our company website; I get emails all the time from men with an interest in furniture making wanting to meet me. I suppose I'm a bit of a novelty in their world.'

'Don't you think it's very dangerous meeting up with strangers?' Tara asked.

'I think I can take care of myself, Inspector, but I appreciate your concern.'

'Did you ever speak with Maurice Young?'

'I'm not sure. I may have done. If he was a potential customer, we might have spoken on the phone. But I don't remember anyone identifying themselves as Maurice Young.'

'But did you make any arrangements by telephone to meet him?'

'No. What was he like?'

Tara ignored the question as Murray asked another.

'Do you use the internet a lot to meet people? Are you registered with any dating sites?'

The woman removed her glasses and smiled at Murray.

'Not really, do you, Detective Sergeant Murray?' He flushed again, but to his credit, Tara thought, he persevered.

'Ever access the dark web?'

'I don't know what that is.'

Tara was not amused by the woman's attitude, but Murray had a smirk on his face suggesting that he had enjoyed the flirt. All they had come away with was the woman's business card, although Murray behaved as if he might return to see her again on a less formal basis. But on the way back to the station something still irritated Tara. She examined the business card. When she got back to St Anne Street, she would get Wilson to check out the company.

CHAPTER 71

Angela had put off travelling back to Cornwall. The weather was poor, cold and wet, and she didn't relish driving a hired car down the motorway in such conditions. Her own car had remained at her cottage when the police had come for her. But it wasn't just the journey that was putting her off. Somehow, and suddenly, her cottage had lost its appeal. It was no longer her secret place, her sanctuary, her bolthole. How could she have been so stupid, leaving the address lying about her house for those coppers to find when they came snooping? And it hadn't taken them long to do just that. The house in Worsley had been empty. Lottie had gone to visit her mother. But why had Janet, her close friend, shopped her? Maybe she had to. Maybe her kids, Peter and Sandra, had found out what really happened to their father, and they had forced their mother's confession. Worse than that. Perhaps they were out to avenge their father's death. Maybe they had killed Maurice and poor Dinsdale.

That young detective, DI Tara Grogan, was a clever lass, despite her baby face. She'd somehow managed to untangle the things that happened so long ago when those creeps Bailey and Jones were sacrificed. Her own attempts to muddy the waters with stories of CND and Greenham Common hadn't put Grogan off. And if this copper was correct now in her assessment of these latest killings, then she too was a target. Somebody had taken issue with Vera Deitate. She could only hope it didn't involve her. After all, she'd left years ago when Mary stopped going because of her illness. They'd done some very wild and, at times, wicked things, but in the end, it still came down to friendships, to personal relationships. She'd loved Mary, admired her, saw her commitment to her beliefs, however strange and out of keeping with the norm. They had enjoyed wonderful sex together, even when Charles had joined them. But who had they hurt, and hurt so badly that after all these years they were seeking retribution?

This house was too big for her and Lottie now. Strange that she felt that way also. That her freshly aroused fears could cast shadows over every aspect of her life. Mostly she and Lottie confined themselves to one sitting room, the kitchen and their bedroom. But this evening she was drawn to the lounge to the right of the hallway, a place where they often welcomed their friends. She sat in a deep cushioned sofa, a strong black coffee in her hand, gazing in the dim light of a single table lamp at the picture on the wall above the mantelpiece. Three stars in gold over a black sun. Mary had come up with the symbols. Only she and Mary would ever know their meaning. Three stars: Charles, Mary and her, reigning over chaos.

She should move to Cornwall permanently, end things with Lottie. Lottie was much too young to be wasting her life living in an old house with an old woman. She should be with someone younger, someone closer to her own age. Besides, if there was trouble ahead then she would never forgive herself if Lottie were to get hurt. Maybe she should retire from working, start to write again perhaps. But what on earth was she thinking? If DI Grogan continued her digging, she might come up with definite proof of who had hammered nails into the hands and feet of those excuses for men. That she had handed the axe to Mary as she had done many times, even if it were only for the sacrifice of a lamb.

Her doorbell chimed. She froze. She wasn't expecting callers. Lottie had her own key and wasn't due back for at least another couple of days. Her hands trembled, and silently she set her cup down on the coffee table. Why did she feel the room growing colder? Relax. Could be anybody; it wasn't late, just gone half past six. With a growing expectancy that she would be faced again with the police and DI Tara Grogan, or maybe someone from the press, she padded to the front door. By the time she'd released the lock, she felt resigned to her fate. At least in police custody she would be safe. She opened the door wide.

'Hello, Angela.'

CHAPTER 72

'So how are you settling into the new job?'

'Dead on,' I replied. 'Gets me out and about. That's what I like. Couldn't stand being closed up in an office all day.'

Collywell raised an eyebrow and smiled. Then I realised what I'd just said, him doing exactly that.

'Definitely better than the kitchen job,' I added.

'Good.' He wrote something into his file. 'And how is the social life?'

I shrugged. Didn't know how and didn't really want to answer that question.

'Any outings? Join any clubs?'

'Na. I've been going down to a pub in the city centre some nights. Good atmosphere and music sometimes.'

He didn't seem overly impressed with that, but as usual he didn't try to judge me, just nodded and wrote in the file. I felt obliged to say something that might impress him.

'I'm thinking of taking up fishing again. Used to do it when I was a kid.'

'Good idea.' He wrote in the file again. 'You know, James, filling your time usefully is the key to it all. Setting a few targets, having something to aim for will keep you out of mischief.'

I certainly had plenty of targets, loads to aim for, but it wasn't going to keep me out of mischief. He gave me some more leaflets on men's health and well-being. What to do if I thought I had mental health problems. I began to wonder exactly what this man thought of me. He was very professional, I suppose, just following procedures. Probably hated my guts, but who gives a shit? As soon as the dust settles over the missing Ella and Vicki, I'm going to get everything ready for another crack at Tara. She cost me my freedom once; she's not going to do it again. And I never walk away from a challenge.

CHAPTER 73

First thing, before going to St Anne Street, Tara made a quick detour out to Bootle. Her car had been valeted and returned to her the previous evening. Murray's car had been resprayed and also returned. Norman Pritchard was still in his dressing gown when he answered the door.

'Sorry for calling so early, Norman, but if you don't mind, I have a couple more questions to ask you.'

'Our Molly's not up yet, so come in, love, and I'll put the kettle on.'

She followed him into the kitchen and watched as he filled the kettle, got two mugs ready and a teapot. She realised just how difficult she had probably made his life in recent days. It can't have been easy coming to terms with the finding of your daughter's remains, and tragically only the head, after more than twenty years. He was aware that Kelly had passed from natural causes, but the removal of her head in a religious ceremony would be difficult for him, or any family, to bear.

'How have you been coping?' she asked him.

'OK, love, OK. My family have been good. They've arranged a small funeral for our Kelly. Seems right to give her some sort of Christian resting place even though she weren't that way.'

'Let me know when it is. I would like to come.'

'Very good of you, love. Can't have been easy for you finding all those things at that house. Glad I don't have your job.'

When the tea was made, she followed him into the sitting room, looking exactly as it had on her previous visit except for Molly's vacant chair in front of the telly.

'I wanted to ask you a couple more questions, Norman.'

'That's fine, love, go ahead.'

'Can you remind me of the names of Kelly's children?'

'You haven't found them as well, have you?'

'No, I was just wondering about their names and where they may have ended up.' She could hardly explain her nebulous thoughts that she might well have found his granddaughter and then to break his heart by suggesting that she was a murderer.

'There was Corey, the young lad, and Aeron was the girl.'

'Do you know what surname they took?'

'Never really thought on it, but I suppose they took their dad's.'

'Keron, wasn't it?'

'That's right, Keron Fogge.'

Something still gnawed at her about these children.

'And you said that Keron moved to the States and took the children with him?'

'Far as I know, love.'

'You've not heard anything since Kelly died?'

'Not a thing.'

'Do you know where he came from originally before he met Kelly?'

'Yorkshire. He was a Yorkshireman as plain as day.' Norman seemed to drift off in his thoughts as he sipped his tea. Tara drank some from the mug, but the old man had sweetened it like his own, with three spoonfuls of sugar. It tasted like hot syrup.

'Any idea where in Yorkshire?'

'He was a Leeds United supporter, so I think maybe he came from there. I don't know the address. Never did have a lot in common with the lad.'

'Thank you for the tea, Norman. I'll let you get on.'

'No problem, love.'

She hurried to the station, and encumbered John Wilson with yet another research task.

'Can you check if there is a Keron Fogge living in the Leeds area? It's a long shot, but I need to ask him about his children.'

'Yes, ma'am.'

'And let me know when you've got something on that furniture place.'

She went in search of Murray who, by this time of the morning, was likely to be filling his face with scones, toast or sandwiches.

'I had a word with Norman Pritchard this morning. I wanted to confirm the names of Kelly's children.' Murray was working to clear his mouth. Tara sat opposite him in the station canteen nursing a mug of coffee. 'The girl's name was Aeron.'

'What about the surname?'

'If she took her father's, it would be Fogge. Wilson is trying to find an address for Keron Fogge.'

'I thought he'd gone to the States?'

'I know, but it's worth checking that he hasn't come back again.'

'Bit of a long shot.'

Tara sipped her coffee, and her thoughts drifted. Murray continued with his full English.

'Do you think it's too much of a coincidence that the person Maurice Young tried to meet up with might be the daughter of Kelly Pritchard?' she asked.

'When you put it like that, yes. Different name for a start. And it's a big assumption to make that somehow these kids are out there waging war. And why? Kelly died of natural causes.'

'What if the kids don't know that?'

CHAPTER 74

'What if it's true, Corey?'

'It isn't. I know what I saw.'

'But you were only eight years old. Maybe she got really sick and then she died.'

'I saw what they did to her. That bitch Sanders handed an axe to Mary, and she cut off our Mam's head.'

'But Angela was adamant that Mam was already dead. She said they just gave her the funeral that she wanted.'

'No, Aeron. Mam was only sleeping. We'd only just left her; we kissed her goodnight before Dad took us out of the bedroom. It was a sacrifice, like all the rest of them. I saw others killed, too. I saw what they did to Simeon. You were too young to remember. Simeon was good to us. He looked after us better than our dad. It was after they killed him that I decided to get out of there. And then on the night they killed our Mam, I took you by the hand and we ran away.'

'But we may have killed people for nothing?'

'No! I've told you, Aeron. These animals did things to us and to other kids. They deserved to die.'

'And what about the others?'

'The others are just the same. They're scum. They've hurt so many people. We have a duty to deliver God's justice.'

Aeron sat on a sofa, her knees pulled close to her chest. There were tears in her eyes. Corey fiddled with the TV remote, flicking through channels, checking for news of the latest kill.

'You know I've always been right, Aeron. I've always looked after us, haven't I? You're too young to remember that place, what went on there.'

'I remember some things,' she said, wiping a tissue across her nose. 'I can still remember Simeon reading to us, telling us stories from the Bible. And I know things went bad. I know he was taken from us. And I can remember our Mam, just a little bit. She was always laughing.'

Corey came and sat close to his sister, placing his hand on her head.

'There you go, see? It was people like Sanders and Young who took Simeon from us. Then they took our Mam. And Fat Dinny did unspeakable things to you and the other girls, particularly the older ones. He got what he deserved, Aeron.'

She snuggled her body into her brother as he stroked her hair.

'I can never forget what they did,' he continued in a quiet voice. 'It is our duty to remove this evil. Only one more to go from our time at Vera Deitate and then we can concentrate on the filth who walk the streets. I need you to be strong, Aeron. I can't do it without you.'

She put her arms around him and squeezed him tight. He kissed the top of her head.

'We need to make plans for your latest friend,' he said.

'He's kind of cute, don't you think?'

'Don't go soft on me, Aeron. You know what he's done. The anger of the Lord is upon him.'

'I know he deserves to die. But I can have some fun with him first. And what about this girl cop? She's finding out a lot of stuff.'

'We'll have to keep an eye on her. Don't want her getting close.'

He kissed his sister again on the forehead, and she hugged him like she always did. He got to his feet, held his hands out for her; she rose, and he led her to their bed.

CHAPTER 75

Tara's alarm sounded. It felt like she'd never been asleep. Too much coffee the day before and too many theories running through her head, she knew she had been still wide awake at half past three. And recently she'd suffered terrible bouts of loneliness, particularly after a poor night's sleep. She longed for someone to talk to first thing in the morning. Exchanging texts with Kate or Aisling as they hurried to work or with Kate as she came off a night shift helped, but it wasn't a person beside her, touching her, whispering a good morning or even a shout of wake up, we've slept in. She scolded herself for being so damned silly. Alan Murray was clearly not the man for her, and yet they spent so much time together. Mostly it was rushing from one crime scene to the next, from one suspect to another, a snatched lunch or a coffee at the station. But they did talk and on occasion not just about their work. She reckoned she knew him as well as any woman currently in his life and vice versa.

Physical attraction was hardly the determining factor when you knew a person as well as she knew Murray. He wasn't unattractive to her, but she was his boss for goodness' sake. She had never regarded him as a friend.

Maybe now she was thinking of him because she was beginning to wonder if the only man who could ever share her life, and understand her, had to be a cop. Should it be someone who shared her experiences, who knew what it was like to deal with horrible scenes of violence, who had encountered difficult and violent people, who had felt in danger and had suffered in their private life because of their job? Should it be someone who had adjusted to the bizarre world of the police officer and in doing so had become maladjusted to ordinary life?

She wiped away her tears as she padded to the shower.

* * *

On arrival at St Anne Street, somehow, she'd expected to find a change. Surely things could not be the same after her ponderings of the morning. But life didn't work that way. It didn't matter if you were a police officer or a checkout girl beeping groceries at a supermarket. Things don't happen simply because you want them to. If you want things in your life to change, you must be proactive.

Murray was nowhere to be seen. Not that she was suddenly going to rush into his arms, but she did want, in some way, to show that she appreciated having him in her life. How she would accomplish such a feat, she hadn't a clue. Wilson, as often was the case, was first to greet her. Inevitably he had information to impart.

'Ma'am,' he said. 'Only one Keron Fogge in the whole of Yorkshire, according to the electoral register.' He handed her a Post-it with the address.

'Thanks, John. Here's hoping it's the right Keron Fogge. Any idea where Alan is? Or maybe that's a silly question.'

She found him in the canteen, full English before him and chatting with two young women from the office, one of them was Paula Bleasdale. A strange pang of envy jabbed her conscience. At that moment she wanted to be the one sitting with him, flirting and giggling at his jokes. Why the hell was she feeling this way?

After breakfast she and Murray headed for Yorkshire and for the address of what she hoped was the home of Keron Fogge, father to Corey and Aeron. She realised that it may well be an entirely different individual, and the Keron Fogge she needed to speak with was somewhere across the Atlantic.

Norman Pritchard hadn't been far wrong in suggesting Leeds. The address she had was for a house in Batley, seven miles south-west of Leeds, and close enough to Elland Road to perhaps confirm Norman's view that Fogge had been a Leeds United supporter.

They stopped outside a grey-brick council house, within a small estate. Most of the surrounding houses were occupied, but there were a couple with bricked up windows and doorways, and walls daubed in locally flavoured graffiti. Tara went alone and knocked on the front door, gazing around the overgrown garden as she waited. An old man with little hair and a pair of thick-framed glasses answered her knock.

'Good morning, sir. I'm Detective Inspector Tara Grogan of the Merseyside Police. I'm looking to speak with Keron Fogge?'

'I'm Keron Fogge, but you'll have to speak up, love. Haven't got me hearing aid in.'

'Are you the Keron Fogge who was once in a relationship with Kelly Pritchard?'

'Can't hear you, love. You better come in.'

He shuffled into his sitting room, and Tara followed. The room was small and cluttered with books, vinyl records and video tapes. A worn velour sofa of olive green was set close to an electric fire. The old man fiddled with his hearing aid, while Tara waited with a patient smile.

'That's more like it,' he said. 'Now who did you say you were, love?'

She showed him her ID.

'DI Tara Grogan, Merseyside Police. I'm looking for the Keron Fogge who once had a relationship with Kelly Pritchard.' By this point she was certain she had the wrong man. Norman had never suggested that Kelly's partner had been much older than she was. Twenty-five years ago, however, this man, in whose home she now stood, would have been at least sixty.

'Kelly who?'

'Pritchard. She had two children, Aeron and Corey.'

He sat down on his sofa and indicated that Tara should sit also.

'Cup of tea, love?'

'No thank you. Have I got the right person, Mr Fogge?'

'That would be my son who had those kids. Hasn't lived here for years.'

'Do you know where I might find him?'

The old man shook his head with a grave look on his face.

'No, love. He calls me from time to time, visits once or twice a year, but he's always on the go that one. America, Canada, Spain, all over the place. Not like my daughter. She only lives round the corner in the next street. Calls in every day on her way home from work. On my own now, you see. Our Maggie's passed away, ten years ago.'

'It's good to have your daughter close by.'

'It is, love, it is.'

'What about your grandchildren, Aeron and Corey? Do you ever see them?'

He gave her a look to suggest she'd asked a question with such an obvious answer, then a frown as punishment for asking in the first place.

'What's this all about, love? Why are you asking all these questions?'

'I'm trying to find out what happened to Kelly's children after she died.'

'Both dead, love.'

'What happened?'

'Killed in a storm in America.'

CHAPTER 76

Harold Tweedy called her on the phone. It was well after two in the morning, although yet again she hadn't been sleeping soundly.

'Apologies for waking you, Tara, but we have an incident to attend.' Only her boss could make it sound like something rather innocuous when it was likely to be something horrendous. He didn't call her out in the middle of the night unless there was good reason.

'What's happened?'

'Scant details at the moment. Manchester Police are on the scene, but it has relevance to your spate of recent murders. I'm on my way there now.'

'What's the address, sir?'

'I believe you already know of it, the home of Angela Sanders.'

As she got dressed, she roused Murray on her mobile and asked him to pick her up. She always felt a little safer with a companion when she was called out in the middle of the night. Besides, lately she had a strange feeling that someone was watching her movements to and from Wapping Dock. She told herself it was just paranoia after her experience at the hands of James Guy, but she couldn't help it. Then, of course, someone connected to this case knew where she and Murray lived. Her car had been doused in blood, Murray's with acid. She was right to be cautious.

A full police incident had been declared at the home of Angela Sanders in Worsley. Part of the tree-lined avenue had been sealed off. There were a dozen police vehicles parked on the road outside the house. Tweedy was already there and waiting to brief them.

'It is Angela Sanders, I'm afraid,' said Tweedy.

'The same MO?'

'Seems like it. I'm waiting to have a look.'

The night air was cold and damp, the sort of cold that penetrates clothing, skin and then bones. They waited for three quarters of an hour, while the SOCOs from Greater Manchester police examined the scene. Tara was glad to have worn a pair of boots and a long coat over her jeans. A beany hat was pulled tight over her ears. She realised that the scene was worth a look, but at the same time she wondered what else she could possibly learn. This was the fourth killing, presumably by the same perpetrators. What more to see? She was convinced of who was responsible. She just had to find them and gather some proof. Poor old Keron Fogge. She didn't believe for a second that his grandchildren were dead. Another twenty minutes went by before a Detective Chief Inspector Browne approached them. He was a tall man, balding and with a dishevelled appearance in a T-shirt beneath a plaid shirt and grey zipped hoodie.

'You guys can take a peek now,' he said, his accent as thick Mancunian as Murray's was Scouse. 'Superintendent Tweedy, sir, if you would keep us informed of your investigations that would be great.'

'Of course, DCI Browne. And thank you for the call.'

'No problem, sir. My DS was aware of the connections to your case. You'll find the victim on the ground floor, first room on the right-hand side.'

All three of them donned the requisite hooded coveralls and shoe protectors. Tweedy led the way inside; the hallway and all adjoining rooms had lights on. A couple of forensic guys moved to the side to let them view the scene.

Even at first glimpse this was so much worse than any of the others. Tara didn't think it possible. She looked at the body of the victim, spread-eagled on the carpeted floor. The head of Angela Sanders was displayed upon her mantelpiece. Blood had seeped and dripped onto the fireplace. The eyes had been forced to stay open with gaffer tape stuck to the eyelids and fixed to the forehead. Her gaze had been fixed so as to look down upon her naked body. Her clothes had been ripped off and scattered around the living room. Her hands and feet had been nailed, through the carpet, to the wooden floor to create the now familiar pentacle. Blood had flowed from the shoulders creating a dark semicircle upon the carpet. But the killers this time had gone further, sunk to lower depths of depravity. The torso of Angela Sanders had been sliced open, from her throat to her pubic bone. Her intestines, liver and spleen had been pulled out and lay beside the body, blood and bile having soaked into the carpet. Laid between the feet, a sheet of A4 held yet another inscription.

The curse of the Lord is in the house of the wicked.

Tara glanced at her boss to see if he had noted the phrase. No doubt he had already committed it to memory. But he was staring at the picture on the wall above the fireplace. They had seen that image before in the basement of Dinsdale Kirkman's home and in the lower room at the Vera Deitate farmhouse. Three stars over what Tara now recognised as a black sun. The significance remained a mystery. A strange piece of art to have hanging in a sitting room. But Tara was dealing with strange people with unconventional beliefs. She wondered why Angela Sanders had been subjected to disembowelling and whether it had taken place before or after she was beheaded. Had she been visited with greater evil because the killer knew of her past? Or was the killer simply upping his game?

CHAPTER 77

'But the old man, Fogge, told you his grandchildren are dead.'

'What if they're not, Alan? What if these kids were raised by their father? Just because we can't find him, doesn't mean the kids aren't alive.'

'But according to Pritchard, Fogge went to the States and took the kids with him. They're just as likely to still be living there. One of the grandparents has to be right.'

They carried on their discussion into the station and up to Tweedy's office. After a long cold night, the pair of them were surviving on coffee. Tara felt irritable. Neither one had returned home. Instead, they'd eaten breakfast at a motorway services and tried to freshen up as best they could. Tara could feel the bags below her eyes and Murray needed a shave.

Tweedy looked better rested, having at least had the opportunity to get home and manage a fresh change of clothes. DC Wilson was the perkiest of them all, bidding each one of them a cheery good morning. Tara and Murray grunted their replies and resumed their debate.

'What about the Bailey kids? More likely to be them seeking revenge?' said Murray.

'I know, Alan. I think we need to speak with that family again. Janet Malcroft told us that she saw Angela Sanders nailing Alastair Bailey to the wheel. Now Sanders is dead. Have Malcroft's children only just learned about what Sanders did to their father?'

'Seems probable to me. And less likely for the Pritchard kids.'

Tweedy had allowed his officers to finish their debate before taking charge of the meeting.

'I see you have already formed an opinion of who is responsible for this latest killing.'

'Someone is embarking on a campaign of revenge, sir.'

'You believe that, Tara?' Tweedy asked. 'What about Derek Greasby? You haven't yet connected him with this Vera Deitate church or with any of the other victims.'

'But the MO is the same, and all the recent killings have that similarity to the murder of Alastair Bailey. Dinsdale Kirkman had an association with the Vera Deitate church. And now Angela Sanders is dead. Whatever is going on it must be linked to that church and to what occurred twenty-five years ago. For me that points to the Pritchard or the Bailey children.'

Murray came in again with a counter argument.

'Or Janet Malcroft, or Trudy Mitchell, or to anyone else that we don't yet know of who has a grievance against this organisation.'

'Malcroft has already confessed her part in what happened when Bailey was killed. I don't think she would be likely to continue killing people after what she told us. As for Trudy Mitchell, her only involvement seems to have been her association with Dale Hargreaves and the bizarre lifestyle they led. As for others unknown, we didn't find much regarding Simeon Jones.'

'And there are still the two unidentified heads found at the farm. Not to mention the ashes and bones of countless bodies that may be scattered in the woods. Any one of their relatives could be out for revenge.'

'OK,' said Tweedy, trying to lower the heat in the discussion. 'Please concentrate on what we do know. Are we able to eliminate any of these people from our investigation?'

Tara and Murray answered together with opposing answers. A no from Murray and a yes from Tara. Poor Wilson was a bystander as the argument continued to rage.

'Yes we can, Alan. I believe Sloan, Greenwood, Mitchell and Malcroft are not the killers.'

Murray shrugged an unenthusiastic agreement.

'What about the Church of the Crystal Water?' asked Wilson. 'Are we any closer to identifying present-day members?'

Tweedy, Murray and Tara had no answer for the detective constable. Wilson proffered one of his own.

'The brother of Simeon Jones?'

No one in the room could raise an argument against the suggestion, but there remained a reluctance in pursuing the theory. Tara was coming to only one conclusion, but she knew she had a long way to go to convince her colleagues that she was right.

An hour later, Tara reluctantly agreed to pursue the connection between the Bailey children, their mother Janet Malcroft, and the events at Vera Deitate twenty-five years ago. Murray and Wilson were more convinced that if the recent killings were directly linked to Vera Deitate then it had to be through Malcroft and her family. Tara struggled with a very different scenario. That the girl who had been in contact with Maurice Young was somehow a Pritchard child, she hadn't figured how that could be, hell-bent on avenging the death of her mother. It seemed her long shot was a very long one indeed, and while Wilson looked into the background of the Oak-bespoke furniture company, she and Murray returned to the home of Janet Malcroft.

* * *

Fortuitously, when they entered the sitting room of the house in Grassendale they were greeted by a young woman, roughly Tara's age. Sandra Bailey forced a smile but glanced nervously at her mother when the police officers were introduced. When she stood to greet them, she was a good six inches taller than Tara although she wore heels and Tara was still wearing her flat boots. Sandra's face was quite pinched. She had dirty fair hair that hung down each side of her face like a pair of curtains. She wore a green skirt and cream jumper with a round neck.

'Mum has told me what's been going on,' she said in a soft voice with only a trace of Liverpool detectable.

Tara knew she had to handle this delicately. Recalling her last meeting with Peter Bailey, he, understandably, wasn't taking the news that his mother had been present when their father was murdered terribly well. But she needed to find out how much Sandra Bailey knew of those times and how much resentment she had stored, a resentment that might give her motive to kill those she thought were to blame for her father's death.

'I would like to ask you, Sandra, how much you know regarding your father's death and your mother's involvement?'

Janet Malcroft was already pressing a tissue to her eyes as her daughter listened to the question.

'I don't remember anything from the time Dad died. Only the day he left home.' She again looked at her mother.

'Has your mother explained what has been going on recently?'

'Yes.'

'And you are aware of her involvement with Vera Deitate?'

'Yes.'

'How long have you known?'

'Only since you arrested her.'

'And how do you feel about that?'

Sandra Bailey rose from the sofa and went to her mother, sitting on the arm of her chair and taking her hand. 'I don't see that she has ever done anything wrong, Inspector.'

'You don't blame her for your father's death?' Murray asked.

'Absolutely not.'

'What about these recent murders?'

'What do you mean? You think Mum has something to do with those?' The girl was close to yelling at Murray. Janet tried to calm her daughter by clasping her hands in hers. Yet again, Tara realised, her colleague had weighed in with his usual lack of sensitivity. But the damage was done; she allowed him to continue.

'How do you feel about them? Some of the victims were around at the time your father was murdered.'

'So, now you're asking if we have killed these people? To get revenge for Dad? That's ridiculous.'

'Is it?'

Sandra looked pleadingly at her mother.

'I've told you everything I know,' said Janet. 'Believe me, Inspector, I have lived with the guilt of what happened to Alastair and what I did to him for twenty-five years. The people who killed him are long dead. I have no reason to kill these others.'

'Does that include Angela Sanders?' said Tara. 'You told us that she nailed Alastair's hands to the wheel and she handed the axe to Mary Kirkman. And yet you have remained as a member of this church.'

'So why would I want to bring suspicion down upon my church by killing these people? You need to start looking somewhere else for your killer, Inspector. Leave me and my children alone.'

'What about your present husband?'

'He works abroad. He knows very little about what's going on, and he's not likely to stay with me when he learns the rest. So, you see, your investigations can wreck lives just as easily as a murderer.'

Those last words from Malcroft stung as Tara got back into the car beside Murray. The thought that their attempts to bring a killer to justice might destroy other lives in the process wasn't one that she'd considered before. She felt genuinely sorry for the Malcroft family if all she had done was to bring them more pain. But then, unlike Sandra

Bailey, she didn't believe that Janet Malcroft was completely blameless for the death of her first husband.

Murray had taken details of Sandra and her mother's whereabouts on the dates around the deaths of each of the recent victims. If the daughter's checked out, then she was nowhere near Liverpool when any of the murders had taken place. That only served to get Tara wondering again about the mystery surrounding the Pritchard children. What had really happened to them?

CHAPTER 78

With a cool glass of wine set beside her, she perused the collection of leaflets and pamphlets spread across her coffee table. Most of them had been gathered from Carl Sloan and from the Vera Deitate farmhouse. Some resembled religious tracts like those handed out by born-again Christians on a Saturday in Pembroke Street. Except these leaflets stated the reasons for the non-existence of God. Scientific evidence mixed with conspiracy theories over how the Earth was created, why Jesus had not risen from the dead, how he'd fathered a child of Mary Magdalene, and how cultures from much further back in time had understood that only the seasons, the sun and stars ruled over the Earth. But many of the more detailed booklets dealt with strange energy sources within the human soul and how they may be harnessed. To Tara it seemed that much had to do with bizarre sexual practices, the use of mind-altering substances and peculiar rituals to summon these forces. She really didn't understand much of it and certainly could not agree with any of it. Often it was said that religion was the cause of most wars and yet here was one that claimed to do good by ritual sacrifice.

Some of those sacrifices she now realised involved the murder of innocent people.

Her door buzzer sounded. It would be Aisling and Kate over for a catch-up night. Quickly, she swiped the papers together and slipped them into her bag. Devil worship was not a topic she wanted to discuss with her best friends.

'Hiya, love,' said firstly by Kate, followed by Aisling.

'Wine is open already,' said Tara. 'Glad you guys are here. I could do with some light-hearted chat.' As soon as she'd said it, she hoped it hadn't sounded condescending. She was always conscious of trying not to burden her mates with her problems at work. And tonight, she was more than happy to hear about the latest offers at Harvey Nic's or what Kate was up to with her daughter.

When she awoke next morning, it was to the feeling that she'd had a decent night's sleep. The first night in weeks. The wine had helped, of course, but she considered it had more to do with an evening's relaxation in the company of her friends. The news that Aisling had a new man in her life, and one who seemed to fit the bill, both rich and handsome, left her with a bittersweet feeling though.

Once at her desk at St Anne Street, all thoughts of Aisling and her new man were swept to the back of her mind as she deliberated on what to do next regarding these 'Pentacle Killings' as one local paper had named them. One question had been niggling since the death of Angela Sanders. Why had the MO changed? Why had the killer gone further this time? Did they consider that Sanders was deserving of such mutilation, or were they becoming crazed, their anger boiling over? Her thinking was soon interrupted by the assiduous John Wilson.

'Morning, ma'am. Some info on Oak-bespoke for you.'

'Morning, John, thank you.' He set the paper on her desk and wandered off. Tara glanced at the sheet briefly and then turned her attention to the forensic reports on each of the killings.

Firstly, she read the file on Derek Greasby. The body had been left in a wooded area, arranged as a pentacle, the head removed, hands and feet nailed to a wooden circular frame, and a biblical inscription from the Book of Proverbs left at the scene. His head was discovered on railings at Stanley Park. Why? She could only think it was done for shock value, to publicise the execution. The killer wanted the public and the police to know exactly what was going on. Still, she had no motive for Greasby's murder. So far, he had not been linked to either the modern-day *de Ecclesiae in Vera Divinitate* or to the church of twenty-five years ago. The killer, of course, may have known differently.

Secondly, she read about Maurice Young. According to Carl Sloan, he may have been a member of the old church community, but it remained unknown whether he was present at the time of Alastair Bailey's killing. His head had been found on the railings of the Anglican cathedral. Again for public display? she wondered. Or did the cathedral hold some significance? Certainly, the placing of Young's body within the grounds of the Vera Deitate farm suggested that the victim had a connection to the cult. Dinsdale Kirkman's murder appeared as a direct swipe at those who were involved at Vera Deitate twenty-five years ago. His parents, according to Janet Malcroft, killed Alastair Bailey, Simeon Jones and perhaps countless others, including the two victims whose heads were found in jars at the farm and who remained unidentified.

Finally, she considered Angela Sanders. Tara dared hope it was the last killing. Sanders had been identified again by Janet Malcroft as having taken part in the murders of Bailey and Jones. Sanders' murder differed from the others by the degree of mutilation of the body. And still the same question remained for Tara. Were all the killings a swipe at *de Ecclesiae in Vera Divinitate* or revenge for the killing of Alastair Bailey and perhaps Simeon Jones? Revenge for Bailey suggested Malcroft or her children. But if it were revenge for Simeon Jones or for those victims still unidentified, she had nothing. She had no clues. And then there was the death of Kelly Pritchard and the mystery surrounding her children. If they were still alive, would they be seeking retribution for their mother who, by all accounts, died of cancer?

And what of the Church of the Crystal Water? It existed twenty-five years ago because Bailey and Jones had been members, but was it still active? How many people were involved? Was someone of a Christian background embarked upon a campaign of terror against a satanic cult? If so, then she should expect to see more victims.

Tara's gut instinct told her that someone was out for revenge, but for what? She couldn't help dwelling on the question of what happened to the Pritchard children. Murray, thankfully, interrupted her thinking.

'Are we paying another visit to this furniture place? Wilson said he'd dug up some info on the owner.'

Tara gave a loud sigh and pushed herself away from her desk and the files on it.

'Yes, I suppose so. At the very least it might cut off that avenue of thought about the murder of Maurice Young.'

Wilson had provided a home address for the registered owner of Oak-bespoke. They drove to Melling, and not far outside the village they came to a stone cottage, partially hidden from the road by trees and hawthorn. It was a higgledy-piggledy array of two-storey buildings adjoined to a single-storey block which had a large conservatory attached. Behind the main house were two further buildings, one resembling a garage or workshop, the other for accommodation, a guest flat perhaps. The gardens were lavish and well-tended, with a beautiful sweeping lawn and several flower beds. Murray parked across the gateway to the house to avoid leaving the car obstructing the narrow road. As the pair started into the drive towards the house, they came across a woman who was gathering leaves scattered over the front lawn. She called out a hello, and Tara stepped off the drive and came towards her.

Wearing jeans and a green fleece jacket, the woman looked around sixty, perhaps a little younger. Her face was clear and lively, with blue eyes and tightly-curled brown hair.

'Good afternoon. I'm Detective Inspector Tara Grogan, Merseyside Police.' Tara showed the woman her ID.

'Hello, Inspector,' the woman replied, immediately looking concerned. 'I'm Daphne Collywell. Is there something wrong?'

CHAPTER 79

'I wanted to ask you about your company, Oak-bespoke.'

'It's really my husband, Alec, you should speak to, but he's at the workshop today.' Tara recalled seeing a middle-aged man who had been polishing a table when they had visited the workshop.

'It is a family business then?'

'Yes, our daughter, Jemima, takes more to do with running the place than Alec nowadays, although he likes to think that he's still in charge. Still the owner in name but it will all belong to Jemima one day. Has something happened, Inspector?' Daphne Collywell's face looked grave. 'You haven't brought me bad news?'

'I'm not quite sure, Mrs Collywell. Can you tell me about Jemima, please?'

The woman looked uneasy.

'If there's something wrong, I'd like to know before we go any further.'

It was another bitterly cold day, and standing in a garden, no matter how splendid, was not the place to carry on a conversation.

'Perhaps, if we may go inside, I can explain,' said Tara.

'Yes, please do. I'll make some tea.'

In a spacious kitchen, over a cup of tea and some chocolate biscuits, much to the delight of Murray, Tara explained the reasons behind her visit. She approached the subject of Jemima by explaining her concern over the young woman arranging to meet men on her own through the internet that she hadn't met before.

'I do worry about her at times,' said Daphne. 'She has never really had a steady boyfriend. Neither has Jason had a serious relationship with a girl.'

'Jason?'

'Jemima's older brother.' The mention of a brother sparked a fresh hope in Tara that her instinct was correct.

'A number of email messages were traced to Jemima's computer at work. A man had tried to arrange to meet with her. She told us that he was merely a potential customer. Shortly after his last communication to Jemima he was murdered.'

The woman's eyes widened in horror.

'Oh, my goodness. Do you mean to say that Jemima could have been in danger if she had met this man?'

At that moment Tara was thinking more that Maurice Young might still be alive if he had never been in contact with Jemima. She ignored the question and decided to ask what she had been guessing at for the last few days, certainly since they had narrowed things down to a suspect hell-bent on vengeance.

'Are Jemima and Jason your natural children, Daphne?'

'Why do I get the feeling, Inspector, that there is something you still haven't told me? You don't think

Jemima had anything to do with this man's death? Please tell me the answer is no.'

'Did you adopt Jemima and Jason, Mrs Collywell?'

The woman was on the verge of tears. Murray fetched her a glass of water. Her face had paled; she no longer looked the bright woman they had met in her garden ten minutes earlier.

'The two of them are so close. Jason would never let Jemima get involved in such things. Why do you think she is connected to this man's death?'

'You need to tell me, Daphne, are your children adopted?'

'Alec and I tried for years you know. Just a matter of time, we thought. But I never did get pregnant. We started out by fostering. A couple of years on, Jason and Jemima came to us. Orphans. They were the most grateful and loving children, and they were so happy with us. We had to fight tooth and nail to finally adopt them. That was twenty years ago. Please tell me Jemima hasn't done anything wrong, Inspector. Our children are everything to us. Our heart and soul.'

Tara placed her hands on those of Daphne Collywell. They were freezing cold and shaking. She found it hard not to shed a tear for this woman. She prayed now that her instincts were entirely wrong.

'Did you ever hear the names Aeron and Corey mentioned by either of your children?'

'No. Why? Their names have always been Jemima and Jason. Social services confirmed it although they never could trace birth certificates. Jason claimed to be eight years old at the time and Jemima was four. They were found living on the streets in Manchester. Apparently, their natural parents were both dead. As far as I know neither Jason nor Jemima have ever made attempts to find out what happened. They never speak of those times.'

Tara looked at Murray for help. Everything seemed to fit, but she needed reassurance from him that she was doing the right thing in sharing her theory with this poor woman. But if she was right then Alec and Daphne Collywell had so much more pain to endure. Murray seemed to sense what she was intending. He gave a nod of approval.

'Daphne, we can't be certain just yet, but we think that Jason and Jemima were the children of a young woman called Kelly Pritchard who died twenty-five years ago. No one can account for the children's whereabouts since that time. Their names were Aeron and Corey.'

'But that's good news. You've found out what happened to them before they came to us.'

Tara couldn't help squeezing the woman's hands. She felt her own heart pounding and her temples pulsing. This was not a pleasant task, breaking the heart of an innocent woman.

'Kelly Pritchard was a member of a satanic cult at the time of her death. It is possible that Aeron and Corey believe their mother was killed, that she didn't die of natural causes. If that is true, then they may be responsible for killing the people who they believe killed their mother.'

'Oh my God! Please no.'

Tara came round the table to comfort Daphne, the woman reaching out to her for support. They hugged each other.

'Do you know where we can find Jason and Jemima now, Daphne?'

'Should be at work,' she sobbed.

Tara nodded to Murray who took it as his cue to order a car to call at the workshop of Oak-bespoke. 'Alec should be there, too. He's not going to understand what's happening.'

Tara felt the whole world sagging on her shoulders. She was running with her theory. If she was wrong there'd be hell to pay. She'd already caused great upset in one family, and now she had devastated another. They couldn't go after anyone themselves. Tara couldn't leave this woman alone. Murray would have to organise the arrest of the Collywell children.

'Where does Jason work, Daphne?'

'In the city. He's a probation officer.'

CHAPTER 80

Uniformed police were unable to trace either Jemima or Jason Collywell at their workplaces. Tara and Murray returned to St Anne Street having left Daphne in the arms of her husband, Alec, when he'd arrived home from work. He'd telephoned from Oak-bespoke when the police had called looking for Jemima. Daphne had immediately summoned him home. Tara was saddened by the heart-rending sight of the husband on his knees beside his wife trying to comfort her while at the same time struggling to comprehend the situation in which his family now found itself. Tara wanted to be wrong about this case, if only to spare the sorrow of this couple. Before leaving, they prised a short list of places from Alec and Daphne where the Collywell children might be found. Tara had somehow convinced herself that not only was she right that they were the killers, but she worried also that this evening the pair may be in the process of selecting another target for their brand of murder.

'Any news, sir?' she asked Tweedy, who had taken personal charge of the emergency at the office.

'No sign of the woman at the furniture workshop, or of the male at his office. I've sent a car to the address you gave me for their flat. I'm waiting to hear.'

'John, what have you found on Jason Collywell?'

The young officer sprang from his chair, and with his usual efficiency presented some notes to Tara. He commentated as she read.

'Probation officer for the last six years. Before that he studied law and theology at university. But we've got our man, ma'am. Look at the list of offenders assigned to him over the years.'

Tara could hardly believe the names in front of her. Dinsdale Kirkman, Maurice Young and Derek Greasby were there amongst a list of dozens. But the name leaping out of the page, yelling at her to notice, was the man she perhaps feared most. The man who had taken her, drugged her and stripped her naked. The man who may have taken her life had not her friends, Kate and Aisling, along with Murray, rushed to her rescue. James Guy, recently freed from Liverpool Prison, was now free on licence and under the supervision of Jason Collywell.

'I need their flat, the furniture workshop and Collywell's office searched now,' she called out to Murray. 'We have to assume they know we're onto them. I'm quite sure the parents have tried to contact them. For all we know the reason we can't find them is that they're in the process of another killing. Either that or the parents have told them to run.' She passed the paper to Murray and watched him as he skimmed down the list. He raised his head and looked at her.

'You saw the name, ma'am?'

'James Guy? Yes.'

'I suppose we'll need to contact all of these people. Organise an Osman warning letter to inform them that their lives may be in danger.'

'Yes, you'd better get someone onto that. We need to find them, Alan, before anyone else dies.'

'Are you any clearer on a motive, Tara?' Tweedy asked.

'Not entirely, sir. We have still to confirm that the Collywell brother and sister are the children of Kelly Pritchard. If they are then they must have a reason for

232

killing past members of the Vera Deitate church. That includes Dinsdale Kirkman, Maurice Young and Angela Sanders. So far, we have no reason to believe that Derek Greasby was connected to Vera Deitate. I can only think their motive is connected to the death of their mother.'

Tara couldn't help her unease at the thought that the longer they remained untraceable the more likely it was that the Collywells were embarked on another killing. But against who? Was Jason Collywell simply working from his list of charges or were all their victims firmly connected to the time of his mother's death?

When neither sibling could be found at their place of work or at their flat, Tara and Murray seized the opportunity to have a look inside each location.

The furniture workshop gave no real clues that it had been used for murder except that here lay the means to construct the circular wooden frames upon which each victim, apart from Angela Sanders, had been nailed. She reckoned that forensics would be able to come up with such evidence perhaps by comparing the various woods used on the premises, the tools and the company van, if there was one. The computer used by Jemima Collywell was taken away; Tara wondered what gruesome secrets were stored upon it.

With the search ongoing at Oak-bespoke, they rushed to the South Liverpool probation office at the end of Falkner Street, close to the Liverpool Women's Hospital. The modern low-rise office building had already closed for the evening, but a keyholder had been summoned to the premises. Tara and Murray were directed to the office used by Jason Collywell.

His computer terminal had already been removed and any locked drawers and filing cabinets had been opened. There was little to be seen at first glance to indicate that Collywell was anything but a professional employee of the probation service. Murray studied the collection of pictures of various Liverpool squads over the years that hung on the wall behind Collywell's desk. One dated back to the eighties showing the likes of Dalglish, Hansen and Grobbelaar. Tara examined the desk, free of files or clutter in keeping with the service's clear desk policy. In the lockable drawers anything of a personal nature, correspondence, etc., identified only Jason Collywell and not a man named Corey.

Lying at the bottom of one nearly empty drawer, she found two photographs. One showed Jemima Collywell in a bikini, one hand on her hip, and clearly somewhere on a sunshine holiday. The other showed a landscape of open fields and hedgerows. It was not an expertly taken shot, a telegraph pole ran down the centre of the picture and it was a dull, cloudy day. She didn't immediately recognise the place, but after gazing for a while she decided that it resembled the area close to the Vera Deitate farmhouse. The house itself was not visible. She already knew it could not be seen from the road. It was the closest thing she'd uncovered so far to link Collywell with the killings.

'I don't think we'll find anything obvious here,' she said to Murray, who had begun to skim through a drawer in one of the two filing cabinets.

'Yeah, it'll take days to go through all these records.'

'And we don't have days. I can't help thinking the pair of them are up to something this evening.'

* * *

Murray drove them to the apartment shared by brother and sister. It was a ground-floor flat of an Edwardian block on the A561, south of the city in Cressington, ironically not that far from the home of Janet Malcroft and from that of the deceased Dinsdale Kirkman. The apartment occupied the entire ground floor, access to the flat above was by a separate outdoor entrance. The sitting room was spacious, minimalistic, with bookcases surrounding two large sofas arranged at a right angle to each other. A gas burner was set into the original fireplace, a coffee table sitting in front with a couple of furniture trade magazines lying on top.

The kitchen was very modern with expensive-looking fittings and a coffee machine sat on one of the benches. There was nothing in either of these rooms to indicate that the occupants were murderers or that murders were planned here. Tara left Murray, who was going through the collection of books, shaking each one in the hope that something incriminating would drop to the floor. She had a cursory look in the bathroom and the smaller of the two bedrooms. Curiously, she couldn't decide which of the siblings slept there. The room was clinically clean, a bed with a plain white duvet, a bedside table and a small wardrobe which, Tara guessed, had been made at Oak-bespoke. Inside it she found some male clothes, trousers, shirts and ties. A cardboard box sat at the bottom. She pulled it out and opened up the flaps. There was a pile of papers and photographs inside, and as she leafed through them, she soon became certain that not only were the Collywells the killers but that they were the children of Kelly Pritchard. She gazed at family pictures, in happier times she assumed, of Kelly with her children and Keron Fogge, a long-haired and bearded man, a throwback to the hippies of the sixties. There were a couple of pictures of the kids with their grandparents, Norman and Molly Pritchard. They had been happier times indeed with Molly smiling, full of health and vitality.

She moved on to what was the master bedroom. It was quite spacious and with a bay window overlooking a long and narrow garden. A strange feeling arose in Tara as she looked around. There was no definitive stamp upon this space. She couldn't say for sure that this was the room used exclusively by either Jemima or Jason. The cream colour scheme wasn't particularly feminine, neither was it masculine. Clothes within the built-in wardrobes seemed to belong to both brother and sister. Grooming products, fragrances, make-up and aftershaves all sat upon the dressing table and, gazing at the king-size bed, she wondered for a second if it was shared.

Sitting on a bedside table to the left-hand side was an old-looking rag doll. An embroidered face with black pigtails. The green flowery dress it wore had the name Jemima crudely written in felt pen across it and was now faded. Turning it over, the name Kelly had been stitched into the material of the dress. On the opposite bedside table sat a large Bible. It was huge, a lectern-style volume, King James version as opposed to a modern translation, a sturdy cover of brown leather, mottled with age, with brass clasps and a reinforced spine. Tara opened it at a place where there was a leather bookmark inside. She should have guessed. The Book of Proverbs. Verse 12 of Chapter fourteen had been underlined in red pen.

> *There is a way which seemeth right unto a man, but the end thereof are the ways of death.*

She wondered if the verses had been chosen specifically for each victim or had there been a progression either through the Book of Proverbs or in the motives of the Collywells. Following what Tweedy had told her about Solomon being the writer of this book – his use of pentagrams, his wisdom, his sense of justice – had these children of Kelly Pritchard, no matter how bizarre it appeared, set out to better the world, to dispense justice to wrongdoers? Was it a justice not available to police forces and not condoned by normal society?

She had all the proof she needed to confirm most of her thinking, but of greater urgency was finding out where this pair of killers performed their deeds and to discover where they were at this moment.

CHAPTER 81

This time I didn't have long to wait. I'd hardly started into my pint of Guinness when in she struts. Black is definitely her favourite colour. Apart from her blonde hair that is. She wore a leather biker jacket, black satin blouse and a short, black pleated skirt. Finished it off with black tights and black knee boots. She walked right up to me. No hanging about by the door this time. No talking to other blokes. Right up beside me. Hand on my arm, she says, 'I'll have a large glass of white wine please, babe.'

Babe she called me. Was this Christmas or what?

'How've you been, the girl with no name?' I asked her.

'Oh, I'm fine. And it's Aeron. But fancy meeting you the other day. A girl might start thinking she had a stalker?'

'I was thinking the same about you.'

'In your dreams, love.' We both laughed. I ordered her drink, and when it came, she took a healthy gulp.

'You look as though you needed that.'

'Mmm. Been looking forward to it all afternoon.'

'So, what else have you been looking forward to?'

She smiled a devilish smile. I reckoned I'd found me a real naughty girl. At long last, I thought. Someone who thinks just like me. Someone who stalks just like me. She gave my arm a little squeeze but didn't reply.

'You want to grab something to eat?' I asked.

'That would be nice, but let's have a few drinks first.'

I ordered a pint for me and another glass of wine for her. We found a small table in a corner, sat down opposite each other and chatted away. The whole time she had her hand on mine as she told me all about herself, and I lied through my teeth about what I'd done with my life. She asked me loads about Belfast and what had brought me to Liverpool. The whole time I'm thinking I'd died and gone to heaven. I was looking into the eyes of an angel. OK, I bloody know it sounds cheesy, but I couldn't remember if anything like this had ever happened to me before. I watched her every movement as she spoke. Her blonde hair had been straightened, a centre parting so that it fell down each side of her face. Her nose had a bit of a bump in the middle which didn't do much for her profile, and she had a narrow mouth and short chin. Not classically pretty but bubbling with sex appeal. She definitely had something.

I hardly noticed that I'd drunk four pints and we were still chatting, gazing into each other's eyes. A couple of times she leaned over the table and gave me a brief kiss. I took it as a promise of what was to come later. With all the beer, I dragged myself away from her and went for a slash. When I got back, she stood up.

'Want to get something to eat now? I know a nice Italian place not far from here.'

'Great,' I said. I downed the remainder of my beer. 'Lead the way.'

It was pissing down when we stepped outside. She hurried along the street with her bag over her head, laughing. Then she stopped by a shop doorway and pulled me inside with her. Boy, she could kiss. Let's leave it at that. When she'd had enough of my tongue, she pulled me into the bistro which wasn't busy, and we took a table by the window. And here's a line I never heard from a girl before. She said it to me when I returned from another visit to the toilet.

'Don't order dessert, you can have it at my place.'

Can you believe it? How lucky was I?

After a pizza we strolled, hand in hand, through the damp night until we came to a street corner where I was going to hail a taxi for us. I was beginning to feel a bit knackered, though. I'd only had a few pints and a couple of glasses of wine in the restaurant, but my head was spinning.

'No, we don't need a taxi,' she said.

'You live close by?'

'I have a driver.'

'A driver? What, do you mean, like a chauffeur?'

She laughed at me. Not so much because of my question, more the way I had slurred my words. I was conscious enough to know I was leaning into her, but she didn't seem to mind.

'Not like a chauffeur, an actual chauffeur.'

'What are you, fecking royalty?'

'No, I'm just reasonably well off.'

She took out her phone and made a brief call.

'We're ready,' she said. I was dumbfounded. Visions of my time with Lady Victoria, the daughter of a duke, swept before me. But I'd had to take her the way I take all my girls. And now she was at the bottom of the Irish Sea. But this Aeron was different. What the hell had I found? She pulled me close, and we snogged.

Everything suddenly went pear-shaped. I can remember seeing a car pull into the side of the street. A black Mercedes. There was a man driving, but I was too drunk to make out his face. Too drunk to realise the significance of the black Mercedes. The last thing I remember is stumbling into the back seat with Aeron. We started kissing again as the car moved off, then all went black.

CHAPTER 82

I was foundered. Couldn't fucking move. I woke up staring into the night sky. I could see the clouds moving across the moon and the branches of trees swaying in the wind. My head was thumping, and it took me a while to figure out what I'd been up to. Last thing I could remember was kissing Aeron. Didn't know where. Didn't know when. Just that we were kissing. I couldn't figure anything out. I looked at my hands. They were tied to a wooden thing, a frame or something. I thought maybe Aeron was into all this bondage shit. Couldn't see my feet, but I couldn't move them either. I was splayed out like a fucking chicken at a barbecue. All my clothes were off me except for my boxers. It was bloody freezing. I called out her name but got nothing back.

'Aeron, love, this is great fun, but do you not think you're ripping the ass out of it? Come on, do something, get me out of here. I'm bloody freezing to death.'

Nothing. I tried shaking to get my hands free, but the wee bitch had used the same gear as I do. Cable ties. Then I realised something. She must have spiked my drink. Why else would I have passed out? Only had a few pints and a couple of glasses of wine. My God, she'd got me just like I got all of my girls. But why? What had I done to her? I'd been the perfect gent. What the hell did she want from me?

'Aeron! Stop pissing around, love.'

'Aeron!'

I was getting seriously hacked off lying on this bloody thing. Started thinking what I would do to the wee bitch when I got free. Then my mind wondered. I'd heard about these strange killings in Liverpool recently where the victims had their heads cut off. What if that was about to happen to me? For the first time since I was a kid, I was scared shitless.

'Aeron! Please, love. Get me out of this frigging thing.' Then I heard something move, a rustling, like somebody was walking through a pile of leaves. But it was dark, couldn't see fuck all.

'Good evening, Mr Guy.'

I couldn't entirely make out the face, but I recognised that smooth voice.

'Collywell, what the fuck?'

CHAPTER 83

Alec Collywell assured Tara and Murray that their adopted children had not been in touch. Devastated by what was befalling their family, he was just as eager to trace Jemima and Jason as the police. Tara felt more uneasy by the minute. She'd convinced herself that these killers were in the process of executing another victim.

She stood at the front door of the Collywell home in Melling. Daphne had taken to her bed, and Alec was trying his best to get some answers from the detectives.

'I don't understand,' he kept repeating to Tara's explanations.

'It all happened before they came to you, Mr Collywell. I can't give you the whole story just now. I really need to find them. Is there anywhere you can think of where they might be? Friends? Might they just be out at a concert, the theatre?'

The man was shaking his head at each suggestion.

'No friends that I know of. They've always been very close to each other. As far as I know they don't go out to shows or anything like that. Church maybe.'

'Which church?'

'I'm not sure. It's in Grassendale, that's all I know.'

Murray was on his mobile straight away getting someone at the station to check out churches in Grassendale.

'Get a car out there,' he said. 'Any open church buildings go in and see if they're inside.'

'Are they religious, Mr Collywell?' Tara asked.

'Yes, go to church every Sunday, Bible studies and the like.'

'It is a Christian church then?'

'Of course.' He gave her a look to suggest she'd asked a stupid question.

'Is there anywhere else? Please, Mr Collywell, think.'

'Sorry, love. I don't know of any other places they might go. I can't understand why they haven't called. I've left messages on their phones.'

'What vehicles do they drive?' Murray snapped in.

'Well, Jason has his car that both of them use.'

'What type of car? What's the registration?' Murray was firing out the questions now. Tara's frustration was growing as this man continued to fumble through his replies. The longer it took the more she was convinced they had an imminent murder to stop. Collywell gave Murray the registration of a 1985 black Mercedes-Benz 3000. A classic car. Tara rang the details through to St Anne Street.

'Any other vehicles?'

'Just the company van.' Again, Murray had to drag the information out of the man.

'What type? Registration?'

Collywell slowly revealed details of the Oak-bespoke van, an Iveco Daily Box, white with the red logo and lettering of the furniture company. As they were about to leave, Daphne Collywell came to the door holding her dressing gown closed around her, firstly admonishing her husband for not inviting the police to come inside and secondly to ask of any progress in tracing her children.

'I'm sorry, Daphne, we have nothing yet,' Tara replied. 'We will try to trace both vehicles.'

'Alec, did you tell the inspector about the old wood store. Jemima keeps extra stocks of oak there. Pieces of old trees mainly.'

'They wouldn't go up there, Daphne,' said Alec. 'Not at this hour.'

'Where is it?' Tara asked, her voice raised in annoyance at the bungling man.

'Not far. Up by Melling Mount.'

They called for backup as they rushed to the wood store. On the way Murray posed yet another awkward point.

'Three of the victims, ma'am, the bodies were found in woods. If they are doing someone else tonight, they could be anywhere.'

'I know, but they must use somewhere for all the preparations. This store might be the place where they make those damned circular frames.'

Murray pulled over opposite the entrance to a narrow lane that stretched into the darkness. It was just possible to make out the roof of an old barn in the distance. Suddenly, lights appeared in the lane.

'Down,' said Murray. They slid down in their seats. Tara watched the two lights of a vehicle gradually approach on a straight part of the lane. When the car reached the junction with the road, it halted briefly then turned right. As it did so she saw only a darkened figure at the wheel.

'That's the Merc,' said Murray. 'What now?'

'Follow it.' As they moved off Tara instructed the backup unit, on arrival at the lane, to proceed all the way to the barn.

Murray followed the Mercedes at a safe distance. There was little traffic at this hour and on this road, so he had to hang back further than he liked in case the driver became aware of them and got suspicious. It was now well after midnight and, with another glance at her watch, Tara felt that time was running out if the killers had taken another victim. The Mercedes wasn't travelling at speed, and Tara tried to imagine where it might be going. They passed through Maghull, and soon it was clear they were headed toward Sefton, but suddenly the Mercedes slowed and, without signalling, turned right. Murray drove on by for a few yards then pulled over.

'That's no more than a lane,' he said.

'Give it a minute and then we'll follow.'

No lights were visible when Murray pulled into the lane. The gravel soon petered out and they rumbled along on little more than a dirt track with grass growing up the centre. Hedges came and went to either side, but it was impossible to gauge exactly where they were. But for the headlights on their car, there was no other artificial light around them. The Mercedes had disappeared into an even deeper darkness. At one point Tara reckoned they were close to a river as she glimpsed moonlight bouncing off water. Then Murray slowed the car when they came to a narrow bridge.

'Where do you want to stop, ma'am? We'd be better sneaking up on them rather than letting them know we're coming.'

'Is there no end to this damn lane?'

'It's leading into those trees ahead of us.'

'Call for some help. We can't just assume there are only two of them. For all we know we might be dealing with a gang of bloodletters.'

Murray stopped the car while he made the call for assistance. Tara felt her stomach rise and her heart pounding. She was now certain that someone was about to die at the hands of the Collywells.

CHAPTER 84

'What the hell are you doing here? Can you get me off this bloody thing?'

'I'm afraid I can't do that, Mr Guy.'

'Why the hell not? You're my supervisor, you're supposed to help me.'

'Tonight, I'm not here to help you. I'm here to kill you.'

'What?'

'You're a curse on normal society, a cancer, an evil being. You have a debt to pay.'

'I've done my time, you frigging eejit. Get me off this thing. Where's Aeron? What have you done with her?'

'My sister will be along any minute.'

'Your sister?'

It was then I realised that I'd been set up. Aeron hadn't just walked into that bar and taken a shine to me. The two of them had planned it. But what the hell was their game? I hadn't done them any harm. Then I began to wonder if they were the relatives of one of my girls. That somehow, they had figured out I had taken their sister.

'If you have no further questions, I'll leave you in peace and quiet until Aeron arrives.'

He fucking disappeared again, me yelling my tits off.

'Collywell, why are you doing this? Where are we?'

I got nothing.

Felt like bloody hours, lying there in the dark, freezing cold. I had pains in my arms and legs, and my neck was cramped. All I wanted was for Aeron to show up so I could talk to her. Get her to listen to reason, to see some sense and get me off this bloody thing. I didn't understand what this man was about. Was he some kind of vigilante? Charles fecking Bronson? I couldn't stop shivering. If somebody didn't come soon, they wouldn't have to kill me; I'd freeze to death. Then I heard voices, quiet, whispers even. I called out, hoping it was somebody else, some random person passing by who could help me. That maybe that prick Collywell had buggered off. Though what kind of passer-by do you get in the middle of nowhere at this hour of the night? I guessed it was the middle of the night. Really, I hadn't a clue, I might have been out of it for days. Then I recognised her voice. Sweet.

'Aeron, love. Come on, what have I ever done to you? Get me out of here.'

'James, I'm glad you're awake. Wouldn't want you to miss anything.'

She stepped over me and stood astride my waist, hands on her hips. In the darkness I couldn't make out her face, just the outline of her trim body.

'What is this? We were having a good time. What did I do wrong?'

'You need to ask the victims of your crimes.'

'I don't know what you're talking about. Your brother knows I've done my time.'

'That's not enough, James. We have a duty to remove the likes of you from this world.'

'You're fucking nuts, love. Off your bloody trolley.'

'Now, now. Don't get angry. It's better if you're calm. It won't take long.'

'Calm? For God's sake, Aeron, wise up!'

'Please don't take the Lord's name in vain, Mr Guy,' said Jason Collywell.

I watched as he handed something to his sister. I couldn't make out what it was until suddenly a torch was shining at my left side. It looked like a big drill or something. Then Aeron crouched down and pressed it into my hand. I yelled liked a smacked child when the damn thing clicked and something sharp went right through my hand and into the wood. Hurt like fuck. The whole time I was trying to figure out how they knew about me, about all the things I'd done, the women I'd had. No way could they have known everything.

'No, please don't! I haven't done anything.'

She stepped around me, the torchlight now shone to my right, and again she crouched down. This time I didn't hear the click, I was screaming so much. The fucking pain was crazy, and I don't know why but I tried to bring my hands close to me. The pain shot up my arms and next I know I was throwing up. I felt her touching my right foot, pushing it sideways against the wooden frame. Another click and I screamed again. A nail went through my bloody foot. Tears flooded my eyes, and the slabbers came down my nose. She took hold of my left foot, and a nail went through it, the pain shooting up my legs, and as my body jerked the shock raced through my arms. My whole body throbbed. Somehow my screaming stopped. I had no energy left, and I was trying to get the vomit out of my mouth. Either that or I would choke. I knew now that I would soon be dead.

'Not long now, sweetheart,' said Aeron, leaning over me. She stroked my forehead. 'Anything you'd like to tell us? Confess your sins before you stand before God?'

'Fuck off!'

'Just a few final words. I'll say goodbye, sweetie.'

I saw the torch shining down upon a book that Jason was holding. Then the cruel fucker started reading aloud.

'Our final reading, James, is taken from the Book of Proverbs, Chapter twenty-one, reading from verse 15.

It is joy to the just to do judgement: but destruction shall be to the workers of iniquity. The man that wandereth out of the way of understanding shall remain in congregation of the dead...'

CHAPTER 85

They'd brought torches from the car and stepped off the lane into the trees. The ground was soft, but it helped muffle the sounds of their feet. Murray led the way, choosing the route, although it was merely a guess that the Collywells had come in this direction. They'd found the Mercedes in the lane and had parked up right behind it.

The Oak-bespoke van was parked a few yards further along. Tara was sure she'd heard screams as she'd climbed from the car, but they were some distance away. She had no idea how far the woods extended, it was unfamiliar territory, but Murray whispered that it couldn't be more than a couple of hundred yards from one side to the other. Going was slow and difficult. They met a patch of brambles and tried edging through. Thorns ripped at her jacket, snagging her jeans and tearing her skin. Then suddenly a few yards distant she caught a glimpse of light.

'Did you see that?' she whispered to Murray.

'Yes. It seems to be static. Don't think it's coming towards us. You move to the left a bit, and we'll try coming at them from two directions.'

She did as he'd suggested but soon encountered more thorns and brambles. Murray's light seemed to be moving faster. He called back in a whisper.

'Turn off your torch.'

Now it was impossible to judge her steps or what lay in front of her. She could see little more than the outline of trees and the pinprick of light ahead. As they edged closer to the light, Tara heard a man's voice. It sounded dull, low monotones as if he were reading. She wondered how best they could tackle them. They had no weapons. She fumbled around her, searching for a branch, anything she might use to defend herself. She couldn't find anything. They should have waited for support but then they may already be too late to save whatever poor soul had been taken. Murray waited for her to draw level. They stood side by side, she feeling precious comfort from the touch of his arm. A few yards in front she could make out the figure of a man, head down and reading by torchlight.

The wicked shall be a ransom for the righteous, and the transgressor for the upright...'

Murray and Tara shouted as one.

'Police! Stop where you are! Police!'

They rushed towards the man, flicking their torches on as they went. Only then did she notice the body prostrate on the ground.

Jason Collywell was startled by the shouts as Murray rushed him. The big-framed cop thundered into him, pushing him backwards. Collywell stumbled then fell. The wind knocked out of him.

'You're too late,' he gasped.

Tara caught Jemima Collywell in the beam of her torch. She had raised a huge axe above her head ready to bring it down on the body beneath her. Tara flung her torch. It hit Jemima in the face. She yelped, and the axe fell behind her as she collapsed on the ground.

'Take him,' Tara said to Murray. 'I'll get her.'

Jason Collywell seemed resigned to his fate. As he attempted to regain his feet, Murray, with a shoulder charge, thrust him down into the damp earth.

'It's all right, officer, no need for any more violence. My work is done.'

Jemima was not so passive. Getting to her feet, she charged off into the darkness. Tara retrieved her torch and followed. Ahead of her she saw the woman fall several times, tripping over tree roots and stumbling into potholes. Soon, though, she was clear of the trees, into an open field, and her speed increased. Tara kept her in sight as she ran. As they approached the edge of the field Jemima suddenly dropped from view.

Tara noticed the light of her torch shimmering on water. The river. She ran the last few yards. When she reached the bank, she saw a drop of at least four feet to the water's edge. Sweeping an arc with the torch, she caught sight of the woman below her and a few yards to her left.

'Stop, Jemima! Don't go in the water. You won't make it.'

Ignoring Tara's warning, the woman waded into the river. Tara caught her again in the torchlight. Jemima began to swim towards the far bank, but in a few strokes, she was floundering. Tara could either leave her to it or go in after her. There was no way the woman was making it to the other side. Tara slid down the grass and ferns of the bank and met the water feet first. But as she tried to wade in, she was instantly out of her depth and, like her quarry, had to swim. The cold took her breath. Gasping, she forced herself towards the woman. Grappling in the darkness, she was guided only by the splashing of Jemima's arms. By chance only, she caught hold of the woman's hair and pulled.

'Leave me alone! Let me go.'

'No, Jemima. You're going to live, and you're going to pay for what you've done.'

Tara grasped the woman's hair and slipped an arm around her shoulders as she felt them both being swept along by the current. The pain from the cold shortened her breath as Jemima struggled to break free. At times Tara was forced under and couldn't avoid gulping the water. But somehow, she gathered the strength to control this woman, and she did so by pulling ever tighter on the long blonde hair. The struggle sapped Tara's energy, but Jemima too was growing weaker. Then suddenly her feet scraped over rocks and stones. She could touch the bottom. They came to rest where the land flattened out and the river became shallow. In the darkness, Tara reached out for the reeds at the river's edge. Shivering uncontrollably, she dragged Jemima to safety and pushed her down into the long grass. Finally, she no longer felt any resistance. Jemima, in a trembling heap, coughing and fighting to draw breath, had at last surrendered.

CHAPTER 86

Soon the area was awash with police officers. Lights from cars and ambulances cast a different hue on the woods. Jason Collywell, in handcuffs, was marched towards a police van. Tara watched him go. He tried his best to look all around him. It was clear he was searching for signs of his sister. Jemima was receiving attention in the back of an ambulance for a cut to her head and for mild exposure. A team of paramedics were working in the forest to remove the latest victim from the deathly circular frame. He had been lucky, relatively lucky.

She met up with Murray at their car. Her wet upper clothing had been removed and she snuggled under a blanket.

'Well done, you,' she said. She was so happy to see him again.

'Thanks. You didn't do so badly yourself, jumping into the river. I'd have let the bitch drown. Was she really so important to you?'

'Absolutely. Hopefully we can get the full story now. If she'd drowned, we might never have known.'

'There's the brother?'

'Mmm. For some reason, though, I'd like to hear her side of things.'

A young female uniform brought them two plastic mugs of tea, and Murray asked her if she had anything to eat.

'Polo mints,' she said, walking on.

'Gee thanks.'

'Did you get a look at the poor sod on the frame?' Tara asked.

Murray looked at her but didn't reply at first.

'He's been nailed hands and feet to the wood. Paramedics are trying to get him free.'

'Did you recognise him?'

At that point Superintendent Tweedy appeared, his face as grave as ever.

'Good work, Tara and Alan. You saved a life, I believe.'

'Sir,' Tara replied, trying to hold the blanket around her and at the same time manage her cup of tea.

'We'll talk in the morning. Get yourselves off home to bed. You've done more than enough for tonight.'

Torches and brighter lanterns emerged from the darkness of the trees. A group of paramedics carrying a stretcher were assisted by several uniforms. She walked towards the ambulance to catch a glimpse of the man whose life she and Murray had saved. As they waited for the rear platform of the ambulance to be lowered, she squeezed through the group of medics and stared down on the conscious face of the man lying on the stretcher. He had an oxygen mask over his mouth and nose, but still she could not help but recognise the face.

'You!'

Clearly in pain, and now under the influence of some pain-relieving drug, he managed to fix his gaze upon her.

'Hello, Tara. Fancy meeting you here.'

CHAPTER 87

They sat around the desk in Tweedy's office, the superintendent, for a change, also seated. A lot of work remained for his team to do in this case. Evidence had now to be assembled in clear and unambiguous form. Not only had they to review statements given by Jason and

Jemima Collywell and all facts connected to their actions, but there were cases pending against Janet Malcroft, Elsie Greenwood and Carl Sloan. Much work had to be done, in co-operation with Cheshire police, concerning the unidentified remains, including the two human heads found at the Vera Deitate farmhouse.

A week since the arrest of the Collywells and Tara had finally managed to establish the true motive behind their actions. Jason Collywell had been very co-operative and proud to tell their story. Jemima was less so, deep remorse having taken over, particularly her realisation that she had destroyed the lives of her much-loved adoptive parents. Her devastation was compounded when Tara had told her that her real mother, Kelly, had most likely died of natural causes. Jason repudiated the suggestion and insisted his version of events to be correct.

'I saw them,' he said. 'They lifted her from her bed, carried her outside and Mary Kirkman cut off her head. They threw her body into the fire and continued with their party.'

'Isn't it likely that she had died in her bed? That what you saw was her funeral? Your grandfather told us that she was terminally ill.'

'No, no. Mum spoke to me just before they came for her. She told me that she loved Aeron and me very much. That one day we would be together again.'

'Did you also witness the killing of Alastair Bailey and Simeon Jones?'

'Yes, but that was before Mum died. Simeon was good to us, to all the children at the farm. He told us that one day he would get us out of there and we could live normal lives. After they killed him, I knew we had to get away.'

'What about your father, Keron?'

Collywell's eyes widened on hearing the name. He gave a conceited smile.

'He didn't care about us, or Mum. He was like the rest of them. Drunk or stoned, at the centre of things.'

Tara explained further to those present in the office, Murray, Wilson, Tweedy and Paula Bleasdale.

'Jason Collywell harboured the desire to avenge the death of his mother and the murder of Simeon Jones. The recent killings were triggered when he was allocated Dinsdale Kirkman to supervise during his probation. When Jason did his research, he confirmed for himself that Dinsdale was the son of Charles and Mary. He said that he had only a faint recollection of Dinsdale at Vera Deitate. Most of it concerned his spending time with the young girls who were there and what he was allowed to do with them.'

'And the method of killing?' Tweedy asked.

'He wanted them to suffer in the same way as his mother and Simeon Jones. In particular, he singled out Angela Sanders for special treatment since she had actually participated in the ritual killings. He showed no remorse for disembowelling her while she was still alive. He holds no belief in the occult except to say that it is evil. He has a faith in God which stems from his near obsession with the Book of Proverbs. Curiously, he had no knowledge of it being used to label the body of Alistair Bailey. He sees it containing all the true wisdom of God. That's also his reasoning for killing Derek Greasby and attempting to kill James Guy. They had no involvement with Vera Deitate, but Collywell viewed them as evildoers. Since Jemima had been a victim of sexual abuse at Vera Deitate, he was determined to rid the world of sex offenders. Jemima went along with it.' Tara had spent the most time interviewing the woman and taking her statement. 'Her brother has protected her all her life. She is completely obedient to him.'

'You mentioned, Tara, that their relationship was incestuous?'

'Denied by Jason, sir, but Jemima admitted they slept together. They are a couple completely devoted to each other.'

Harold Tweedy, in sombre mood, thanked his team for all their endeavours. In particular, he praised the actions of Tara who had but a second to save the life of James Guy.

'I am very proud and feel privileged to have you all in my team,' he said. 'As you are aware there was an element of personal connection to the death of Alastair Bailey. He was a close friend. Thank you for the way in which you approached this aspect of the case. Perhaps if I had taken more interest in Alastair's difficulties all those years ago, I may have been able to prevent his death.'

Tara felt deep sympathy for her boss as he spoke. She realised this case had hit him hard, but she refused to believe that twenty-five years ago he hadn't done everything in his power to help his friend. Harold Tweedy was simply that kind of man.

'Tara, may I have a word?' The others filed out of the office, while she remained in her seat. She imagined he had some further instructions for her regarding the preparation of the case against the Collywells and others.

'I realise how difficult it must have been for you coming across James Guy.'

'Yes, sir. It was a shock, but you just have to do your job. I'm glad that we saved his life. It would have been very hard to take if he had died out there.'

'I understand. You've made a great partnership with Alan. I'm very proud of you both.'

'Thank you, sir.'

Tara returned to her desk to get ready for going home. She glanced across the office to where Alan Murray was rising from his chair and slipping on his jacket.

'Fancy a pint?' she called. Maybe Tweedy was right, they did make a good pair.

He crossed the room to her desk, smiling.

'Love to, ma'am, but can't tonight. I've got a date.'

'Good for you,' she said, trying her best to suppress her disappointment. 'Who's the lucky girl?' She leapt immediately to the assumption that it was someone from the station. Paula Bleasdale, maybe. After all, they spent so much time here, how could he possibly meet a girl elsewhere? Then she noticed him beaming, a roguish smile on his face. Still, he hadn't replied.

'What?'

'I am going for a drink with Trudy Mitchell.'

'Wow!'

'Don't look so surprised. I'm not all bad, you know.'

'It's not that. I just didn't imagine she was your type or you hers.'

'Thanks very much. And just what do you think is my type?'

She couldn't answer, didn't want to try. Murray then seemed happy to explain.

'I gave her a call yesterday. She thought I was about to ask more questions on her past. I told her the case was solved. When I asked her out, she came over all soft and gentle.

Tara smiled and truly wished the best for him.

'You never know.'

'Good night, ma'am.' He swaggered to the door.

* * *

She turned up the volume on the television, another bland American sitcom in full swing. A bowl of tortilla chips in her lap and a glass of orange squash on the table beside her. There were times when it felt good to be alone.

CHAPTER 88

I thought I was tatie bread. Tara saved my bacon. Who'd have thought it? If she hadn't thrown her torch at yon crazy bitch, I was finished. She was about to cut my frigging head off. And what had I ever done to her? Nothing. And Jason Collywell, my supervisor, up to no good. Easy to see how you can lose your faith in people.

Can't do much at the moment. My hands are healing well, but I have to stay off my feet for a few days. Bloody nails went right through just below the ankle. Lucky thing that they didn't sever my Achilles tendons. Would've been totally buggered. The pain is not too bad, eating the painkillers though, but the most important thing is to avoid infection.

The police came to see me in hospital. Wanted to get my story on how I got mixed up with this girl, Aeron. They already knew that Collywell was my supervisor. Turns out he'd bumped off a few of his other charges who were sex offenders. I wasn't really surprised when Tara didn't show. I suppose me and her have a bit of history. A big lad called Wilson asked me a shitload of questions about how I met Aeron, what we did, where I was taken, what was said, and all the ins and outs of what they did to me in that forest. He told me some stuff as well. About how lucky I was. Apparently if it hadn't been for Tara sussing out what this pair of numpties were up to I would have met my maker.

Never thought I'd be glad to get back to my dingy flat, to a bit of peace and quiet. A nurse calls on me every day to dress my wounds, and I've had a shrink of some kind come to see if I'm suffering from post-traumatic stress disorder. Am I fuck? I'm going to milk this for all it's worth. I'm a victim, you know? I've suffered at the hands of crazed killers. I should have been protected. Compensation, that's what I'm looking for. Do you know they had the brass neck to appoint another probation officer? Didn't take them long. Funny, but if I'd needed to see a consultant at the hospital I bet you a pony I'd still be waiting a year later. And yet here's my new supervisor come to visit me. Just to put a face to the name, she tells me. Then I had to go over it all again for her benefit. What if she turns out to be another axe murderer or the mad poisoner of Bootle? Ugly cow as well. Fecking Sumo Spice, that's what I call her. With her big arse she should be done for cruelty to chairs.

'Anything I can help you with, Mr Guy?' she said. Not likely to ask her for any favours. Not going to trust any of them fuckers again.

* * *

My left foot healed quicker than my right. It means I can walk a bit now using a stick. Makes me feel like I'm sixty instead of in my thirties. I see people staring at me when I hobble onto the bus. And then I notice a nice piece of skirt, a wee girl who takes my fancy. But what am I going to do about it? Nothing for now. How many stalkers are there limping about the place with a stick? Just have to be patient. There's nothing else for it.

I've taken a bus down to the Albert Dock a couple of times when it hasn't been raining. Usually in the early evening. I wrap up nice and warm and maybe take a seat along the promenade close to the Echo. Twice now I've seen her. Jogging by, earphones in, ponytail lolloping behind her as she runs, her lovely tight bum looking great in the leggings. She doesn't notice me. Or if she does, she's an even better detective than I think she is. I'll always be grateful that she saved my life, but I haven't given up on her. No way José. Truth is, I want her even more.

EPILOGUE

Tara stood between Murray and Wilson, rain beating down upon their umbrellas. Darkness was closing in early under the tall trees, bare of foliage now in deep winter.

Unprepared for the call out, she stood in ballet pumps and a dress she kept for nights out with the girls. A party frock. Bright and cheerful. A silk scarf around her and a light jacket hanging over her shoulders. The cold could do her no more harm as she watched the guys examine the scene. Were there really places within this city that people did not go? Places where a body could lie for weeks or months undisturbed, undetected? Then one morning, a couple walking their dog meander through the woods only to discover the poor soul who had come to grief. At least she hoped that was the way of it. She hoped it was not such a fresh kill to suggest another killer on the loose. How could she possibly explain it? How could she reason with herself that someone could be doing the same thing? Have the same motive? Have the same warped morals to justify taking a life in this manner?

The naked and headless body was nailed to the frame and set upside down against a tree. The inscription placed between the legs. She'd wasted no time in reading it and didn't have to guess that it came from the same book. Presumably, some unsuspecting citizen would discover a human head somewhere in this city, a city vibrant with life yet capable of coughing up its tragic dead.

Somebody would find the head of Keron Fogge.

Character list

DI Tara Grogan – Main investigating detective.
DS Alan Murray – Tara's colleague and assistant.
DC John Wilson – Junior detective.
DC Paula Bleasdale – Junior detective.
Superintendent Harold Tweedy – Senior detective and Tara's boss.
Rosemary Black – Retired detective who investigated the murder of Alastair Bailey 25 years ago.

James Guy – Serial killer and sex offender. Served prison sentence for the abduction of Tara.
Jason Collywell – Probation officer to James Guy. AKA Corey Fogge/Pritchard son of the late Kelly Pritchard.
Jemima Collywell – Sister of Jason. AKA Aeron Fogge/Pritchard, daughter of Kelly Pritchard.
Alec Collywell – Adoptive father of Jason and Jemima.
Daphne Collywell – Adoptive mother of Jason and Jemima.

Janet Malcroft – Former wife of murdered Alastair Bailey. Member of the Vera Deitate cult.
Peter Bailey – Son of Janet Malcroft and Alastair Bailey. Car mechanic.
Trudy Mitchell – TV personality. Former member of Vera Deitate cult and mistress of Dale Hargreaves.
Angela Sanders – Writer, celebrity, activist and former member of Vera Deitate cult.
Elsie Greenwood – Owner of Goth shop, tenant of Vera Deitate farmhouse.

Dr Carl Sloan – University lecturer, owner of Vera Deitate farmhouse and present-day leader of Vera Deitate cult.

Deceased characters:

Derek Greasby – Sex offender and first present-day victim of pentacle murders.

Maurice Young – Sex offender and second present-day victim of pentacle murders.

Dinsdale Kirkman – Sex offender, son of Mary and Charles Kirkman and third present-day victim of pentacle murders.

Alastair Bailey – Murder victim from twenty-five years ago, ex-husband of Janet Malcroft and former friend of Harold Tweedy.

Simeon Jones – Murder victim from twenty-five years ago.

Terry Lawler – Murdered journalist relevant to Tara from a previous case.

Kelly Pritchard – Deceased mother of Jason and Jemima Collywell.

Keron Fogge – Father of Jason and Jemima Collywell.

Dale Hargeaves – Deceased actor, former partner of Trudy Mitchell and a former member of Vera Deitate cult.

Charles and Mary Kirkman – Deceased parents of Dinsdale and former leaders of Vera Deitate cult.

Minor characters:

Lorraine Tweedy – Wife of Superintendent Harold Tweedy.

Ms Greasby – Mother of victim Derek Greasby.

Tina Jeffries – Victim of Derek Greasby.

Joanne White – Rape victim of Derek Greasby.

Don Mason – Partner of Tina Jeffries with a caution for assaulting Derek Greasby.

Brian Witney – Medical officer.

Kate – Close friend of Tara's.

Aisling – Close friend of Tara's.

Norman Pritchard – Aged father of the late Kelly Pritchard

Carol Sherman – Elsie Greenwood's solicitor.

Michael Coombes – Carl Sloan's solicitor.

Ella, Vicki and Thai – Victims of James Guy.

Trevor Jones – Brother of murdered Simeon Jones.

Keron Fogge #2 – Father to Keron Fogge (the partner of Kelly Pritchard).

Sandra Bailey – Daughter of Janet Malcroft and Alastair Bailey.

If you enjoyed this book, please let others know by leaving a quick review on Amazon. Also, if you spot anything untoward in the paperback, get in touch. We strive for the best quality and appreciate reader feedback.

editor@thebookfolks.com

ALSO IN THIS SERIES

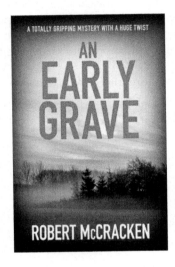

AN EARLY GRAVE (Book 1)

A tough young Detective Inspector encounters a reclusive man who claims he holds the secret to a murder case. But he also has a dangerous agenda. Will DI Tara Grogan take the bait?

Available on Kindle and in paperback.

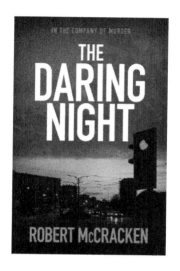

THE DARING NIGHT (Book 2)

Liverpool is on high alert after a spate of poisonings, but DI Tara Grogan is side-lined from the investigation. Yet when she probes into the suicide of a company executive, she becomes sure she has a vital lead in the case. Going it alone, however, has very real risks.

Available on Kindle and in paperback.

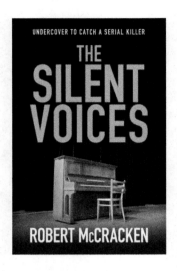

THE SILENT VOICES (Book 3)

When bodies turn up on a Liverpool council estate, DI Tara Grogan goes undercover to get inside information. But she risks everything when the cover story she adopts backfires. Can she work out the identity of the killer before she is exposed and becomes a target?

Available on Kindle and in paperback.

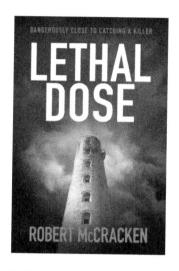

LETHAL DOSE (Book 4)

Investigating the death of a journalist, DI Tara Grogan stumbles upon his connection to a number of missing women. Is it possible the victim was actually a serial killer? As Tara closes in on the truth can she evade a fatal jab?

Available on Kindle and in paperback.

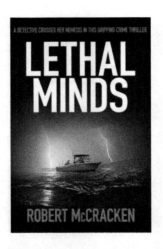

LETHAL MINDS (Book 6)

Following a murder, a drugs feud in a notorious Liverpool
estate is kicking off when a missing woman's body is
found in the Irish sea. DI Tara Grogan has her attention
divided, and someone with a grudge to bear has her in his
sights.

For more great titles, visit

www.thebookfolks.com

ALSO OF INTEREST

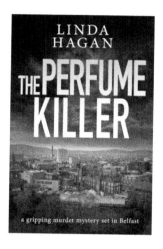

THE PERFUME KILLER by Linda Hagan

Stumped in a multiple murder investigation, with the only clue being a perfume bottle top left at a crime scene, DCI Gawn Girvin must wait for a serial killer to make a wrong move. Unless she puts herself in the firing line…

Available free with Kindle Unlimited and in paperback.

Printed in Great Britain
by Amazon